The Cutting Room

LOUISE
WELSH

CANONGATE

Edinburgh · London · New York · Melbourne

This paperback edition first published in 2011 by
Canongate Books

First published in Great Britain in 2002 by
Canongate Books Ltd,
14 High Street, Edinburgh EH1 1TE

www.meetatthegate.com

1

The author wishes to thank the Scottish Arts Council
for a writing bursary in September 2000,
which enabled her to spend time on this novel

British Library Cataloguing-in-Publication Data
A catalogue record for this book is
available on request from the British Library

ISBN 978 0 85786 086 6

Typeset by Hewer Text Ltd, Edinburgh
Printed and bound by Clays Ltd, St Ives plc

To Ena and John

Contents

1

Never Expect Anything

> *'Beauty is truth, truth beauty,'* — *that is all*
> *Ye know on earth, and all ye need to know.*
>
> John Keats,
> 'Ode on a Grecian Urn'

NEVER EXPECT ANYTHING.

An old porter told me that my very first day. We called him Cat's Piss. Mr McPhee to his face but always Cat's Piss, or sometimes C. P. McPhee behind his back.

'Never expect anything, son. They'll tell you they've got the crown bloody jewels in their attic and all you'll get's guff. But sometimes — not often mind, just now and again — you'll go to the pokiest wee hole, a council estate, high-rise even, and you'll find a treasure. So keep an open mind, try and filter out the nonsense merchants, sure, but never look at a map and think there'll be nothing there for us, because you can be surprised. I've been here thirty-five years and I'm still surprised at what we find and where we find it.'

'Yes, Mr McPhee,' I'd said. Looking all the while at a pile of furniture reaching almost to the ceiling and thinking, You stupid old git, thirty-five years in this place.

I'd not been thinking of McPhee as I drove to the call. I'm twenty-five years at the auction house, forty-three years of age. They call me Rilke to my face, behind my back the Cadaver, Corpse, Walking Dead. Aye, well, I may be gaunt of face and long of limb but I don't smell and I never expect anything.

I didn't expect anything driving along the Crow Road towards Hyndland. I hadn't taken the message myself but the call sheet said, *McKindless, three storeys plus attic, deceased, valuation and clearance*. I didn't need to know anything else except the address and that was in my pocket.

I hate Hyndland. You'll find its like in any large city. Green leafy suburbs, two cars, children at public school and boredom, boredom, boredom. Petty respectability up front, intricate cruelties behind closed doors. Most of the town houses have been turned into small apartments. The McKindless residence was the largest building in the street and the only one still intact. I parked and sat for a while looking at it. It dominated the road, a dark, sober façade intersected by three rows of darkened windows. No clue of what lay inside except you could bet it would be expensive. Tiny casement windows peeped from the slanted roof of the attic. More like five storeys in all including the basement. If we were lucky and the executor took our quote, this call might supply a whole sale. I was getting ahead of myself, there was nothing to say there was anything of use at all in the place – but the odds were for it. I turned the van into the driveway, noting the remnants of a garden. Last year's crocuses pushing through the long grass — whoever had lived here was well enough last spring to organise their garden, this spring it was them that was planted.

Never expect anything.

Cat's Piss should have added, 'But be prepared: anything may happen.'

I slicked back my hair and wondered if I should take Joan-in-the-office's advice and have it cut short. I had a feeling that perhaps a short-back-and-sides could be the prelude to romance for Joan — well, if Joan had been Joe I might have thought about it but the way things were I might as well keep my locks. Sure they were grey but they went with the look.

I took off my shades — it's only polite to make eye contact on the first meeting — rang the doorbell twice and waited. I was about to ring a third time when I heard footsteps. I had expected someone in their forties — wealth of this kind usually finds a fair few relations willing to help with the burden of tying up the estate — but when the door was opened it was by a woman who wouldn't be seeing eighty again. She was dressed like the respectable women from my childhood. Single string of pearls, heather twin-set, long tweed skirt, thick woollen tights and brogues. Her hair, though sparse, was set in stiff egg-white curls. Age had withered her. There was the beginning of a bend to her spine. She leant the whole of her weight, a good seven stone, against a plain wooden walking stick.

There was a crooked man and he had a crooked house.

'Mr Rilke, Bowery Auctions.'

I handed her my card and let her look me up and down. I could almost hear her assessment: hair bad, tie, shirt, suit good, cowboy boots bad. Well, she had a point, but they were genuine snakeskin.

'Madeleine McKindless. Come in.'

Her voice was young, with the authority of a school-teacher.

The stained glass of the front door cast a red glow across the hallway, a staircase with an ornately carved mahogany banister was to our left, the parquet floor laid with thinning Turkish rugs; this family had been rich for a long time. A heavy mahogany table stood to the right of the door. It was bare, none of the usual family photographs, and I guessed she'd been doing some clearing out already.

I knew in an instant there was no way we were going to get the job. It was just too big to trust to a local auction house. She was a fly old bird getting us in to do a valuation then playing us off against the big boys.

'Let's go into the kitchen. It's the only place I feel halfway comfortable in this mausoleum.'

She led me through the hallway and I followed her, slowly, down a set of stone steps worn thinner in the middle, by generations of McKindlesses no doubt. She favoured her left leg. I wondered if she was due a hip replacement and why she was making things hard for herself. Why take these stairs, with a whole house to choose from? The kitchen was on two levels, scullery on the lower level where I could make out an open door leading to the garden. A flask of coffee, some mugs and a plate of biscuits were already laid out on the huge kitchen table.

'My brother's home help laid out a refreshment for us. I suffer from arthritis and angina, among other things. I like to save my strength for non-domestic tasks.'

'Very sensible.'

A smell of burning drifted in from the garden. I walked to

the door and looked out onto a well tended lawn at the end of which burnt a bonfire. A gnomic gardener jabbed at the flames with a long rake. He caught my stare and raised his free hand in a half-defensive wave, like a man staving off a blow. He lowered his cap over his eyes and fed papers from a black refuse sack into the flames. Madeleine McKindless's voice brought me back to the table.

'You come well recommended, Mr Rilke.'

'That's good to know – we've been doing business in Glasgow for over a hundred years.'

Her eyes glanced me up and down like the quick click of a camera shutter. A brief smile. 'I can believe it. My brother Roddy died three weeks ago, neither of us married, so I am left alone with rather a large task on my hands. You'll be wondering why I've called you in – you're a respectable firm but you're a small firm and it might have made more sense for me to go with one of the London houses.'

'It's an obvious question.'

'I want it done quick.'

'I want it done quick.'

Blue eyes that used to be bluer looking straight at me.

I should have stopped right there and asked her why, but I was already making calculations in my head, adding up time, manpower and money, wheeling straight into business as she knew I would.

'I'll need to take a look around before I can give you a preliminary estimate of how long it'll take. I'll provide you with a rough valuation by the end of the week.'

'I want the house cleared by next Wednesday. That should give you ample time to pack and warehouse it. I want it empty. If you can't do it in a week tell me now – I've chosen you, Mr Rilke, but there are others that could do the job as well.'

And I believed her. I stood my ground half-heartedly, telling her she'd not get top price, that there was only so much possible in a week, but we both knew it was a useless dance.

'I'm too old to discuss things, Mr Rilke. Either you can do it or you can't. I know it's a big job. I'm asking a lot, so there will be a commission paid directly to you on top of the auction house fee as a token of my appreciation – if you manage to get the work done on time.'

She had me.

'I'll telephone the office and have them send over some people to start valuation and packaging this afternoon. You realise we're going to have to work through the night for probably most of the week?'

'Do whatever you have to. I'll allow you unlimited access.'

She slid a jumble of keys across the table.

'Come and go as you need. I'll trust you to secure the house.'

'Well, if it's going to get done, I may as well start now. What about personal effects – papers, letters, anything of a private nature you might want to keep? Have you been through them with someone already?'

'My brother had a study on the ground floor. I'll continue to work through that myself.'

'Okay. If there's anything we think you may want to see we'll bring it to you there.'

I turned to go. I wasn't looking forward to the phone call I was about to make; three weeks' work to be done in one and the usual sale only three days away.

'Mr Rilke.'

I halted, my hand resting on the door jamb. She was staring at me hard, hesitating, as if she was trying to make up her mind about something.

'My brother had a second office at the top of the house. He had the attic floored and worked up there when he wanted total peace. It's one of those pull-down-ladder arrangements, too much for me. I would be grateful if you would work on that yourself. I don't think there will be anything of interest to me, more fuel for the bonfire I suspect, but I would appreciate your discretion.'

'You have it.'

I gave her my best smile, the one that flashes gold, and made my way upstairs.

I hate a death.

Especially a recent death with the grief – or greed – still fresh.

Dealing with the bereaved is a strain. As the man said, you never know what to expect. I have packed away lifetimes while daughters watched me and cried. I have seen siblings feud over trifles, the earth still fresh on their parent's grave. How Miss McKindless felt about her brother's death I wasn't sure.

I made my phone call. It went no better than I'd anticipated. I promised to come in at five and explain myself. The rest of the afternoon would be spent on a rough inventory – furniture, paintings and miscellaneous *objets d'art* to be removed first. Rule number one: always move the good stuff first; that way you won't lose it or drop it, and if the deal falls through, you may still get something.

The crew arrived at two, mutinous at the prospect of double

shifts. I jollied them into a semblance of good humour – told them I was sure it would be thirsty work. I could see my commission ending up down their throats come the end of the week. When they saw what we had, they quietened down. The job was big. It was a while since we'd had a whole town house and the tight schedule meant we'd need extra hands – the usual unemployed sons, brothers, cousins, dragged away from their beds and daytime soaps for cash in hand.

And it was good. Better than good. Antiques of that calibre hadn't seen the inside of a Glasgow saleroom for years, hadn't seen Bowery Auctions ever.

My apprenticeship had been served in an atmosphere of regret. The regret of my elders at the passing of 'the good stuff', the Georgian silver, treasures and spoils of empire that according to CP had littered the salerooms of his day. I'd rolled my eyes and cursed him for an old man. Now I mourned junk-shop Victoriana and art-deco bibelots. I missed the street hawkers and book barrows of Paddy's Market's prime, shook my head at what passed for quality, and pitied youth. The best was not yet to come. It had vanished for ever.

Or so I had thought.

I wandered through silent rooms, whistling under my breath. Scribbling an inventory dotted with stars and ex-clamations. Trailing my fingers along the perfect grain of furniture old when Victoria was a girl. Opening drawers to reveal trays of rare coins, stamp collections neatly hinged in albums, jewellery pouched in velvet bags, faceted crystal wrapped in tissue, good silver and fine linen of a sort found only in old houses. His sister must be the last of the line, crippled by taxes or on the lam. She was selling the heirlooms too fast, too cheap. It should have smelt wrong but my senses were overwhelmed. I kept right on going, as pleased as

Aladdin when he first rubbed that lamp and discovered his Genie.

Still, impressed as I was, I did notice an absence. Usually you get a feel for the person who used to live in the house you're clearing – little things, style, a mode of living. You find photographs, souvenirs and keepsakes. Their books reveal interests, and inside their books are clues: tickets for a train taken every day; cinema stubs; theatre programmes; letters. I've found pressed flowers, leaflets from Alcoholics Anonymous, birthday cards, the bottle behind the wardrobe, love notes, cruel letters from the bank, baby's curls, the leash of a dog long dead, neglected urns, whips, library books years overdue, size-twelve stilettos in a bachelor's apartment. Of Mr McKindless I was no wiser by the end of the day than I'd been at the beginning. There was a sterility to the collection, an almost self-conscious expense about the dead man's possessions. Everything said: *I am a very rich man*; nothing more. I found one crimp-edged photograph. A black-and-white image of a stern, ba'-faced man. His eyes looked out at me piercing, frozen. I shivered. Well, I didn't take that good a photograph myself. The inscription on the back read *Roderick, 1947*. I put the photograph absently in my pocket, then left the crew under the tutelage of my head porter, Jimmy James, and made my way back to Bowery Auctions.

It was dusk. Not five o'clock yet, but the light was fading, streets lamps glowing into life, small squares of shop windows illuminated. I crept the van along the Great Western Road, an inch behind the car in front. In the window of Zum Zum Fabrics three high-quiffed dummies cut dance poses, sheathed in silks and brocade. A couple had rung the bell of the jeweller's next door and now stood rapt over trays of dowry gold. African drumming gone funky drifted from Solly's Fruit & Fine Veg. The traffic eased onto the bridge and me with it. Beneath the orange U of the underground hot air turned to steam. Commuters disappeared into the sudden mist, some reappearing on the other side, others taking the glowing caterpillar tunnel that leads beneath the river and disappearing from view. The cab radio drifted from music to news . . . Things were still bad in Ireland, they were still fighting in Palestine, and Tories and Labour still disagreed. A boy had been stabbed outside a football ground, a toddler lost, a prostitute murdered.

I looked across the bridge and into the darkening afternoon. The last shades of light were fading into grey, night beginning to veil the park-land. I thought of my boyhood when chemicals foamed the Clyde and every sunset had been a tainted, pyrotechnic blaze. Bowery Auctions stood outlined against the sky like the hull of a mammoth upturned ship, four red-brick storeys swelling into the curved flank of tiled roof. The third floor was lit. Rose Bowery would be waiting for me.

It had started to rain; water dripped into the well at the bottom of the ancient elevator shaft. I hailed the lift and listened to the clamber of clattering chains as it descended. The tired grille creaked as a hand from within concertinaed it back.

They were the perfect couple, a rare balance of fat and thin which weighed together would equal two right-sized men. Their worn complexions, dirt-grained collars and creased jumble-sale suits spoke of late-hour, long-drinking nights and blank stumbles into unmade beds. Fats carried a sheaf of papers stuffed carelessly into a folder. Skinny made do with carrying himself. They stepped by me, lowering guilty eyes. I watched them go, wondering who they were collecting for, and if this would be the day the lift stranded me between floors. If it was, Rose Bowery would probably leave me there until an object of value came along. The lift juddered to a halt, I eased back the metal grille, the heavy outer door crashed open and there was Rose.

If Maria Callas and Paloma Picasso had married and had a daughter she would look like Rose. Black hair scraped back from her face, pale skin, lips painted torture red. She smokes Dunhill, drinks at least one bottle of red wine a night, wears black and has never married. Four centuries ago Rose would have been burnt at the stake and some days I think I would have been in the crowd cheering the action along. They call her the Whip; you might think she likes the name, she encourages it so. Rose and I have worked together since Joe Bowery died twenty years ago. I have never been so close to a woman, never wanted to be.

'So, Rilke, tell me why we are about to do three weeks' work in one?'

I settled myself on the edge of a 1960s dressing table and fingered a black hollow where a cigarette had burnt away the veneer.

'No choice, Rose. It's good stuff. We'll do well. It was take it or leave it.'

'And you thought that was a decision you could make on your own?'

'Yes.'

'Rilke, when my father left me his share in this auction house it was little better than a junk mart and organised fence. What is it now?' I raised my eyebrows; never interrupt the litany. 'It's the best auction house in Glasgow. But it'll not stay the best if you do things like this. There is no way we can shift that amount of stuff in a week.'

'Wait till you see it. We can shift it, Rose.'

'*We can shift it, Rose*. There's no *we* about it. You made this decision all on your owney-oh. What if I'd arranged something else?'

'But you haven't.'

'Lucky for you. But I could have. You've never grown up — if anything you regress a little every year. It's going to be a real push to manage this job in the time allocated. What if I *had* got something else? Whenever I think you're calming down something happens and I'm visiting the police station or the hospital. Sometimes I think you're the reason I never had kids, I've been lumbered with you since I was eighteen.' She turned away. 'Jesus, it's been some bloody afternoon.'

'The reason you never had kids, Rose, is you would strangle them in the first week. But if you've changed your mind we could probably have them together. I owe you that much. You're forever getting me out of trouble and I never have to hit anyone in your defence or mind you when you're on a tear.'

'Ach.' She waved my words away. 'Do you not think I should have been consulted?'

'It was take it or leave and it's unbelievable stuff. Christ knows why they've called us in, but be glad they have. This could make us, and if we pull our finger out we can do it in a week. Look around you. What's in here right now?'

The room had the dead feeling common to public buildings when empty of people. Without the activity of a sale it was a ghost of itself, an echoing shell. There was a junk of heavy oak furniture, monstrosities too big for modern apartments, boxes of soiled napery and bric-a-brac. Six large wardrobes stood like upright coffins against the far wall.

'For God's sake, Rose, look at those wardrobes. The Sally

Ann had a sign in their window last week, *Buy one wardrobe, get another one free.*'

'We've had better sales.'

'Woolworth's has had better sales. It's sad, Rose, sad. Crap furniture for DHSS landlords and it's been like that for weeks, months. This is good stuff, the best. I've seen it, you've not. We can shift it, but only if we stop arguing and get moving.'

Rose had taken out her cigarettes while I was talking and was searching in her handbag for her lighter. I caught a glimpse of make-up, black nylons, a packet of tampons, a sheaf of unpaid invoices, a dog-eared paperback, before she caught me watching and gave me a quick, sharp look. I took out a book of matches and sparked her up.

'Thank you.' Her tone was not entirely sincere.

'I saw your visitors leaving.'

Rose took a long drag on her cigarette, and shook her head. 'When I was a girl I thought all sheriffs would look like Alan Ladd.'

'Problem?'

'The usual. We turn over a lot, but the money we get stays the same while the price of everything else goes up. I asked the council for time to find last quarter's rates. They told me, no favours.'

'This could solve that.'

Rose took a deep breath and dredged up a smile. I knew her well enough to know she was miserable, and I appreciated the effort.

'All right,' she said, 'shall we have a drink while you tell me about it?'

'I thought you were giving up during the day?'

'It's been a hard day. Anyway it's after five.' She went into the back office and returned with a bottle of wine already two glasses low in the mark. 'Here, you're allowed one when you're driving, aren't you?'

She polished a tumbler on the edge of her skirt and handed it to me.

'Rose, did you just take this out of one of the boxes?' I nodded towards the cartons of bric-a-brac under the centre table.

'It's clean. Christ, I remember a time when you weren't bothered whether you had a glass or not, so long as there was some alcohol on the go. Now drink up and tell me all about it.'

And I did. Pleased with my prize, laying it at her feet, never once thinking where it might lead us.

2

Say Cheese

The roses every one were red,
And all the ivy leaves were black.
Sweet, do not even stir your head,
Or all of my despairs come back.

Paul Verlaine, 'Spleen'

I WAS BACK at the McKindless residence by six. I dismissed
the squad at ten with instructions to be back by eight. I had a
good, rough idea of what was in the place and knew we could
do it in a week – just. I was about to leave when I
remembered the attic.

Miss McKindless had retired some time during the
afternoon, presumably to her brother's ground-floor study.
Places look different after dark. An hour ago the house had
been full of the shouts and jokes of the porters as they
packed and shifted stuff into the vans outside, now it was

deathly still. It was strange climbing the stairs to the upper floor unsure of whether I was alone in the house. I had no wish to frighten the old lady – there's a spectral aspect to me: it's not for nothing they call me the Walking Dead – and so I sang softly to myself as I climbed, a bit of Cole Porter,

> It's the wrong time,
> In the wrong place
> Though your looks are lovely,
> It's the wrong face,
> It's not her face,
> But it's such a lovely face,
> That it's all right by me.

I thought I heard laughter, so faint I couldn't be sure whether it had come from downstairs or above me. Miss McKindless still busy at her work and amused by my rendition, no doubt, but it spooked me a little. I knocked on the door of the spare bedroom at the very top of the staircase and when there was no reply entered.

The room was the sparsest in the house, empty except for a bed, a small bedside cabinet and half a dozen chairs. The walls were a glaring white, as if they had recently been repainted. None of the chairs matched; a harlequin set, we would call them in the trade. I had been in the room earlier in the day and dismissed it as not worth a second inspection. Perhaps it was the late hour and tiredness but now there seemed something sinister about the arrangement of the chairs. They were grouped round the bed as if six people had kept vigil. Perhaps they had: this was a house of death, after all. Perhaps Mr McKindless had requested a spartan room in his last days.

Still, the arrangement gave me the creeps. I moved the chairs into a row against the far wall, opened the drawer of the bedside cabinet and looked in. At the very back was a small white object. I slid my hands in and retrieved it. It was an intricately carved netsuke. The ivory was cool, smooth against my hands, responding to the heat of my flesh, growing warmer as I turned it in my palms. At first I couldn't make out what it was meant to depict. There was a confusion of limbs, a complex jigsaw of bodies that formed a perfect sphere my eye found difficult to disentangle. Then, as puzzles do, it all came into focus and I dropped it on the bed. There were three bodies, two female, one male. The blade of the carver had rendered them round and chubby, but athletic never-theless. They gripped each other in an erotic combination impossible in actual life, but that was not what had shocked me. What made me drop the ball was the look on the face of the carved man, a leer that pulled you in, a complicit stare that drew attention to the dagger in his hand, for as he penetrated one girl with his cock, he stabbed the other through her heart. The features of the stabbed girl were caught between surprise and pain. Her companion as yet knew nothing of her fate: her expression was of simple delight in the game. It was a truly horrible object and worth several hundred pounds. I took out my silk handkerchief, wrapped the netsuke in it and placed it in my pocket.

The ladder to the attic was folded against the ceiling, as Miss McKindless had described. I found a pole behind the door and hooked it down. I could see why the old lady would find access impossible. I hadn't mentioned it, but despite my height, I'm not good at altitude. I put my foot on the first rung, the aluminium rattle sounding loud against the silence of the house, and climbed. The trap had a Yale and a mortise lock. I struggled for a minute or two, holding the ladder with one hand, fumbling around in my pockets for the keys with the other, changing hands, finding the keys, then searching for the right ones in the anonymous jumble. The ground started to slip away. I reeled against the ladder, realising I was about to lose balance, then a key turned smoothly in the mortise, the Yale beside it clicked home, I pushed open the trap door and hauled myself in.

I stood for a minute in the dark, half crouched, my hands on my knees, trying to catch my breath, then, unsure of the height of the ceiling, cautiously straightened and felt for the light switch.

I was standing in a long, thin room perhaps half the length of the house. Bare floorboards, clean for an attic. The ceiling began midway up the walls, angling to a peak. Three small windows that would let in a little light during the day. Along the right-hand wall were racks of metal shelving holding tidily stacked cardboard boxes. The left wall was covered in waist-high, dark oak bookcases, books neatly arranged. In the centre were a plain office desk and chair, to their left a high-backed armchair, comfortable but scruffy, inherited from some other room, beside it a bottle of malt, Lagavulin. Dead man's drink. I unscrewed the cap and inhaled a quick scent of iodine and peat which caught the back of my throat. It was the good stuff, right enough. There was no cup so I took the end of my shirt and rubbed it along the mouth of the bottle before taking a good slug. I was curious about the contents of the cardboard boxes but turned first to the bookcase.

It is revealing how people arrange their books. I was once in a house where the couple, man and wife, committed collectors of first editions, had placed every book in a sealed plastic bag, then on the shelves, spine in, pages out. 'That way they won't get sun-damaged,' they explained. Others arrange books according to height, the tallest first, top shelf, left-hand corner, tapering down to the tiniest at the very bottom. Me, I have them willy-nilly, on suitcase, shelf and floor.

Mr McKindless had employed the age-old method of alphabetical by author, with the occasional grouping of publisher. Regimented over three shelves was a large collection of Olympia Press. Little green and white paperbacks pressed together – *The Sex Life of Robinson Crusoe, Stradella, White Thighs, The Chariot of Flesh, With Open Mouth* . . .

I have always admired Maurice Girodias. He founded the Olympia Press some time in the 1950s in Paris. Pornography was in the family, but before he put his profits into a hotel and lost he was a master of the art. Girodias would invent (un)suitable titles, advertise them as available for sale, and then, depending on the response to his advertisements, commission a writer to produce the book. Many a penurious writer subsisted on his cheques and not a few successful ones lost their royalties. He claimed that some tourists came to the city simply to purchase his titles. I agreed. The Olympia Press concentrated on the avant-garde, particularly sex, and people will travel further than Paris for that. Like many collectors McKindless seemed to have been compelled to own every title. I scanned through the novels. Yes, here it was, the first edition of Burroughs's *The Naked Lunch* in its slip case. I had never handled one before. All the Henry Miller was here, too. The Olympia novels were just a start. Shelves and shelves of erotic fiction. It was a library that would fetch something. I took a rough note, glad it wasn't me who would have to manoeuvre the boxes down the ladder. Here was the private man. The personality I had missed below stairs, confined to the attic like a mad Victorian relative.

I pulled open the drawer to the desk and had a look inside. Stationery, some nice pens, nothing much. Out of habit my fingers skimmed the underside of the drawer. There was something taped there. I took out my penknife and slit it free. A simple white card. `⊘PM camera⊘club` Cryptic. I replaced the drawer and slipped the card into my pocket.

I considered stopping. Almost left right there. It was the whisky that drew me back. One more drink, leave the van in the driveway till morning, last orders at the Melrose, then a walk through the park and see what gave. It was the good stuff. A reward for working so hard, being clever enough to arrange a big deal, a pat on the back from me to me.

I should know myself: that bottle was too full and I was too empty. I took it with me and started on box number one, the kind of thing all good citizens leave behind, paperwork, old documents, things that really could have been thrown away and kept for why? The next two boxes were pretty much the same, old magazines, records, more paper, my progress was slowing, the bottle halfway lower in its mark than when I began. One more box I decided – leave it on an even number, while I could still negotiate the ladder. At first it looked like more of the same. The general detritus of life, bumf, short for bum fodder, bills filed then kept to no purpose, bank statements – all showing an impressive balance – insurance policies never claimed on.

To anyone watching, my investigations would have appeared haphazard, but I have the skill of the searcher. Without looking I can sort silk from cotton velvet, cashmere from angora, I can tell with my finger tips an etching from a print. And I can turn base metal into gold. I think that if there is anything good in a box I will find it. Who knows what's passed me by?

It was an envelope. Just a buff-coloured, thick-papered, document envelope. Straight away I knew it held photographs. I could feel them, the weight, the uniform size, photos not good enough for an album. Two thick rubber bands secured the folds, one pink, one blue. Pink for a girl. Blue for a boy. I pulled the bands off, slipping them tight round my wrist, they caught in the hairs of my arm, swift visions of mad nights. I kept them there, a taut reminder, and slid the photographs into my hand.

Mr McKindless is wearing a white shirt and bow tie. His hair has lost some of its Brylcreemed bounce, it lies damp and plastered across his forehead. His attention is focused on the young girl in his arms. She is pretty, pale-faced and lipsticked. Her head thrown backwards in his embrace, her dark curls, ringlets almost, tumbling away from her face. She is naked except for suspenders and stockings, and seems almost asleep. McKindless looks as if he is talking, trying to rouse her. Still she gazes, sleepy and smiling, not at him but towards the man who is entering her. This second man is half out of frame, a torso of chest and arms and erect cock, his right hand pointing towards his member, his left on his hip like some music-hall queer. A second girl, dressed like the other, sprawls carelessly to his right, her cunt revealed. She lies watching McKindless and his companion, her left leg under the other's left arm. She looks bored. I have seen factory girls look that way towards the end of their shift.

The background was anonymous, a black and white stripe of wallpaper, a door frame, but I guessed they were in Paris. These, no doubt, were what had required my discretion. I wanted to go home. I took another tilt at the whisky and turned the photograph over. Written on the reverse, in pencil, was *Soleil et Désolé*.

I began to flick through the rest. More of the same. Mr McKindless in sweaty action, his thin, pigeon chest, hairless and neon white – well, even a spider has a body. Then girls, girls, girls. Some holding power in their gaze, others wretched, sad.

A housewife, head bent, lifts her dress, hiding her face, revealing her sex. Two girls undo their clothing, look into each others eyes, and, laughing, touch. Breast to breast, tongue to tongue. A woman is sprawled on a bench. White gloves lie next to her on the seat. She pulls her jumper up over her head, hiding her face, displaying her breasts.

I could date them roughly from the clothes. Stockings held just above the knee, patterned day dresses in cotton and crêpe de Chine, suede shoes with high, thick heels. Postwar, but only just. Had Mr McKindless been a Tommy with a Box Brownie? The background varied, different rooms and studios, but they had poverty in common.

A girl stands in a bath, soaping herself before the lens.

Now she is climbing out of the tub, bending, exposing her rear like some Degas beauty.

The room was stark. It reminded me of the high-ceilinged, linoleum-floored, kidney-chilling bathrooms of my youth.

A woman fingers her crotch in a kitchen, a broom is propped against the wall behind her, she is wearing felt slippers.

Now Mr McKindless again, face flushed with drink and pleasure. A more formal arrangement this time. McKindless and another man, undressed sentinels, a naked lady reclines on the crest of a sofa, posing between them. Her arms are raised above her head in an arch; she has the flourish of Anna

Pavlova. McKindless is half supporting her, one arm round her thin waist, the other on her thigh. Beneath them, on the seat, a man and woman embrace. The woman breaks the clinch, saying something to a person out of view, something drunken and funny and strident. Whoever she addresses it isn't the photographer. Her look is directed away from the lens. Each man wears a fez at a jaunty angle. Everyone is laughing.

A long time ago these people had moved and talked and laughed. The photographer had pressed the button, the shutter had clicked, their shadows captured on film. Forever young, debauched and laughing. What had she said, the woman at the front of the photograph? I could feel her energy. The instant the photograph was taken she had leapt to her feet and . . . If I could look with the right eyes I would see her move. Her tiny frame would stand, sashay across the room, turn to me and . . .

There was someone downstairs. It wasn't so much a noise as a slight change in the atmosphere, a draught perhaps as the door had been opened, but I knew someone was in the room below.

I slipped the photographs back into their envelope and put them in my inside pocket. I had almost killed the bottle. I took a hit for courage and walked over to the trap.

'Hello?'

Even to my own ears my voice sounded shaky. Beneath me someone took three swift steps to the door, then closed it gently behind them. The footsteps faded down the stairs, the front door slammed. Had it been left unlocked when the squad had finished earlier in the day? Christ, we get the biggest call we've had all year and it's burglarised under our noses. The old lady was probably dead in her bed, murdered by some psycho we'd invited in with open door. I rattled down the ladder, forgetting to be afraid of the height.

Everything was as I had left it, the chairs neat against the wall. Out in the hallway all the doors were shut. I made my way down to the ground floor, where we had stacked most of the good stuff. It all looked pretty much the same. Finally I checked the front door: locked. Whoever had been creeping around in the middle of the night had a key. I went upstairs, secured the attic, put the ladder back in its resting place and left.

3

A Walk in the Park

O Rose, thou art sick!
The invisible worm
That flies in the night,
In the howling storm,

Has found out thy bed
Of crimson joy:
And his dark secret love
Does thy life destroy.

William Blake,
'The Sick Rose'

OUT IN THE STREET I looked at my watch: a quarter to three.
For a second I considered going to the pool room for one last
drink and some company, but instead turned my back on
Hyndland and walked towards the West End.

It was raining. A faint drizzle that was almost a mist. The pavements were shiny with rain and the reflected orange glow of the street lamps. I trudged solidly on, putting the cod respectability of Hyndland further behind me with every step. I felt in need of an exorcism. The smell of bad beer hung in the air outside Tennents Bar, even three hours after closing. The lights were on, the staff inside having a lock-in. I could stop, give the knock and Davie boy would let me in for a final few before bedtime, but it wasn't drink or bed that I wanted. I crossed the lights at Byres Road. Still busy, even at this time in the morning. A drunk careened past me, hands in his pockets, head down, making his way home with drunk man's radar. 'Ahway ta fuck, you auld poof' he muttered.

I pulled up the collar of my raincoat and walked on. Climbing the rise of University Avenue, towards the illuminated towers of the university, their haze clouding any view of the stars. It was getting quieter now. I descended towards Gilmorehill Cross, then turned right into Kelvin Way, avenue of dreams.

Kelvin Way is edged by park-land and university grounds. Mature limes line either side of the road, towering above the street lights. Their roots escape the concrete, gnarled talons, making a journey along the street a negotiation of puddles and fissures. The tops of the trees danced gently in the rain, Arthur Rackham silhouettes, branches clutching at each other, casting crazy shadows and darkness. After a straight boy was mistaken for a queer and murdered, an attempt had been made to make the street brighter, stringing lamps across the centre of the road. They only added to the charm, bobbing negligently in the wind.

A car passed me slowly, a BMW, lights dimmed. The driver moved slightly in his seat, glancing towards me, looking without looking, me seeing him, no eye contact. It wasn't a walking corpse he was after. He stopped ahead of me. A slim figure detached itself from beneath a tree and got into the car.

If you like a bit of rough and have drowned your fear and your conscience, this is the place to come.

'Looking for business?'

It's like a mantra on The Way. A boy leaning against the tree in front of me. How old? Fourteen? Sixteen? He was wearing the current uniform of shapeless sports gear. White cap, white top, blue sweat pants. I think of him as a ghost. A whey-faced spectre. He had found a short cut on that road we all travel. His head was nodding, falling forward gently, then just as gently straightening, as if the weight of his head and gravity together were too much for him. Jellied. Gouching. Glazed eyes seeking mine.

'Looking for business, Mister?'

'No, son. Not tonight.'

He stepped back to his post, passive, as if he had forgotten me already. Junkies and whores are used to waiting.

I crossed the street and slipped into the park. The dawn was beginning to slink in, black drifting to grey. I took the hump-backed bridge over the Kelvin. The rain was heavier now. I could hear it against the rush of the river. Damn it, I was going to be soaked. Christ, only the desperate would be here tonight and, while I was desperate myself, it wasn't desperate company I was seeking. I veered right and took a turn round the fountain. It had been erected as a tribute to the man who brought fresh water from Loch Katrine to the city of Glasgow. It stood there dry, derelict and neglected. Rain, beating an irregular tattoo against the rubbish, gathered in its trough, graffiti sprayed across its statuary and enamelled zodiac plaques. I examined the most recent legends. *God is*

Gay, SEX Credit cards acepted, Nicholson bangs monkeys. Well, Nicholson, I thought, I've been there. Sometimes you just have to make the best of things.

I turned my back on the fountain, walked past the kids' playground and towards the duckpond. Litter lined its border, shreds of the day. Crisp packets, juice bottles and no doubt not a few condoms. Everywhere I could sense decay. The pigeons were roosting on a skeletal willow poised above the water. Grey, tattered feathers fluffed out to protect them from the rain. Winged rats.

A figure moved ahead of me, breaking from the cover of trees, into the no man's land of the pathway, light-coloured jacket unveiling him against the early-morning shadows. 'Good man,' I whispered to myself, 'wear white at night.' He walked towards the war memorial. The sculpted kiltie rested above the lists of dead boys' names, gazing towards a world without wars. He paid us no mind. My quarry turned his head slightly, making sure I was on his trail and I knew we were going to be fine. He led me up a pathway towards a bench sheltered in the lee of a tree. My eyes had adjusted to the darkness. When he turned I saw a well-set man of around thirty. I couldn't make out his features entirely yet. Don't let him speak, I thought walking towards him, making eye contact. His right hand was in his pocket, I thought I could make out the bulge of his erection. I was so close I could hear his sigh, smell the faint odour of beer on his breath. I reached out, meaning to touch him, and he took my arm in a firm grip:

'You've got something I want.'

The words were close enough to a menace. I tensed, and my free hand formed into a fist. Then he was on his knees and it was the usual routine.

I was fishing around for a condom in my pocket – it's only etiquette to reciprocate – when I heard it. The ear-splitting, propeller clatter of the spy in the sky. Light flooded the park. My new friend ran towards the top path and out towards the deserted office quarter of Park Circus. There were footsteps everywhere around me, enchanted shadows made whole, men fleeing across the grass and the scree of the pathways, and there I'd been afraid of not getting a click. I turned to run in the direction of Woodlands. There was a gate by Caledonia College I could scale at a leap. Then there was a hand on my shoulder and a torch in my face and I knew the game was up.

We were a sad crew, the half-dozen of us in the police van. After we'd each been cautioned for lewd behaviour nobody spoke. I took out my tobacco and rolled myself a smoke. No one stopped me. We hadn't reached the camaraderie of the jail-house yet and I didn't offer them around. I was thinking about what I had on me. Rule number one of cruising: remember the dangers. You may be mugged or arrested. Do not carry anything that may incriminate you or get you into more trouble. In my pocket was a wrap of speed, a quarter of grass so good it might be class A, a packet of extra-thick condoms and a selection of pornographic photographs I hadn't fully perused.

At Partick police station I made myself last in line. I hadn't seen a mirror but I guessed I didn't cut quite such a dashing figure now. The rain had soaked through my raincoat, into my suit, and through my shirt. My hair hung long and lank against my face. My only hope was that I looked so bad they wouldn't bother to search me. Looking at the going-over they were giving the unsavoury collection in front of me I knew there was no hope. I did the only thing you can do in circumstances

like these. I kept my head down and waited for something to
turn up.

I'm not new to the routine. Name, address, date of birth.
The things they always want to know. Then,

'Empty your pockets.'

One thing after the other; wallet, penknife, notebook;
pushing the wrap and the deal into a hole in the lining of my
suit jacket; my keys, the McKindless keys, loose change.
'Speed it up or I'll do it for you.' The netsuke. 'C'mon, get
on with it.' I reached for the envelope of photographs. The
ones I'd seen were this side of legal, and they might keep the
sergeant's attention long enough for me to get away with the
drugs. If they took a notion to search my flat I was in trouble.
'We don't have all night.' I smiled, pulled the envelope from
my pocket, then beside me a slim, dark man in a blue suit.

'Been misbehaving, Rilke? All right, Sergeant, Mr Rilke's
just coming into my office for a little chat.' I shoved the
envelope back in my jacket before it could be taken from me.
'You keep his things safe for him. Except this, let's have a
closer look at this.'

He picked up the netsuke and walked on with me, meek as
a rescued felon, behind him. My companions followed us with
their eyes, cursing me for a grass.

'In here.' We entered an office at the end of the hall and I
tried to gather myself together. 'Sit.' He indicated a hard
chair opposite his desk. 'And will you take that bloody
raincoat off – you're dripping all over the place.' I peeled
it from me and bundled it under the chair. 'So, Rilke. Can you
not learn some discretion? Are there not clubs you can go to if
you want to do that kind of thing? Would it not be pleasanter
for you? A wee gin and tonic, a trot around the dance floor
then back to a bachelor pad for whatever it is you want to do.

Are you not getting a bit old for skulking about in bushes?'

'I'm not much of a dancer, Inspector Anderson.'

'Always quick with the answers, though. You were the same at school. Look at you. What a bloody state to get yourself into.' He picked up the phone, 'Two cups of tea through here quick as you can.' Turning back to me, 'I probably should have just let them search you there. Aye, you always had interesting things in your pockets, Rilke.'

'The guy I met in the park certainly thought so.'

'It would maybe be as well to remember that I'm the law. I've rescued you from an embarrassment. Why not? We go back a long way. But don't take the piss.' He picked up the netsuke and turned it over in his hand. 'This is a horrible wee relic. I tell you, if this isn't against the law it should be.' A uniform came in with the tea, thick porcelain mug for Anderson, polystyrene cup for me. 'Now tell me about this thing.'

He placed it on the desk between us with a quick squint of distaste at the grinning murderer.

'It's a netsuke. Japanese, probably nineteenth-century though hard to date. They were originally a carved toggle – a posh version of those buttons we had on our duffels all those years ago. Japanese gents would have used them to tether their purses, which they wore dangling from their waists. They developed into ornaments popular in the export market. They're generally made of wood or ivory. This one, as you can probably see, is of the ivory variety.'

'I didn't stop you there because I found that genuinely interesting. But I think you know what I meant. Where did you get it?'

'A job I was on today. I'm clearing a house up in Hyndland and I came across this last thing. I just wrapped it in my hanky and shoved it in my pocket. It's worth a lot of money.'

'This kind of thing depresses me. You've got a craftsman, no, an artist, he can create anything he wants and this is what he comes up with, a piece of filth. You know, half the blokes I see in here, they're not clever. They're fuck-ups for the most part. No wits. No chance. You feel sorry for some of them, but mostly they just bore you. There's too many of them. Now and again though you find an evil, clever bastard and that's what the guy who made this was. Tell me about the man who owned this.'

'What, you on a slow night tonight?'

'Just humour me. I've got this predilection – you could say it goes with the job. I'm used to people answering my questions. I find they generally prefer it to the alternative.'

'I'm beginning to wish you'd left me out there.'

'It can be arranged.'

'Okay. I can't tell you much so there's no harm in telling you what I know. I started clearing a house in Hyndland today. A death. Natural causes, as far as I'm aware. Party by the name of McKindless.'

'McKindless.' He turned the word over in his mouth like he was feeling it with his tongue, savouring the syllables. 'McKindless.' The vowels soft then hard. 'That's a name with a history.'

'Tell me.'

'I don't know yet, but it rang a bell in the old police belfry. Leave it with me and if I think it's interesting I might look you up.'

'I'd appreciate it.'

'Aye, you're interested aren't you? Makes me wonder what else you found in there.'

'I was only called in today.'

'Well, let me know if you find any bodies. C'mon then. Believe it or not, there's actual crime going on in this city. I'll get you past the front desk.' He stood and led me towards the door. 'And Rilke.' I turned towards him. 'You did me a favour a long time ago. I've not forgotten. But mind yourself, there's only so much I can do.'

I looked at him, the middle-aged policeman in a suit, and remembered the boy he'd been.

'I'll mind myself.'

'Good lad.'

I collected my paraphernalia from the duty sergeant and then went out to face the day.

4

The Final Frame

I could not love except where Death
Was mingling his with Beauty's breath.

Edgar Allan Poe,
'Introduction' (1831)

WHEN I WOKE IN the morning I lay and stared at the ceiling for a long time, then leant over and reached for my jacket lying damp on the floor near my mattress where I'd flung it the night before. I felt in the pocket to see if my tobacco and papers were dry enough to roll a smoke, and came across the envelope, stiff with its bundle of photographs. The tobacco was passable, the papers stuck together and useless. I rooted around the room until I found another packet, then got back beneath the covers to smoke. I unfastened the envelope, flicked through the images I had already seen, pulled the next photograph from the pile and stopped.

There are three people, two men and a woman. They are in a basement or cellar; on the wall behind them rough plaster gives way to bare bricks. The men wear monks' habits, coarse robes secured by cord, long-sleeved and hooded. The hoods throw shadows across their faces, concealing their features. The woman is young, thin, and naked, save for a delicate silver bracelet round one wrist. Her hands and feet are bound together and secured to either end of a long bench. Her calves and the small of her back lie against raised bars, the bars shot through with spikes which cut into her flesh. The rope that secures her wrists is attached to a ratchet, the monks are engaged in turning a wheel which pulls the rope taut, stretching her body and pulling her down further onto the spikes. They have her on a rack.

The flash had been overexposed, rendering the woman a bleached white against the dark background. The monks were in sharp focus but she was almost a negative. Her features had vanished, save for the anxious dots of her pupils and the open gasp of her mouth. I looked at the photograph a long time. Did she want them to do that to her? There was no way of telling. It was too long ago. There were only a few photographs left in the pile. I turned over the next one.

The same girl, still naked, lies on a wooden pallet. Hanging on the wall behind her is a hessian sheet. It has been put there to act as a backdrop, but falls short of the edge of the frame, exposing a rough brick wall. I stare at the wall for quite a while. The woman has been cruelly treated. There are the raised marks of a whipping on her stomach and thighs. Her ankles, calves and knees are bound with bristly rope which digs into her flesh. Her hands are tight behind her back, presumably secured. She lies slightly on her right side, towards the camera. Her breasts have been roughly bound, the rope twisted three times round them, distorting their shape, crushing them to her. Her head lolls backwards. She is still the whitest thing I ever saw but I can distinguish her features now, distorted, ghastly. Pupils unfocused and far back in her head, a mouth that ended with a scream. Her throat has been cut. Blood flows from her wound, slicks its way across the pallet and drips onto the floor. I wonder if it stains the photographer's boots.

For the final photograph the photographer has stepped a little closer. The girl lies on the same wooden boards. Now she is wrapped in a white sheet, only her bare feet exposed. A rope is coiled round her length from neck to ankle, securing her shroud, defining the shape of her body. A gag is tied, on top of the sheet, round her mouth. I can see her arms lying straight against her hips.

I'm not sure how long I sat there after that. I felt peaceful. A little boat on a calm ocean. My mind was completely empty. I could hear my neighbour's tread on the floor above me. Four steps from his bed to the hallway, the click, clack, tap of the Rottweiler following in his wake. Perhaps I should get a dog. I was tired of people. I took my baccy and rolled myself another cigarette. My hands had a bit of a tremble on but they remembered what to do. I sat and smoked it in silence. Then, though I didn't feel like it, looked at the photographs again. Were they real? They felt authentic, but that meant nothing. I put them back in their envelope, fastening them once more with the elastic bands. I wanted to think about what I had just seen. If there had been a murder, she'd been dead a long time. There would be hours to spend in a police station at some point, no doubt, but even with Anderson's backing Partick constabulary might have me confessing to a Parisian sex crime committed when I was a wee boy. Still, there was no way I wanted a casual search finding these in my inside pocket. I lifted the loose floorboard under my mattress and placed them beside the revolver. Then I glanced at my wristwatch lying on the floor beside me. Eight-thirty. I should have met the crew at the McKindless house half an hour ago. I managed a quick cold shave, dressed and left.

I was back in Hyndland for nine. The squad were outside waiting for me, half a dozen of them, two Lutons. One empty, ready for today's load, the other full of yesterday's loot. The back of the second van was raised, the crew sitting in a parody of a living room, among the furniture we had packed the day before. Nobody greeted me. Disapproval hung rank in the air. I could see the unfurled *Daily Records*, the front-page photograph of the dead callgirl, smell the sweet, milky coffee and hot rolls. Before I rounded the corner this had been a merry scene, with my defection the main topic. Now they looked at their feet and chewed on their breakfasts. They'd had an hour to ruminate on my faults as an auctioneer and as a man. Jimmy James, the head porter, shook his head slowly. Niggle, the youngest of the crew, excited by my folly and not wise enough yet to bide his time, broke the silence.

'You're awfy late, Mr Rilke.'

'And you're awfy kind to get me my breakfast, Niggle.'

I relieved him of the potato scone and egg roll he had been about to raise to his mouth and helped myself to a foam cup of coffee that was marking a ring on the polished surface of an occasional table. His expression buckled.

'Oh, dinnae greet, son. Someone give him another roll

before he starts bubbling. And the rest of yous, what are you waiting on?'

I set them to. One squad up to the warehouse to empty the first van, the other filling the second. They would go like this all day, keeping a steady pace, Jimmy James in charge. I didn't intend to be there for long. There was the usual sale to be attended to. In the normal course of things this would be a courtesy call. Just stick my head round the door and make sure everything was going smoothly. No upsets or squabbles. The householder happy, the team polite, but today there was something else I needed to do.

Miss McKindless was in the downstairs study. I chapped on the door gently and she bade me enter in her young, schoolteacherish voice.

'Mr Rilke. You look as though you've been working hard.'

Getting picked up by the police tends to have an ageing effect.

'Are you satisfied with your progress?'

'So far we're on schedule. Accidents barred, I'd say we'll be out of your hair in a week's time as requested.'

'You're hovering.' She laid down her pen and removed her spectacles. Those blue eyes bored through me. 'Is there something particular you'd like to discuss?'

'Well yes . . .'

She leaned back in her chair.

'Take a seat.'

I settled myself in front of her. Now was my opportunity. My chance to get rid of the photographs. Pass the whole sorry mess over to someone else.

There was a framed portrait photograph on her desk. A black-and-white image taken a long time ago. I lifted it. Dark eyes stared malevolently from the past. I felt that, had I met this man, I would have known myself in the presence of evil.

'Your brother?'

'That's Roddy, yes.'

'A handsome man.'

'I'm sure that's not what you wanted to discuss.'

'No, I'm sorry.' I wondered if the portrait had always lived in this room or if she had moved it there herself in an attempt to keep her brother close. Her devotion touched me. I wondered how much she knew of his life. 'You told me you'd never been in your brother's upstairs study.'

'I believe I told you that on our first meeting, yes.'

'I wanted a word about its contents.'

'Get to the point Mr Rilke. You don't have time for hovering or havering if you're going to get the job done on time. Tell me what it is that you found.'

'It contained a significant library.'

'I see.' Her voice remained calm. She lifted her pen and drew a small cross on the blotter in front of her. 'My brother was always a keen reader.'

A second cross marked the page, followed by another.

'These were books he may have wanted to keep private.'

She laughed.

'Mr Rilke, the moment I saw you I knew you were the man for me. A born diplomat. Yes it is possible that he might have wanted to keep them private. Do you think that explains why he kept them in a locked attic inaccessible to the rest of the household?'

I levelled my hands on the table. 'It seems a reasonable hypothesis.'

'It does, doesn't it? Dispose of them.'

At first her meaning eluded me.

'I was going to suggest that you might want to enter them for a specialist book sale. They could realise an impressive sum if there was the right interest in the room. It would mean Bowery storing them for a month or two but I think you might be impressed by the return and—'

She levelled her gaze. 'I want them burnt.'

I spoke before I thought. 'Miss McKindless, this is a significant collection. I know the nature of the material may offend, but some of these books are worth a great deal of money.'

Her pen scratched across the paper.

'I am an old lady. I have as much money as I need.'

'They are worth a lot of money because they are rare editions of significant texts. Many of these books were produced in extremely short print runs. There are editions there that you come across once in a lifetime. Once in a lifetime if you're lucky.'

'Look at your right hand, Mr Rilke. It's shaking. Is it the thought of the money or the books?'

'Both.' That and the hangover. 'You don't destroy this kind of material. If you don't want to profit by the library, gift it. I can make arrangements. No one need ever know where it came from.'

'I want it gone. Burnt and no trace left. If you need this sale as much as I think you do, you'll do it for me before the week is out. If you're too squeamish, there are other auction houses, other auctioneers.'

'Apart from anything else, clearing the attic would involve a considerable amount of work. Books are heavy, Miss McKindless.'

'I've already told you. I'm an old lady with too much money and no one to leave it to. Bill me. I'll make the cheque out to yourself or Bowery Auctions, whatever you prefer. Or perhaps cash would be better. "Cash is king." Isn't that what they say, Mr Rilke?'

'They say a lot of things, Miss McKindless. It isn't the money.'

'No? Okay, let's accept that you are a man with your own code of honour.' She drew a final cross. The once white page had been transformed into a graveyard. 'I'm sorry if I'm compromising you, but nevertheless, if you want to hold this sale I'm afraid you must render me this service. I prefer to pay, rather than simply trust you. Experience has taught me that is the best way.' She met my gaze. 'I intend no slur on your integrity. I want you to do it, Mr Rilke. By all means get help removing the contents of the attic, but I want it to be you who lights the fire, your hands that put the books, and any associated material, into the flames.'

'I could prepare an inventory. You wouldn't be required to see or handle any of the material, just to sign a release.'

'I want to know nothing, see nothing. Not a single title. Not a scrap of paper. Render me this service, Mr Rilke. Were I a young woman I would do it myself, but time has caught up with me.'

I looked perplexed, then gave her a sad smile and nodded. In my head I agreed to nothing. *I can smile and smile and be a villain still.*

'Can I trust you, Mr Rilke?'

I thought of the guilty stash of photographs beneath my floorboards. To reveal them would be to lose the sale.

'As you say, Bowery Auctions are very keen to secure your custom.'

'I'd prefer a yes or no.'

'Yes. Yes, you can trust me.' Beneath the table I crossed my fingers like a deceitful child.

'Well, then, let us both get on.' Her voice was brisker, as if she regretted revealing a weakness. 'We've both got things to do and time is of the essence.'

She nodded dismissal and returned to her work.

In the hallway four of the crew were manoeuvring a lacquered Japanese cabinet down the staircase. I paused, admiring the black gleam of the uncrackled glaze, the tiny figures traversing the Bridge of Happiness, painted over and over again on its drawers, its fragile shelves and compartments. A good £4000. Jimmy James halted three boys, carrying a rolled Chinese rug, at the top of the stairs. I ran up to the second floor, nodding to him as I went by. He blew his nose on an old rag and ignored me.

The next floor was deserted. I entered the spare bedroom and pulled down the ladder. There wasn't enough time or privacy for me to give the attic the going over I wanted. If there was a mystery to Mr McKindless, the solution was likely in that room. I took a screwdriver out of my pocket, removed the mortise and replaced it with a new one I'd picked up that morning. It wouldn't hold off the determined, but they'd have to make a bit of a noise and at least I would know someone had been motivated enough to break in. I tidied the mess of wood chippings away and left through the front door without a goodbye to anyone.

Back at the flat I showered, dressed, then dug the photographs from their hiding place. They were no easier to look at and made no more sense than they had the first time. I could see the roughness of the rope, stray fibres escaping the weave. I knew how that rope would feel, but I knew nothing else.

There was a photocopyist's on my route. I stopped by and asked to use one of their machines. The assistant looked too young to guard the shop on her own. She came out from behind the counter.

'We're not busy the now, give them to me and I'll do it for you. How many copies do you need?'

I'd taken the photographs out of my wallet. She held out her hand, smiling.

'I'd rather do it myself if you don't mind.'

She was insistent. 'It's no trouble. This place is like a morgue. I tell you, you could die of boredom in here some days.'

I laid on the patter. 'Thanks for the offer, but I'm an auctioneer and these are delicate, old photographs. I need to copy them for a potential bidder. I'm better handling them myself, that way if they get damaged it's my fault.'

The girl looked impressed. 'Can I have a look?'

I prayed for someone to come through the door and distract her, but she was right, it was like a morgue in there.

'I'd love to show them to you but I'm in a bit of a rush. Do you mind if I just copy them quickly?'

Her bottom lip petted forward. 'Suit yourself.'

She huffed towards a photocopier and switched it on.

I placed the pictures of the tortured girl gently, face down on the machine, closed its lid, pressed the button and watched as the image scrolled forth, the ink still damp, frozen on paper, the outrage revealed, repeated. I did the same with the pictures of McKindless. The machine hummed through its task, sliding out the wretched scenes. I felt myself almost falling into a trance. The photocopier stopped. I gathered my copies, headed to the desk and counted the pages in front of her, taking care not to display the horrible facsimiles.

'Sorry about being in such a rush.' The girl rang the price up on the till, 'You should come round the auction house one day. There's a sale every second Saturday, it's interesting. I'll give you a wave from the rostrum.'

She smiled as she handed over my change. My pal again.

A block from the shop, I realised what I had done, turned on my heels and ran. Too late. The girl stood, motionless, a frightened mannequin, next to the machine I had used. She'd lifted the lid and now stood holding a photograph, a tangle of naked bodies, McKindless at the centre. A spider in a web of flesh. I took the photograph from her limp grip, whispered, 'Sorry,' and left.

I had an idea of what I was going to do next. My game is knowledge and contacts. What your own knowledge can't tell you, your contacts might. Balfour and Sons started taking photographs of Glasgow when busy tugs still chuffed along the Broomielaw and Highlanders conversed in Gaelic on Jamaica Bridge. The black and gold sign above their door dates their establishment to 1882 and their back catalogue covers almost every part of the city through the last century. I'd helped them fill gaps in that catalogue over the years, calling on them whenever I found something I thought they might like. They are known for being a good family firm, close, like all these old business families. No under-the-counter trade there. They'd treated me with politeness and courtesy and I was going to thank them by spoiling their day. But they had been born with silver nitrate in their veins and if anyone could tell me whether these photographs were real it would be one of the Balfour boys. I peered through the window, trying to make out who was inside, hoping for Dougie, the eldest brother, but unable to see the interior for the prints crowding the display. I walked round to the side of the building and entered the shop.

'Well, Mr Rilke, long time no see. How have you been?' Mrs Balfour was the kind of mother every boy thought he might like. Neat, well dressed, a short practical woman. Who knows, she might have beaten her boys every night of their lives with a wire coat hanger, but she made me think of mince and tatties and stories at bedtime. I'm apt to be sentimental about other people's mothers. There was a large sheet of glass on a carpeted workbench, Mrs Balfour was poised over it, halfway through cutting it down to frame size. She looked up at me quickly, the laser-sharp scalpel still in her hand.

'Just give me a minute, son. If I stop now I'll make a mess of this.'

I watched the blade as she guided it gently through the glass, using a steel ruler a foot long to mark the line. I thought of an Arctic vessel creeping slowly under dark skies, skirting icebergs, destined to sink; then, with a final snap, the scalpel broke free. She straightened up and smiled at me.

'Now, that's it. Sorry to keep you waiting. What can I do for you? Is there something in the saleroom you think we might like?'

'Not at the moment, Mrs Balfour. I might have something coming up, you never know. This is more in the way of a social call. Is Dougie around?'

The smile didn't move but there was a quick flicker behind her eyes that told me she thought I'd come to try and borrow money. I'm not in the habit of making social calls, and if it were business I'd be as well talking to her.

'I've not got any Balfour plates, but I've come across some other material I'd like his advice on.'

'Something you'd rather I didn't see?'

She was sharp.

'I'd not be comfortable showing it to you.'

'You're a gentleman, Rilke. Softer than you look. I doubt it's anything I haven't seen before, but I respect your honesty.

Dougie's not here.' She smiled, and there was a bitterness in this smile. 'He's in his office. Why don't you go and chat to him there?' I made a move to walk round the counter. 'No, son, not that office, he's in Lester's, three doors up.'

And I realised she'd not been worried I was going to borrow money, she'd thought I might be due it.

There's a move to make gambling socially acceptable. Dog tracks offer corporate hospitality, the lottery is Saturday night, family entertainment and Internet bets are the click of a mouse away. None of these moves has reached Lester's. The door swung open lightly, oiled by use and I entered into a fug of smoke.

Lester's is a simple arrangement. The concrete floor is littered with old dowts and losing slips. To the right is a booth where the teller sits behind a protective grille, handling wagers and payouts. Penny-ante stuff for the most part, but Lester's has had its big wins. Lester's office is beside her, with Lester himself in constant attendance. Squint sideways through the office door and you'll see his bald pate bent over mysterious paperwork, or perhaps the broad back of a man in a suit as he leans back on Lester's visitor chair. On the opposite wall two large televisions flicker in high colour, showing horse races or football matches. Beneath them is a ledge where punters fill in their betting slips with the small blue pens Lester supplies. It is a busy shop. Men nip in, place their bets and are away again. Only the committed stay to watch race after race.

I spotted Dougie in the far corner, his eyes trained on six horses making a desperate circuit round the park at Haydock. There were two other men beside him, concentration focused on the screen. The commentator reeled out an account of what was happening before their eyes, in a flat accent cut with practised enthusiasm, his spiel faster than any auctioneer's. I waited until the race was over and each man had turned away without a word to the others. None of them made their way to the payout booth.

Dougie spotted me before we spoke. 'Rilke. How's it going?' He patted me on the shoulder.

'Fine, Dougie. Yourself?'

'Been better, been worse.' He had the sad optimism of the chronic gambler and I wondered I had never seen it before. 'You in for a wee flutter, eh? Got a hot tip?'

Aye, I almost said, give it up, but instead I shook his hand and said, 'No. No, actually I'm in to see you. I wondered if you'd look at a few pictures I've come across.'

'My kind of pictures?'

'Very few folk's kind of pictures. I guess you'd call them a select taste.'

'So why do you want to show them to me?'

'I need to find out about them and you're the best man in Glasgow for photographs.'

'Ach, flattery will get you everywhere. Well,' he laughed, remembering my proclivities, 'you know what I mean. I've got a bet on the next race. Hang on while I see how it goes, then we'll go through to the back room and I'll see what I can tell you.'

We waited through three races. Dougie had a three-way accumulator, the first two, favourites, came in, the third, a ten-to-one sure thing, fared poorly on damp ground and didn't even feature. He stood through the show without a change of expression. When he turned at last from the screen his face wore the same cheerful look he had greeted me with.

'Ah well, you win some, you lose some. C'mon, then, show me these snaps.'

He led the way through to the gents' at the back of the shop. There was a smell of piss from the trough, the brown walls were covered in graffiti and the cubicle was locked. Dougie didn't seem to mind: the smile stayed glued to his face.

'They're not what you're used to, Dougie.' I wanted to prepare him before I shattered his day. 'They're nasty.'

'Ach, I can take it, Rilke. Me and Charles went to Amsterdam a couple of years back. There's things there would make your hair stand on end.'

'Aye, I guess so.' I took out the envelope and flicked through it until I found the pictures I wanted. 'What I want to know is are these real?' I handed them over to him. 'You'll see what I mean.' I waited for him to focus. 'I mean, did they kill that girl or is it a set-up? I don't know if you can tell that kind of thing from a photograph, but I reckoned if anyone could it would be you.'

I watched as Dougie looked through them slowly, silently, the light fading from his eyes. He squared the bundle, then took a small magnifying glass from his pocket and examined them again, closely.

'I'll tell you what I can, though it's not much. There's no camera trickery here. It's a simple point and shoot.' The friendly tone was gone now, it was all business. 'The technology was there. Georges Méliès filmed *A Trip to the Moon* in 1902, but this guy's not going to the moon – well, not in our sense. You have to ask yourself what would they be faking? If there's trickery here it's in the set-up, make-up, false blood, acting. Christ, Rilke. I hope she was acting but look at her. For fuck's sake, man, that's an open wound.'

'I know. I'm sorry I had to show them to you.'

'Aye, I'm sorry you did as well.'

'Can I buy you a drink?'

'No. There's one coming up soon I've had my eye on for a while. I'll stick around and see how it turns out. What are you going to do with these?'

'I'm going to try and find out what happened.'

'It was a long time ago.'

'I know that, but I'm going to try anyway.'

'Why do you want to know? Is she something to you?'

'I don't know, Dougie. I've no idea who she was — just a lassie — but she was somebody and I can't leave her there.'

In my mind there was a slam of closing doors and the smell of spilt blood.

'I wish you well, but Rilke?'

'Yes?'

'Make it a while before I see you again.'

I touched his arm, turned and left him there washing his hands. I wondered if his horse would ever come in and if it did what he would blow the money on.

5

Leslie

One foot in the grave, the other on a banana skin.
James Pryde, Head of the Clan Macabre

DOUGIE HAD SAID IT was all in the set-up. So now I needed to find someone who knew about these things. I headed back in the direction I had come, away from Woodlands and towards Park Road. A guy in a donkey jacket waylaid me and asked for money. He looked as if someone had polished him with old chip wrappers. Everything shone except his shoes and his attitude. I paid my Jakey tax, then slipped into a doorway, took out my mobile and dialled.

'Leslie? Rilke.'

'Rilke.' The soft, harsh voice, a bass Marlene.

'I wondered if you were in.'

'And now you know. Can I get back to what I was doing or is there something on your mind?'

'I wondered if I could call round.'

'Terribly formal this weather, aren't we, Rilke? Why did you not just chap the door?'

'I've got something I want to ask you. Are you alone?'

'For the moment.' Suspicion hung between us on the line. 'Why?'

'There's something I want to show you.'

'Rilke, if I'd not given up double entendres as a camp cliché I'd be having a field day. Get yourself over here and tell me what it's about.'

He hung up before I could say goodbye.

It took me fifteen minutes to get to Les's. There was splintering round the lock where the door had been recently broken open and mended. I hit three short Morse dots on the button above a cryptic *L*, and on the buzzer's cue pushed open the heavy close door and made my way to the top landing. The door to Les's apartment was on the snib. I released the lock behind me and went through the darkened hallway to the living room.

Heavy velvet drapes were drawn against the gloom of the day, creating a premature twilight. I hesitated in the doorway, letting my eyes adjust, taking it all in. A wave had hit the room, tilting it quick, one way then the other. Furniture had pitched forward, books somersaulting from shelves, a cabinet jettisoning drawers, drawers spewing their contents. Everything was just so much rubble, a jumble of CDs, papers, clothes, shoes, wigs, objects tumbled together with no respect for tribe or genus. Les himself was sitting on the edge of a displaced couch, dressed in a black pleated skirt and polo-neck jumper, dragging on a roll-up. He had made a start at tidying, righting chairs and the coffee table, but even those looked out of kilter. A painting hung awry above the fireplace, a wide-grinned Mexican illusion in an outsize gold plastic frame. Les's comment on mortality. Look this way, a laughing skull in a tasselled sombrero, sucking on a cigar, turn your head a little, Les with sombrero and cigar. I leant over and straightened it. Les flesh – no flesh – then flesh again. Behind me the real Les laughed his *bandito* laugh, a high bray that ended in a phlegmy cough.

'Cheers, Rilke, that's a real improvement.'

Les was never a pretty boy. In his best phase – say, seventeen to twenty – he had an elfish charm. He was the evil pixie, the giggler behind the bad fairy's skirts urging her on to more wickedness. At forty he has a face that reflects his life. Deep-set, heavy-lidded eyes, high cheekbones, a slender nose just the right side of hooked, and a wide, thin-lipped mouth. As faces go it's too much, overdone, as if he has one feature too many. But dressed, from a distance, he can be anyone you want him to be. He coughed again, a sixty-a-day grandmother's cough, rich and textured.

'Rose just phoned looking for you. She sounded in a right state. I told her I'd not seen you for days. I'm not sure if she believed me, so you better call her and dial 141 while you do it. I don't want that mad bitch coming round making a scene.'

'I thought you two liked a scene.'

He twisted his mouth. 'Outclassed, dear boy. When it comes to scenes, Rose wins every time. Feel like a beer?'

'Aye, all right. What happened here?'

'Ach, what do you think?'

He pulled himself from the couch, awkward, rubbing his hands over the small of his back, straightening stiffly as if he had been sitting there for a long time. Chaos continued in the kitchen, jars of food tipped across the floor, oats and cereal merged with lentils, rice and pasta, drawers upturned, contents scattered, pots and pans tumbled into crockery. Leslie skirted the mess as best he could, reached into the fridge and handed me a chill can.

'I was busted last night. They took the place apart in their usual half-arsed way – you know, books out the bookcase, clothes out the closet, drawers on the floor.'

'Did they find anything?'

'No, of course not. I wouldn't be talking to you if they had, would I? No.' He started to laugh, 'It was in a tartan shopper hooked on the pulley. A fucking bar. Three coppers pulling the place apart and one giving me the once-over: Where is it? they know I've got it; I'm an intelligent guy, why not save us all a lot of time and do myself a favour. He was so embarrassed. I was in a frock. He couldn't even look at me, and all the time it's hanging there above their heads. They had this dog with them, a big German shepherd. It was going crazy, jumping up, whining, practically baying, the poor beast was in torture. Its handler kept on shoving it down telling it to *sit and shut up*. It was the only one there with brains, I'm telling you, man. Christ, it was all I could do to stop myself looking up. A fucking red tartan bag. I swear I thought it was going to start talking to them, open up its zip mouth and shout, ''Here I am, here I am, how do you do?!'' '

'Where is it now?' He jerked his head at the ceiling, no, at the red tartan bag swaying slightly on the pulley. 'Leslie. It's still there?'

'Well, I didn't know what to do with it. I've not been over the doorstep all day. I tell you, man, it's a real worry. That's why I was pleased when you phoned.' I let that one ride. 'Anyway, what's on your mind? You looking to score? 'Cos I'm well supplied.' He laughed until the coughing took over.

'Jesus. *La dame aux camélias*, right enough. It's not the cough that carries you off, it's the coffin they carry you off in.'

'It's a matter of contacts.'

'Oh yes?'

'Leslie, you know a lot of people.'

'Nature of the business.'

'I need to meet someone who knows a bit about the skin trade.'

He sat himself down at the kitchen table, motioned for me to do the same, and took a sip from his can.

'You buying or selling?'

'Buying.'

'Well that's a relief. I thought for a moment you were wanting to get your skinny shanks on celluloid.' He took out the makings and began to roll a joint. 'What kind of stuff are you after?'

'I need some information.'

'Rilke, that's the worst thing you can say to a guy in my game. Information? Now, you can say it to me because we've known each other a long time and I know you can be trusted, but drugs and porn, big-money low-scruples operations. There's those that would kill me for the contents of that tartan bag. Know how much that's worth? Sure you do, a grand. Nothing. But there's folk would do that.' He folded his fingers into the shape of a gun, put the barrel to my temple and fired, 'Pow! Just to get their hands on it.' I recoiled from the blast. Les grinned and blew away imagined smoke, Annie Oakley-style. 'I'm well protected, well connected, but even so, screw up and you're on your own. I'm shitting it over this bust. I've to split that with Gerry and if he doesn't get his money I'm in big shtick. You know Gerry. Crazy man. Normal rules don't apply. I won't just owe him the stake, I'll owe him a share of the profits as well. What kind of info are you looking for, anyway?'

And I knew he was setting me up for a trade.

'I want to find someone who knows about photography. Someone who knows about the snuff set-up.'

Leslie had played a poker face at too many meetings with too many dangerous men to react, but he toyed with the ring-pull of his can before he spoke.

'Want to tell me what this is all about?'

He passed me the joint, I dragged on it, took out the envelope of photographs and slid it across the table.

'I found these on a call I was doing.'

He looked through them slowly, smiling at the early ones, giggling a little, turning them this way and that in an exaggerated attempt to sort out people and positions.

'Just goes to show you, man, nothing new under the sun, eh?'

'Keep looking, Les.'

'Don't you worry, boy. Auntie Leslie isn't squeamish.' Then he hit them. He kept his face straight but there was no laugh. He took a long toke, squinted through the smoke at the last four again, then turned to me.

'Okay, what do you want?'

'I want to find out how these pictures were taken.'

'What do you mean?'

'I need to know if this set-up is authentic.'

'Why?'

'That's my business.'

'True enough, man, but if you want my assistance it might pay to confide in me.'

'I don't know why, Leslie. Let's just say I can't leave her there. I might be able to find out who did this to her and that seems important to me.'

'Well you're wrong, Rilke. If this is real then it's a horrible thing, but it's a long time ago. Who did it doesn't matter. She's long gone and you won't be able to change that. The past is the past. If you ask me – and I realise you're not asking, but I'll give you this one for free – if you ask me, this is as much to do with your past as with what happened to this poor unfortunate. Leave it alone. You've done well, you and Rose, with your wee swag market. Don't start getting yourself mixed up with unpleasantness and unpleasant people for no reason.'

'I appreciate the advice, Les, but I still want to know.'

'Aye, I knew you'd say that.' He put the photographs back in the envelope and handed them to me. The crazed smile was back. 'Well, I gave you some free advice, Rilke, but there's very little free in this world, you're a businessman, you know that.'

'How much?'

'Help me get the dope out and I'll put you in touch with a contact who can help you.'

'No way, Les.'

'Oh come on, man. I've got it all worked out. I've been thinking of it since last night. All I needed was another body and here you are. Just listen, it's foolproof.'

'There's no need for me to listen because I'm not doing it.'

'Rilke, please. I'm between a rock and a hard place. If the soldiers get me I'm looking at three years – more if some polisman's wee lassie kills herself on E the week I go to trial – and if I screw up with Gerry I'll lose my balls.' He laughed again. 'There's not many people I could trust with a bar, Rilke. If you hadn't called me first I would've called you.'

'The thing is, Les, you're desperate. Any plan is going to look good to you.'

'Untrue. If I get caught I'm screwed. You get caught, say I duped you. We go back a long way.' Then he said the six words that should have sent signals flashing. 'You know you can trust me.'

'Look, Rilke, we don't even know that they're watching the building – we have to assume that they are, but who knows what goes on in the life of a polis? I'm small fry. The CID would probably smoke that in a week. No, they did a big production number last night and came up with nix. My guess is that they'll be pissed off and go on with the next thing. Maybe an unmarked out front for form's sake. I go out the front door carrying a suspicious-looking carrier bag. Inside that bag another one, wrapped up inside that, a box in ten layers of newspaper, and inside that thon hideous china Alsatian Frances gave us when I had Nero. By the time they've unpeeled that lot, you'll be well over the back court and away.'

He looked pleased with himself.

'And that's your master plan? You create a diversion while I leg it with the incriminating material.'

'Simplest is best. We'll meet up at yours, I'll get the gear to Gerry and give you the info. Christ, I'll even chum you to the meet. We can go for a pint after.'

'They'll have seen me coming in.'

'Rilke, there's nine flats in this building, six of them multiple occupancy. This area of Glasgow suffers from a preponderance of single, middle-aged men with a drink problem. They'll not have noticed you.'

'Still no way, Les.'

'I'll put you in touch with the person you need to talk to. This boy covers his tracks – you'll never find him without me.'

* * *

Four cans and three joints later Leslie was handing me his keys.

'Double-mortise the front door and make sure you lock the back entrance to the close. I don't want any junkies sneaking in for a smoke.'

He swaddled the cheap china ornament in two newspapers, hunted through the detritus on the floor for tape, then gave up in disgust.

'I hate this, fucking hate it, there's no need for this mess. They could look and put things back as they go along. You know why they do it, don't you?' There was no pause. Les, like Rose, was the master of the rhetorical question. 'Psychological torture. Bloody Nazis. What kind of sick fuck becomes a polisman?'

'James Anderson.'

'You know how I feel about that. A good man gone bad.'

'I saw him yesterday.'

'Oh yes?' Leslie had found the cardboard box his stereo had come in and was cutting it down to size. 'Did he take down your particulars?'

'Aye, he did.'

He stopped, knife poised mid slice.

'Christ, he never. I thought he was straight in every sense. I thought it was just one of those boyish things, you know, quick willy-rub behind the bike sheds.'

'We didn't have bike sheds at our school.'

'Come on. I'm filled with girlish curiosity.'

'Is that what you call it? No, it was nothing like that. I got nicked in the park last night. Anderson called me in from the front desk and let me off with a talking-to.'

'Oh that's great. Fanbloodytastic. You can't even sniff around the park without getting nicked. That fills me with confidence.'

He was wrapping the box in a series of carrier bags, smoothing out creases, splitting the handles and tying them together.

'Maybe you should get somebody else.'

'Look, I'm just a bit rattled. Of course I've got confidence in you. You're a smooth operator, I know that. Just try and not screw up, eh?' He slipped the package into the final bag, patting it affectionately. 'There, that should take a while to unwrap.' He pulled down a swing coat from the back of the door and zipped on a pair of calf-length black boots. He wasn't going to win any beauty contests. He turned and gave me a grin. 'Ready to go?'

'Are you sure you want to go out like that in daylight?'

'Ach I do it all the time. Nobody looks at me and if they do they just think I'm a hacket woman. Anyway, some of us poofy bastards are good fighters. All set?'

'Haven't you forgotten something?'

He paused, swore, 'Christ Almighty!' broke into laughter and lowered the pulley.

'There's no way, Leslie. No way.'

'Come on. It's lucky. It was right above that polisman's head last night and he didn't even notice. It was a fucking miracle. As soon as I get back I'm going to phone the Pope and ask him to consecrate the pulley.'

'It's too conspicuous. It's just not the kind of bag I would carry.'

'For me, Rilke.'

I stepped out of the back door and looked around. Leslie's back court was fourth in a row. To get to the street I had to cross three back yards, scaling four six-foot walls on the way.

Jeremy Bentham invented the panopticon as a means for warders to keep constant surveillance on prisoners. He proposed a circular prison with cells built round a central well from which the watcher could see the watched at any angle. Quite where this fits into his greatest happiness system I'm not sure, but it became popular among designers of schools. Les's back court wasn't circular and it wasn't a true example of a panopticon, but I estimated my journey could be observed from about seventy flats. I managed the first two walls fine, walking as nonchalantly as I could in between, the tartan shopper banging against my leg. In the third, a young boy on a tricycle was cycling circles beneath a line of bilious washing. He eyed my advance.

'Forgotten my keys, son.' I hauled myself over the wall and into his yard trying to look paternal. 'Should you not be at school?'

The child lifted his face and gave me a suspicious look. His baby teeth were tiny tombstone stumps.

'No. I'm no big enough yet. You need to be five to go to school. Kyle goes to school. He's a big boy.' He shifted his gaze from me towards a second floor window and in a voice like a fog horn shouted, 'Mammy! There's a man just climbed over the fence.'

The window slammed open and it became clear where junior had got his voice.

'Right you. Stay where you are while I phone the police.' I could see her grappling with a telephone, dialling 999, shouting at me at the same time. 'I'm onto you. Keep away from that child. Pervert. Knicker-stealing plamph. I know your face now. You'ds best steal your pants elsewhere, bloody weirdo.'

Around the back courts other windows were sliding open. I

shielded my face with Leslie's lucky tartan bag, pulled myself over the final fence, and ran from view.

There were things I should be doing, things that would make me money and wouldn't get me arrested. I slowed my pace, trying to look like a guy who habitually carries a tartan shopping bag, a thin man in a black suit covered in orange brick dust. An ordinary guy on the way back from the Co-op with the week's butcher meat. Out on the street nobody paid me any attention.

Les was waiting. 'You took your time. I was beginning to get the wind up. No probs?'

I let us in. 'No, none at all.' I felt weary. 'You?'

'Easy peasy.' He had a buzz on him. Adrenalin or speed? I didn't care. 'I took a ride on the subway to make sure I wasn't being followed, got off a stop too early and walked the rest of the way. Better not hang about, though. Sooner this is off my hands the better. Cheers, man. That's one I owe you.'

He put his arms round me in a bear hug, relieving me of the bag at the same time.

'I'll collect now.'

Les's face became a question mark, one eyebrow raised, mouth turned down. He moved his feet in a boxer's fast-toed shuffle, still charged with the electricity of the adventure.

'What?'

'The contact.'

'Oh yeah. Sure you want this?'

'I wasn't helping you out of the goodness of my heart, Leslie.'

'Yeah, well, a deal's a deal.'

He took a mobile phone from his bag and started to dial.

6

The Nature of Pornography

. . . though no city has ever been changed
into such a stinking ulcer on the face of green Nature,
The poet says unto thee, 'Splendid is thy Beauty!'
Arthur Rimbaud, 'L'Orgie parisienne'

THE VOICE ON THE telephone had been flat and accentless. The precision of someone speaking a foreign language perfectly.

'Yes, Leslie said you would call. How does five thirty suit you?' He'd given me the address and hung up with, 'Fine, see you then.'

Simple. A date with a pornographer. A man who knew about the snuff set-up.

Pornography is a versatile industry, it moves with the times. When the first caveman discovered he could paint on walls, using dyes fashioned from earth and ash, another dirty little *Homo erectus* saw the chance to draw a bare naked lady. In the days before photography, paintings, etchings, drawings of every imaginable vice existed and, of course, as soon as the camera came on the scene the industry expanded with delight. The advent of cinema inspired undulations viewed in porno picture palaces across the globe. Video closed most of those cinemas, but who cared? There was money to be made. In every high street there is a video store where, for a couple of pounds, you can rent your own show. Of course, there are always some whose tastes are difficult to satisfy and for them there are quiet little shops away from the main drag, hidden palaces of strange delights. It's as if the everyday shopper doesn't see the dreary storefront, the unwashed window that displays nothing, nothing at all. But if you are sympathetic, if you have the motivation, you can be in any town, any city, in the world, a stranger on your first day, and it will sing to you. Some people run from Grandma's house, they long for the bite of the wolf.

The *A to Z* revealed the address to be in an alleyway off the far end of West Nile Street. It was the end of the afternoon; the sky hung dark and heavy, like a lid on the world. I could feel the heat of the day stored under my feet in the sticky tar pavements. Intimations of summer, or environmental disaster. A trickle of sweat drifted down my spine and I worried my shirt might stain.

I set off along Argyle Street, dodging between schoolkids and stacks of cardboard boxes littered with rotting vegetables. Three Sikh pensioners sat, smoking and gossiping, on wooden chairs arranged on the pavement outside a grocer's shop. One of them said something in his own language and the group chuckled. 'Bloody Sair Heids' muttered a harassed woman arcing past them, catching her loaded shopping bag against my shin. The old men's laughter followed me. I didn't mind; people had done worse than laugh.

Outside the funeral directors, black-edged traffic cones reserved a space for the dead. As I passed the aluminium doors scrolled up, revealing the loaded hearse within. Seagulls squabbled on top of a telephone box, hovering, flapping their broad wings, cawing half-human screeches, orange beaks dipping with dainty derision, pecking over something rank. Their presence inland confirmed the approaching storm. A vein on my temple started to throb.

Ahead of me an old man crept a creaking wheelbarrow along the pavement. Derelict factories were under demolition near the quay and he'd collected low-quality scrap, the kind younger, fitter scavengers would ignore. I drew level, took in the rusted cart, his dusty suit, the stoop of his back, and felt the man with the scythe at my elbow. Maybe I wanted to dismiss Death. I should have known better.

'D'you need a hand?'

He hunched further over the barrow, quickened his pace and hissed, 'Fuck off. It's mine. I found it, away and get your own, you fucking bastard.'

'You're an ungrateful old git.' I reached over and rattled a bit of distorted metal. He cringed, bravado gone, dropping his prize, glancing up at me once, covering his head reflexively with his arms, but not before I had seen the yellow spread of fading bruises across his face. 'It's all right,' I said. 'I wouldn't hurt you. I'm not after your stuff.'

I touched his shoulder and he flinched.

'Leave me alone' – a whisper – 'just leave me alone.'

A block later, I turned to look back. He was still there, frozen, whispering, covering his head.

A small posse of boys gathered round the streaming

window of the Finnieston Fish Emporium, eating sweets, transfixed by the ugliness of a gaping monkfish, whiskered sea monster. Across the road a policeman took a firm grip of a shabby suspect's manacled wrists and huckled him from a patrol car to the station. The prisoner, head down, stumbled as if drunk, or too tired to care. The police braced himself with expert ease and checked the descent. Safe in the long arms of the law. Newspaper hoardings propped side by side declared the discovery of the toddler's drowned body and the promise of full details on the slaughtered 'vice girl'.

At Charing Cross I was absorbed into the late-afternoon tide of office workers. Here, then, was sanity. The industrial age had given way to a white-collar revolution and the sons and daughters of shipyard toilers now tapped keyboards and answered telephones in wipe-clean sweatshops. They shuffled invisible paper and sped communications through electronic magic. Dark suits tramped along Bath Street, past the storm-blasted spire of Renfield St Stephen's, home to prepare for another day like the last and another after that. Cars crept at a sluggish pace towards curving slip roads and the motorway miles below, where three lanes of paralysed traffic shimmered in a heat haze. Buses forced their way to obedient queues of defeated commuters, unoiled brakes screaming at every touch. A coach, trapped in the gridlock, opened and closed its pneumatic doors, trying to raise a breeze from the stagnant air. Elevator buildings that inspired the Chicago skyline disgorged men and women crumpled by the day, some barely a step from the door before they lit their first fag of freedom, sucking long and hard, deep inhalations that revealed their cheekbones, smoke curling from their nostrils, working for a hit. And all around me mobile phones. People talk, talk, talking to a distant party while the world marched by.

A gang of youths swooped through the crowds, flinging themselves with an echoing boom against the metal grilles of shut doorways, young Dodgers intent on intoxicating debauch. 'A fucking three-hundred-pound gold chain!' The homebound herd hesitated, for an instant, city radar thrown, then moved on.

A bruised boy with the face of a prophet, stood whispering, 'Any change, please? Any change?' As each one turned from him, he offered his empty polystyrene cup, like a gift, to the next. I tipped him a pound.

'You'll only encourage him,' grumbled a beefy man, sweating in his grey pinstripe, trundling by, without pause for debate.

At West Nile Street I counted down the door numbers until I came to the one the voice had given me. A basement record shop. The front was painted pale blue, a gold on navy sign above the door read SIRENS, flanked on either side by the mirror image of a big-busted mermaid strumming a guitar.

I loped down concrete steps bevelled with years of use – how many footsteps? – into a tiny courtyard choked with litter. The window reminded me of a joke we used to play as kids: 'Excuse me, Mister, how much are your dead flies?' 'I don't sell dead flies.' 'So how come you've got six in your window?' A long time ago someone had stretched nicotine-coloured cellophane across the glass to stop the records warping in the occasional sunlight. It hadn't worked. Albums flopped half-heartedly among the dust, the distorted vinyl bowing their cardboard sleeves. It was almost as if whoever ran the shop didn't want any customers. I had come to the right place.

I pushed open the door, a bell announced my presence, and I was out of the city and into the gloom. A cool, black-painted cave, walls lined by racks half filled with lolling albums. The counter was far forward, maximum storage minimum display, no room for browsers. An arch behind the counter was screened by a fringed, plastic red, white and blue curtain, the kind common to butcher's shops; beyond it the glow of a computer screen. Pornography's new frontier. A sign by the counter read, *We have thousands of items in stock not on display. If you don't see what you're looking for — ask.* Above the records, shelves of videos. I slid one out . . . *featuring real girls from Glasgow.* Why not *Real Girls from Rio?* Taut, tanned buttocks losing out to the Pilsbury Dough cellulite of the girl next door. It cheered me to think that given a choice the average Scottish pervert wanted to wank to the robust Scottish girl in the street. Then I wondered if all straight men liked these big-busted, well-fed young women, or if it was just the perverts. The thought depressed me again.

The curtain parted. A young boy in a khaki shirt stood regarding me from the archway, the fringes draped round his shoulders like a patriotic veil. Youth wrapped in the flag of the Empire. He was handsome. Dark like the black Irish, saturnine. Shoulder-length hair, sensitive mouth, pale-blue eyes, translucent and impossible.

I was too old to call it love at first sight, but I had all the symptoms. People have died for love, they have lied and cheated and parted from those who loved them in turn. Love has slammed doors on fortunes, made bad men from heroes and heroes from libertines. Love has corrupted, cured, depraved and perverted. It is the remedy, the melody, the poison and the pain. The appetite, the antidote, the fever and the flavour. Love Kills. Love Cures. Love is a bloody menace. Oh, but it's fun while it lasts. The world faltered on its axis, then resumed its customary gyration, a place of improved possibilities.

'Can I be of some assistance?' His tone didn't fit the look or the venue.

I smiled, wondering if my face was changing, taking on a lupine stretch. Beware the wolfman. 'My name's Rilke. I have an appointment.'

'My name's Derek. Who's your appointment with?'

He made eye contact, raising his eyebrows slightly. Was he flirting with me? I felt the old stirring in the groin but all that showed was I wanted him.

The straights think that we have some kind of radar, that there are signals we give off, a mode of dress, style of conversation. *'Dear boy' said Francis, fingering his green carnation and smoothing the lapels of his bespoke suit, 'tell me, do you have many Judy Garland CDs?'* Well, of course there is a place for that, but it's never been part of my technique. I prefer a more straightforward approach. What hinders me is the old question: is he queer? I saw this boy and wanted to take him by the hand, lead him out into the street to my room, any room, and strip him naked.

'Is your appointment with anyone in particular?'

'Just ask around in the back, son. There'll be someone there who wants to speak to me.'

I glanced through the stock while I waited. It's a common emotion, a distaste for sex that doesn't turn you on. It was too much for me, the lushness of the images. Big-busted, large-bottomed women bent forward grasping their bosoms, legs stiff, rears raised like stretching cats', glossed lips slightly parted, as if this was the most erotic moment of their lives. For all I knew, it was.

I wondered if there was anyone I knew featured in *Real Girls from Glasgow*. I left the videos and picked up a magazine. The same girls-next-door, this time legs splayed in alarming Technicolor. I was peering through my magnifying glass, trying to discern whether the images had been tinted, when I heard the voice from the telephone.

'You have to be careful where you put the staples in some of these.'

He came forward to greet me, hand outstretched. A thin man in his fifties, about five eight, white hair cut short and natty, tortoiseshell spectacles I suspected might be non-prescription. He was dressed in a dark suit and black roll-neck. Everything expensive, everything anonymous. A man you would forget. A man it might be safer not to remember.

'Mr Rilke.'

'Just Rilke.'

'Rilke. A friend of Leslie's.'

'A mutual friend.'

'Yes, quite so. My name is Trapp. Why don't you come through to the back, and we can have our conversation in private. Derek will deal with any shop business. Bring the magazine if you like.' He indicated my magnifying glass. 'Close scrutiny, eh? Just when I thought there was nothing left to reveal.' He drew back the curtain and ushered me through, nodding to Derek, busy tap-tapping at the computer. The boy left the room without a word. I followed him with my eyes. The man traced my gaze. 'A nice boy.'

'Seems to be.'

I still couldn't place the accent, a touch of the US masking a European clippedness.

'So, Leslie didn't explain why you wanted to see me, but I owe him and I gather he owes you, so here we are to pay our debts. Tell me what I can do for you.'

I took the envelope containing the photographs out of my pocket and laid it on the desk.

'I came across these. I'd like to know more about them. What's going on? Specifically, are they authentic?'

I slipped the pictures of the tortured girl from the pile and slid them across the table.

He looked at each in turn without a change of expression. 'Do you know the girl?'

'No.'

'May I look at the rest?'

I pushed the others towards him. He leafed through them slowly, frowning with concentration.

'Are you familiar with anyone in the shots?' I nodded. 'Could you indicate them for me please.'

I took a picture where Mr McKindless's face was prominent and pointed to him. 'This is the owner of the prints.'

'Ah yes, yes.' He worked his way through the photographs, then sat silently, eyes shut, fingers steepled beneath his brow. 'Excuse me for a moment.'

He left the room and there was a sound of running water.

I looked about me: half office, half warehouse, everything neatly arranged. On the computer monitor a galaxy raced towards me. I nudged the mouse gently and it cleared, revealing nothing. Derek had saved and filed whatever he was working on before he left. My new acquaintance returned, affecting not to notice the clear screen though I felt sure he had marked it.

'Yes. Our Leslie is a naughty boy, isn't he? What made him think I could help, I wonder?' There was a menace in his tone that belied the gentleness of his words.

'I badgered him into it, and you know Leslie, he's more enthusiastic than accurate at times.'

'Yes, a man prey to strange enthusiasms. I will tell you what I can, but first tell me something. What do you know about the origin of these photographs?'

'Nothing, or next to nothing. I know the man who owned them was wealthy, the source of the wealth I don't know. As well as these photographs, he has a large collection of erotic fiction assembled, I would say, over many years. He lived in Hyndland with his sister.'

'Lived?'

'I suppose that's the other thing I know about him. He's dead. I came across the photographs in his effects.'

'You're a lawyer?'

'No, an auctioneer.'

He laughed. 'An auctioneer. Are you planning on putting these *under the hammer*?' He emphasised the phrase as if it amused him.

'I've no plans at all right now.'

'One more question. Why?'

'Why what?'

'Why take the trouble?'

'No reason. I'm interested.'

'A lot of effort to go to for no reason.'

'Nevertheless, here I am.'

'Yes, here you are. Okay. This man' – he pointed at McKindless – 'you say he collected erotic fiction, dirty books.'

'Yes.'

'Anything else?'

'Not so far. Well, I found a netsuke, a carved ivory Japanese ornament. It was pornographic in nature.'

'Sadistic?'

'Yes.'

'Okay, there's a consistency there. This man has the mentality of a collector. He appears himself in some of these photographs, which suggests his passion isn't for photography. These here' – he indicated the scenes of torture – 'are original photographs, but we don't know how he came about them. Is there anything to suggest he didn't simply go into a shop and buy them? Under-the-counter trade. It happens sometimes, I'm told.' He smiled.

'I've a feeling about them. The way they were stored together, the similarity in the style' – I was surprising myself now – 'the length of the shot, the general arrangement. Remember, I spend my life classifying, determining provenance, authorship. No, I take your point and I could be wrong, but I'm certain these came from the same origin. There's something I can't quite put my finger on, but what it amounts to is a consistency of composition and the decision to store them together. There's a connection.'

'Okay. You feel sure somehow that this man is involved in the creation of these pictures. Personally I think there is not enough evidence, but we'll work under that assumption for the meanwhile. What you really want to know is was a young girl murdered for sexual gratification and her corpse photographed?'

'Yes.'

'I would say almost certainly not.' My face must have registered surprise at his quick response, he laughed. 'You're disappointed! I have spoilt your mystery. Okay, how can I be so sure? For the reason you are sure they were taken by the same person. Professional experience. Many people fantasise about sex and death. Eros and Thanatos. The association is as old as time. Repeated over and over, in art, literature, cinema, mythology even. The official line in my profession is that no snuff movie has ever been made. Such a thing could never happen. This is self-protection. We all know, of course, that it has. I have never seen one, I know of no titles, but I know somewhere, there is a film of one person killing another at the point of climax. How do I know? Because reason tells me. Experience tells me. If someone has thought of doing a thing, then someone somewhere has done it. The world is an old and wicked place, Rilke, the dreadful has already happened.'

'So why . . .?'

'Why do I think these are staged? Because very few people ever carry out these fantasies. The mess, the logistics, the jail sentence. No, I said that somewhere someone has done it. I stand by that, but most people can distinguish between fantasy and reality. We meet many people with dubious morals, but we meet very few psychopaths. I do not think these photographs are authentic.'

'But you can't be sure.'

'Who can ever be sure? Let me show you something.' He went over to a filing cabinet and returned with a document wallet. 'Look at these.'

He removed a sheaf of prints and passed them to me. A familiar image repeated, different locations, different personnel, but the same formula over and over, a body wrapped tightly in bandages, some with faces revealed, others with heads so tightly swathed I wondered how they hoped to breathe.

'Look familiar?' He laid my picture of the mummified girl beside them. The resemblance was irrefutable.

'What are they doing?'

'They call it "the Egyptian", for obvious reasons. I would describe it as a form of bondage, a letting go, an abdication of responsibility. In everyday life we fight for power; sometimes, in our fantasies, we relinquish it. Here's an interesting one.'

He handed me a cutting from a magazine. A woman, prone and tightly swathed, her features obscured, body hidden, save for a window at her pubis where tufts of hair sprouted black against the Corinthian white of the bandages.

'David Bailey photographs his beautiful wife.' He laughed. 'Perhaps I, too, am an artist. Here's another.' He indicated an androgynous form encased in black latex, fetish mask zipped at the mouth. 'The same impulse. Well, at least they're quiet.'

'You think this is what's happening in my photographs?'

'What does it look like to you? I think your man liked to get up to naughty games. I don't think he was a killer. Experience is against it.'

'Is there any way I can be sure?'

'Mr Rilke, you are too old for that question. I am sure. Whether you are sure is for you to decide.'

'I think that's as good an answer as I'm going to get.'

I stowed the photographs of the girl in my pocket and began to get up from my seat.

'One moment. What do you intend to do with the pictures now?'

'I've no idea. Strictly speaking, they're not mine, they belong to the estate. I guess I'll show them to his sister. I've a feeling she won't be entirely surprised. What she does with them after that is up to her. She might wish to destroy them.'

'I would give you a good price for them.'

'Why, if they're so . . . unoriginal?'

'Their age, their lack of provenance, invokes a certain frisson that enhances their value. Whether you involve the sister or not is your affair.'

He tried to persuade me some more and I tried not to take offence at the assumption I could be bought. The truth is, I could, but neither of us knew the right price. In the end he wrote down a telephone number on a piece of paper and passed it to me.

'Remember, Rilke, I'll buy them, this week, next week, this year, next year, I'm in the market. Perhaps you don't need money, but there's always something we want. Ask me. I'm a useful person to know.'

I thought he was exaggerating.

I left him filing his prints back into the wallet. The front shop was still free of customers. The threatened storm had arrived and rainwater coursed down the basement steps from a blocked drain on the street above. Grime and dry dust would be washed into the basement courtyard coating the litter in a further layer of silt. Outside, the human traffic had slackened. Now only the occasional footstep passed the window, sober trouser legs, a pair of high heels click-clacking at a quick pace, eager to be home. I could hear Trapp in the back room talking on the telephone, in a language I couldn't identify. Derek leant over the counter reading a paperback novel. He lifted his head and our eyes met. I winked and nodded towards the door. The curtains behind him parted and he lowered his gaze to his book.

'Well, Rilke, I hope our meeting has been of some use to you. Remember my offer.'

The white-haired man placed a gentle hand on my shoulder. The warmth of his touch crept through the layers of my clothing and I turned towards him, holding out my hand, wanting to loose myself of his benediction, his restraint, taking his hand in mine like a man making a deal, looking him in the eye and smiling. I assured him I'd remember.

*   *   *

Outside the rain had a horizontal stretch. I put up my collar, climbed the worn steps from the basement, then the cleaner steps of the insurance offices above. Its stained-glass windows presented a diptych of dangers. A red fire ravaged a warehouse while fire-fighters battled in vain. A young girl turned away from a ship setting sail. The rising breeze caught hold of her yellow hair, coiling it into art nouveau swirls, a smile touched her lips as she walked into the wind and away from the gathering clouds that glowered over the vessel. A lady with her premiums paid up. A golden legend promised *Probity, Equity, Security*. I settled myself in the lee of the doorway rolling a smoke, waiting.

I was on my third damp roll-up when I heard the door below open. I eased myself back, into the shadows, but it was Derek sure enough, swearing under his breath at the rain already plastering his hair, leaving dark stains on his soft suede jacket. *Oh sweet boy, let me towel you dry.* I watched his ascent, marked the slenderness of his hips, the slim-fit black trousers tapering into Chelsea boots. I coughed and he started.

'Jesus fuck!'

He stepped backwards into the basement, sheltering beneath the stairway, brushing away the water that ran into his eyes from his damp hair, peering up at me. I wondered what type of spectre I presented.

Chat-up lines have never been my forte. I've never been able to get beyond . . .

'How're you doing?'

'Fine. I've just finished.'

'It's a wet night.' I was toiling.

'Sure enough.'

In the air somewhere there was a crash of thunder, three

short beats then a flash of lightning and the smell of cordite. He winced and looked at his rain-spotted suede.

'Fancy a pint?'

'Why?'

'Well, this rain is going to ruin your jacket.'

We made a mad dash across West Nile Street, a river now, right enough, blocked drains and streaming gutters. A bus sailed to a stop, fanning a spray of spume across the pavement. We outran its arc and into the nearest pub.

It was a lawyer's howff, advocates and their attendants clustered round the bar swilling spirits, talking loudly and looking like so many devils with their black suits and flushed faces. It was standing room only. I would have liked to get him somewhere quieter, a warm bar with a snug, where I could lull him with drink and words. Here with the hustle of suits around him the boy was liable to drink up and move on. Hell, someone might splash single malt over his good coat. I fetched the drinks, we eased ourselves into a corner and touched glasses.

'Cheers.'

Close to, I could see he was older than I had thought in the gloom of the shop, about twenty-three, twenty-four.

He brushed his damp hair back from his forehead. 'Not much of a place, this, but dry, eh? That's some storm.'

'Aye, it's harsh. Pity the poor sailors at sea. It looks like it might be on for the night.'

His smile broadened. 'In that case best to be home, warm and cosy.'

Was he teasing me? I didn't want him to go home alone. I wanted to lick his white teeth, bite his lower lip until it bled red blood, warm and sticky, coating his mouth like cherry lip-gloss. I sipped my pint against the faint taste of iron in my mouth.

'Well, you never know, in the time it takes us to have a couple of pints it may have dried up.'

Silence faltered between us. Him waiting calmly, me grasping around in my head for words.

'So do you like your job?'

'I've done worse.' He laughed again; this time there was an edge to it. 'It pays a wage, just about, but no, I wouldn't say I like it. It's peaceful, he lets me read – novels, fiction, not the stuff he sells. It's better than McDonald's, but not what you'd call a career.'

'So what would you like to do?'

'A million things.' He looked around the bar. I wondered if he recognised any of his customers. If he did he wouldn't greet them. 'You've got the advantage on me. You know where I work and what I do, but all I know is your name, if it is your name.'

So I told him about myself. Told him about the auction house. The thrill of discovery and the exercise of knowledge. I showed off, recounting pursuits of provenance. Pictures I had traced with my finger on the map of Europe. I told him of art dealers who enhance the value of paintings, inserting a dog or a person into an uninhabited landscape or perhaps a ship going down with all hands on sullen seas. Of daubs that had been enhanced beyond recognition and banished from the sale-room. I told him tales of houses I had visited. Discoveries I had made. Costume jewellery substituted for heirlooms. Death masks, a caul, a withered hand. The sale where every book held a ten pound note snug against the fly leaf. I took him with me through the trade, the feuds and rings, the fist fights and tyre slashings. I held his eyes with an old routine, wanting all the while to push him harsh against the wall and press myself against him.

'Sounds like fun.'

I shrugged. 'It's a living.'

'Aye, but it's interesting. You're working with things you like. So what did you want with Trapp this afternoon?'

'Nothing much. I just wanted him to look at some photographs I'd found. I thought he might be able to tell me a bit about them.'

'You must be well connected to get him to take time out for that. What did he say?'

'That they weren't as rare as I thought. He backed it up with illustrated proof, then offered a decent price for them.'

'And you now want me to cast my expert eye over them. That's what this pint is about.'

Not entirely. 'You've seen right through me.'

'Ach, well, get us another and I'll do the biz. It's not often I get consulted on matters of fine art.'

I lifted our empty glasses. 'Wait till you see them.'

I showed him the scenes of death first. He studied them closely, silently, the crowd around us receding, uproar subsiding, as the images took on their dreadful focus. He held them one by one in his palm, laid them out in a terrible triptych, then returned to each in turn, bringing them close to his eyes – irises expanding, pupils dilating, growing wider to take it all in.

'There's something beautiful about these.' His words broke the spell, and the racket of glasses and drunkenness was around us again. 'I know they're horrible but there's a ghastly beauty there.' I raised my eyebrows. 'Ach, you know your art history – we're trained to enjoy these images. How many annunciations? The Virgin Mary waiting for Gabriel to fill her full of the seed of the Lord, the original *droit de seigneur*. How many wan, prone women laid out like death? This is a step further, a step too far you might say, but it's right slap bang in the tradition of Western art. The innocent drained of blood. The victim of vampires. ''The death of a beautiful woman is the most beautiful thing in the world.'' Edgar Allan Poe said that.'

'That's interesting.'

'But not what you wanted to hear, right?'

'It's just an angle I'd not considered. You look at this and see art?'

'Hey, you're the one showing me dirty pictures. I'm just telling you what I see.'

'Sorry.'

'Aye, that'll cost you another pint. No, no harm done, it's not that I think it's okay – the opposite, if you must know – but you can look at something rotten and still see the beauty in it, right?'

'I take your point. What I'm trying to find out is did this actually happen or is it some kind of weird construct?'

He raised his gaze from the photographs and gave me a distrustful stare. 'Why are you so keen to know? A taste for the low life?'

I fed him the same half-truth I'd been trying to convince myself with. 'This could be a lucrative sale for us. If I show these to the police they'll be forced to investigate, and that means no auction. On the other hand, I don't want to be complicit in covering up a murder. I thought I'd see if there was any real need for worry before I decided what to do.'

He accepted it without question.

'Fair enough. No way of telling.' He looked up from his scrutiny. 'That's what he told you, right?' I nodded. 'You asked me what I want to do. Movies. Mad, eh? I make short films, show them to other folk who make short films, send them in to competitions and get nowhere. It's all I think about; film daft. I see the world through a frame.' He squared his thumbs and index fingers together, peering at me through them to illustrate his point. 'I look at something, I'm trying to think how it would look up on the screen. A bus goes by and I'm calculating angles I would shoot it at. Short cuts? Cut, cut, cut, cut' – he sliced at the air with his fingers – 'or one continuous sweep? I meet someone, I'm casting them in my head – you, for instance.' There must have been something in my eyes because he stopped. 'Ach, never mind. The most depressing sound in the world to me is the sound of a video cassette dropping back through the letter box, another rejection. Who cares? That's my personal tragedy. But this is where my expertise is useful to you. I make horror films. Blood is my speciality.'

'So what do you think?'

'I think Trapp's right. There isn't any way of being sure. But if it is fake, they've done a really good job.' He held the picture of the dead girl up close, scrutinising it with a dread enthusiasm. 'A fine job.' He caught my look. 'That's not nice, is it? I hope not' – he lifted the photograph, her slashed throat, her bloodstained breasts, her sightless eyes rolled backwards in her unpillowed head, and lowered his voice as if he were speaking to himself – 'but it really could be.' He shivered. 'Brrr, enough to give you the heebie-jeebies. What are the rest of? Dismemberment? Cannibal parties?'

I passed over the envelope and watched while he flicked nonchalantly through the remaining prints, their content nothing compared to the magazines he handled every day. He paused, then laid a photograph slowly on the table, as if it was the losing card in a high-stakes poker game. McKindless's panting face looked up at us.

'This was taken a long time ago, but it's him right enough. The dirty wee bastard.'

I freshened our drinks. The after-work crowd started to drift home, the bar grew quieter and we moved to a small table.

'How do you know him?'

'Have a guess.'

'A valued customer?'

'Spot on. Well, to be honest I don't really know. It's a bit like you today. He comes in and I'm banished to the front shop while they get on with business in the back. Suits me fine.'

'Do you think it's healthier not to know?'

'Don't know. Don't care.'

'What's with the computers?'

'What do you think? A web site, databasing his stock. Nothing exciting. As far as I'm concerned, it's dead boring. To be honest, I've been thinking of moving on, getting a job in a proper video shop.' He made a face. 'I've been there too long.'

'So you don't think I'm going to get anywhere looking at these pictures.'

'No. Not on their own. That's the thing about pictures, they hint at more than they show. You might see a shadowy figure lurking round a corner, but you can never go round that corner and discover who it is. Isn't there anything else you could look at?' He lowered his voice conspiratorially 'Clues?'

I shook my head, then remembered the Camera Club card. I slipped it from my wallet and handed it to him. 'Just this.'

'Anne-Marie.' He started to laugh.

'You know her?'

'Know her? Man, she rose from the tomb for me.'

7

Camera Club

THE TAXI'S DIESEL ENGINE began to whine as we climbed the sheer face of Garnethill. The driver shifted down gear and we crept on, slowly. I leant back against the seat, trying to forget the dizzying drop down to Sauchiehall Street behind us. Derek turned towards me,

'You okay?'

'Aye, fine, fine, just not that good at heights. Why don't you take my mind off it by explaining where we're going?'

'I told you I made videos.'

'Yes.'

'Well, they're ten-minute shorts for the most part. Video cameras, the technology's brilliant, we can do things that professionals could only dream of twenty years ago, but it's still expensive, right?'

'I guess so.'

'Anyway, by the time you've rented the equipment,

there's no money left to pay actors and that's how I met Anne-Marie.'

'She's an actress?'

'Aye. Well, in the same way that I'm a director. She's good, but she hasn't had a break yet, so she works for no fee with the likes of me: arty, off the wall, independent, broke. I met her when she came into the shop to put an advert up. We got talking and one thing led to another. She played lead female vamp in my last short. She was good, really good.'

The massive hulk of the art school appeared on our left, illuminated now. Too close for us to see anything more than a glimpse of detail in the monumental structure. The driver dropped gear again and the taxi grumbled on at a slow walking pace.

'So what is it with the Camera Club?'

He smiled. 'Wait and see.'

Derek had given the address as somewhere in Buccleuch Street. He started to sing as we got out of the cab.

'*Oh there's not much to do, in Buccleuch.* Now that, as you will see, is a lie.' He looked at his watch. 'Twenty past seven, we'll be in time.' Then paused. 'I hope Anne-Marie doesn't mind us turning up like this.'

The close door was unlocked, no entry phone. Derek pushed it open and led me into a hallway which smelt of ammonia and homeward assignations. Rubbish littered the stairwell. A bike was tethered to the ground-floor banister by two hefty chains. There was something painted in small pink letters, way down low on a padlock near the ground. I eased myself down, gently and peered at the inscription. FUCK OFF.

'That's Anne-Marie's wee joke.'

'Very droll.'

We met no one on the stairs. But there were signs of life:

lists of names on handwritten cards, cooking smells, a bass
beat pounding, a raised voice, discarded cigarette packets,
burnt tinfoil shavings. Black rubbish bags sheltered in doorways. A dog barked and a shadow passed across the spy hole.
Always anticipate the menace of strangers. At last we reached
the top floor. Here the landing was swept. Pots of plants,
scattered with seashells and pebbles, rested against the wall.
Derek rapped three times on a door and it opened from
within. Standing in the hallway was a large man dressed in
expensive-looking trainers, black jogging bottoms with a red
dragon motif on the right leg and a black T-shirt with *Gorbals
Tae Kwon Do Club* printed across the chest.

'Derek, mate, how's it going?'

'Very fine, Chris. Yourself?'

'Brand new.'

'And Anne-Marie?'

'Down to the swimwear. She'll be finished soon.'

Niceties over, he turned towards me, making it clear that
the time had come for introductions.

'This is a friend of mine, Mr Rilke.'

'So you want to join the Camera Club, Mr Rilke?'

'I'm not sure.'

'Rilke was hoping to ask Anne-Marie about some photos
he's got.'

Chris smiled.

'Well, you know the rules. On Tuesday nights all callers are a
member of the Camera Club. That'll be thirty pounds, please,
Mr Rilke.'

Derek avoided my look. I fished three notes from my
wallet and handed them to him.

'And ten pounds for the hire of a camera.'

No one likes to be a mark. Not the guy walking away from

the halo of autoteller surveillance cameras with a white cross chalked on his back. Not the loser in a shell game. I didn't like it, but the big man's tone invited no discussion.

I handed him another note and he passed me a Polaroid One Step. An instant camera, devised in the 1970s, so party goers could reassure themselves that they really were having fun. Soon adopted by that overlapping category of criminals, kidnappers and antique dealers.

'And another ten spot for film.'

I swapped my last ten for a slim, foil-wrapped packet.

'Why don't you go through, now that you've paid your money.' It wasn't a question. 'Just down the hallway, third door on the right.'

The door to the room was made of dimpled glass. It held a thousand distorted reflections repeated in honeycomb, an impression of people and white light, pink faces and dark suits, a crush of bodies all leaning towards . . . I pushed open the door and stepped through. Six men were arranged in front of a makeshift platform. Before them stood a young girl, in a red and white polka-dot bikini, striking a pose. She was a pretty girl, sparkling eyes and an open smile. A pretty primary schoolteacher, an air hostess, a weather girl. She opened a parasol and peeked cheekily out from behind. Next she placed a large sun hat on her head, angling it, perkily, this way and that. A nineteen-fifties pin-up, naughty, but wholesome. With every change in pose the men raised their identical Polaroids and clicked. The room was suffocatingly warm, silent save for the clicking of shutters and hiss of pictures.

A man turned away from the model and gave me a furtive glance. He was colourless, tired-eyed and balding. His neighbour shifted his feet and lowered his gaze. I was spoiling the ambience. Upsetting the balance, watching the watchers.

The model changed position and I lifted my camera, caught the girl in the square of the viewfinder and held her close. I felt like an assassin. The eye behind the lens. My mouth tasted of ashes. I swallowed, pressed the button and the flash exploded.

The picture slipped out with a mechanical whirl. I watched the black surface transform, the white bikini bleaching into view, the blood-red polka dots seeping through, the girl's face, pale and smiling, her eyes two crimson dots.

She slipped behind a screen and reappeared, as I'd guessed she would, no longer wearing the bikini top. The cameras flashed an *agitato* strobe, but each man kept his place, an almost regulation three inches from the others. The heat and white light were beginning to take their toll. The room smelt of frustrated testosterone and sweat. I sneaked a glance at my neighbour. He had removed his jacket. Damp rings circled his armpits. I took my pictures with the rest, letting the shifting images drop, one by one, to the floor. The girl disappeared behind the screen. A shuffle of reloading film, then stillness. We stood in silence for what seemed like an age. Each man looking ahead, wishing the others away, imagining himself the only photographer in the room. Seven gentlemen callers, awaiting the return of the same sweetheart. Then, just when I thought the show was over, the girl re-emerged, naked. I'd been afraid of what might happen next, but she moved gracefully through a routine of artistic poses, indifferent to the crescendo of flashing light, bowed to the audience and stepped, once more, behind the screen.

The door opened and Chris appeared, He shook each man's hand and retrieved the cameras from them. They left with quiet thank yous, carefully stowing photographs in their pockets as they went.

*   *   *

I'd expected Anne-Marie to be wearing an embroidered silk kimono, but she'd slipped on a tracksuit similar to Chris's. We sat round a table in the kitchen, drinking tea from cheerful yellow mugs. Derek and Chris were eating their way through a plate of gingerbread. I wasn't hungry.

Derek had introduced me and I'd handed Anne-Marie the Polaroids I'd taken. She'd looked at me suspiciously.

'Do you not want them?'

'They're not my thing.'

'You mean you didn't come here to take dirty pictures, but he charged you then pushed you through the door anyway.' She laughed. 'You're a bugger, Christian.'

He shrugged. No one offered a refund.

'Did you enjoy the show anyway?'

'You pose very well.'

'Well, that's a diplomatic answer if ever I heard one.'

She laughed again. She had a pleasant laugh. It was an effort not to join in. Derek sensed my irritation and gave me a conciliatory look. I'd been angry, but it didn't take more than a look for me to like him again. More than like.

'Rilke here is an auctioneer. He came across some horrible pictures, snuff photographs they look like, in some dead guy's attic. Thing is, he also came across your card and he wondered if you might be able to tell him something about the man.'

'Snuff photographs? You mean, like, pictures of a dead person?'

'Yes.'

'Like, you see them not dead, then dead?'

'It looks like the girl has had her throat cut.'

Anne-Marie put her hand to her own throat. 'Ugh.'

Chris reluctantly surrendered his piece of gingerbread. 'Shouldn't you be going to the police with this? I mean, cheers for letting us know he had Anne-Marie's card, but why are you here?'

'From the look of the pictures it happened a long time ago. Mid-nineteen-forties or thereabouts.'

'Aye, but even so, murder's murder. There's maybe someone still alive wonders what happened to their sister, their mother. There's records for that kind of thing; missing persons.'

Derek broke in. 'Rilke's got a photo of the guy. I thought you might recognise him.'

'Even if I did, what could I tell you?' Anne-Marie poured herself some more tea from the large, brown pot on the table. 'I never talk to the clients. I'm the muse, untouchable and silent. I'd lose my power over them if I spoke. I'm a fantasy object. The minute they realise I'm a real girl I've blown it.'

'Have you never spoken to any of them?'

She made a pained face. 'Once or twice, but not if I can help it.'

Chris spoke through a mouthful of cake. 'That's what I'm here for. Make sure everyone behaves themselves.' He wagged his finger in mock admonition. 'No touching the muse. No shouting or whistling.'

Anne-Marie smiled. 'I think they prefer it like that anyway. Most of them are frightened wee mice. That's why they're here and not at the lap dancing or some legit camera club. They take their photographs, then go home and get their rocks off in private.'

Derek looked disgruntled. I wondered if he was unhappy about letting me down. It was a pleasing thought. Anne-Marie reached over and patted his hand.

'Sorry to disappoint you, Deke.'

'Will you have a look at his photographs anyway?'

'Derek' – he was pushing her too hard – 'maybe I should head off. I've to be somewhere later this evening, anyway. Thanks a lot, Anne-Marie, for the tea and cake.'

'No, wait a moment, unless you're in a hurry?'

I shook my head.

'It wouldn't do me any harm to look at a picture of the man, I suppose. He's not standing next to a dead body, is he?'

'No.'

'Well that's all right, then. I'm a bit squeamish.'

I warned Anne-Marie of the nature of the McKindless portraits before passing them to her. She studied them briefly, twisting her face in disgust, then passed them to Chris with a significant look.

'Oh yes.' Chris nodded. He didn't seem to notice that Anne-Marie's face had gone the colour of cold porridge. 'I remember him. This was taken a while ago, eh? But it's him for sure.'

Anne-Marie pulled her fingers through her hair. 'He had the wrong idea.' She took a thin strand in her mouth and chewed on it gently.

Chris straightened in his seat. 'I put him straight. Anne-Marie, there's cake left if you're hungry.'

'It helps me think. Do you want to tell him about it or will I?'

Chris sipped his tea. 'There's nothing much to tell, is there? It happened. It's inevitable. You've been warned often enough. Anyway,' he addressed himself to Derek and I, 'this bloke came a few times, no problem. Then he asked if he could photograph Anne-Marie in private, on his own. He asked me because I'm the front of house. Like Anne-Marie said, she never talks to them. Well, I told him no and he went away peaceful enough. That's all there is to it. He tried his luck and didn't get anywhere. The only strange thing was the amount of money he offered. It was a lot.'

'How much?'

'Let's just say too much just to photograph someone and enough to tempt madam here.'

Anne-Marie looked defiant. 'I only said that perhaps you could be in the next room.'

'He didn't want that. The man was quite specific. He wanted to photograph you, alone in the house. He specifically stated alone. Aye, that'd be right. I told him to sling his hook.'

Anne-Marie looked down at her cup. 'You think you know everything, Christian, but I'm not stupid. I've looked after myself for a long time now.'

'I'm not denying that, but part of the reason you do okay is because you're a bright girl.'

She rolled her eyes towards the ceiling. 'I'm twenty-seven, I've got a masters degree in fine art and I'm trying to complete a postgraduate in—'

'Aye, like I said, you're a clever girl. But you're no physical match against a man.'

'Well, that's why you're here.'

'Aye, and the day that you start letting punters in to photograph you on your own, that's when I know, degree or no degree, you've lost it.'

'Point taken.' She turned to me. 'Will you show me the pictures, the pictures of the other girl?'

I looked at Chris. He shrugged.

'Don't look at him, look at me.'

I slipped the photographs from the pile and gave them to her. Anne-Marie looked through them silently, threading a strand of hair anxiously between her fingers. Chris held out his hand and she passed them to him reluctantly.

'Jesus Christ!' The big man's face distorted in distress. 'Can you understand what I've been going on about now?'

'You've made your point.'

Chris raised his voice. He was holding onto his temper, just. 'I don't see how you can say that when we go through this charade every week. Do you want to end up like this lassie?'

He held the photograph close to her face, so close the focus must have blurred. His hand trembled. I tensed myself for movement, unsure of what might happen next.

'Look at her, Anne-Marie, look. Jesus wept. She's dead.' He placed his face in his hands. 'I can't be here twenty-four hours a day. What you're doing isn't safe. Don't you read the papers? Listen to the news? Even the girls turning tricks on the street don't invite punters into their home and they're getting picked off, one by one.'

'It's fine, Christian. It pays well and nothing's going to happen. Rilke's just told us the man's dead. He's no going to come after me now.' She ran her fingers through her hair again. 'Anyway it might be make-up. She could be acting. People have strange fancies.'

Christian raised his face from his hands.

'Strange fancies, that's one phrase for it. Admit it, Anne-Marie, you enjoy it as much as they do, you get a kick out of it. You like the attention, posing away up there, showing them everything you've got.'

Derek and I sat at the table forgotten.

'Why don't you just get it over with and call me a whore. You get your cut of the wages of sin. You're not so moral when you're opening the door and taking the money.'

Christian sounded defeated. 'If it wasn't me it would be someone else. At least this way I get to keep an eye on you. Christ knows what Mum would say if she knew.'

I looked at Derek and he nodded, mouthing, 'Brother and sister.' A faint smile played around his lips. Embarrassed or enjoying himself? I couldn't tell.

'The only way Mum would find out is if you were to tell her.'

'Or if you end up on a slab like this lassie.'

'You worry too much.' She leant across the table towards him and took his hand. 'I wish I could convince you.'

'You'll never convince me.'

'I'm the one in control. I don't fuck anyone. No one slips a tenner down my knickers. No one touches me. I don't do a striptease. I pose. I make them wait while I go through a whole fashion show. I give them winter wear, day dresses, evening gowns, the lot. It's only after I've modelled the swimwear that I take my clothes off.' She laughed. 'Then the cameras go wild.'

Anne-Marie had returned the Polaroids to me at the door. 'A souvenir.'

She'd given Christian a kiss on the cheek, then handed him his jacket, pushing him out gently, saying, 'Aye, aye,' to his warnings of 'Put the chain on . . . Look through the peephole before you open the door to anyone . . . Remember training tomorrow night.'

He'd stood on the landing until he heard the chain pressed home, then followed us down the stairs.

'Christ, I worry about that lassie. Why can she no be happy acting in your daft films?' He patted Derek on the shoulder. 'No offence, like. I enjoy your movies. Listen,' he turned to me, 'you find out anything, you let me know.' He slipped his hand into his pocket and handed me a fold of notes. 'Sorry about earlier. Just a bit of fun.' I counted four tens and looked at him. 'Well, you did use a roll of film.'

I folded twenty of the money Christian had returned into a small square and palmed it to Derek along with my business card asking, 'Will you phone me if you hear anything interesting?'

'Sure.' He held on to the card and gave me back the money. 'Owe me one.'

'I'll look forward to you collecting.'

He smiled, said, 'See you around,' and walked into the night without giving me his phone number.

I looked at Christian. He sighed, 'I'm going to have bad dreams tonight.'

I patted him on the shoulder and left him standing there, a big man, looking up towards the stars, towards a slim silhouette, moving against the light at a third-floor window.

8

TV Land

Darkling I listen; and, for many a time
I have been half in love with easeful Death,
Call'd him soft names in many a mused rhyme,
To take into the air my quiet breath.

John Keats, 'Ode to a Nightingale'

LATER THAT EVENING I stretched myself across Rose's Emperor-size bed, playing with the glass of wine she had given me, holding it up to the light, watching the flame through the ruby filter and beyond it Rose's reflection, bathed in the dim glow of the trembling offertory candles.

'So good for the complexion.'

It was restful watching Rose metamorphose into herself. She sat at her dressing table shrine, slightly flushed from her bath, her damp hair piled high on her head. I was conscious of a pride that heterosexual men must feel. I was going out on the town with a beautiful woman. It was just a shame about where we were going.

I watched as she felt among the jumble of cosmetics, finding the desired potion without moving her gaze, combining lotions and powders with the skill of the apothecary. She leant towards the cloudy glass, hung with old evening gloves and beads and pat-patted a powder puff that might once have belonged to Jean Harlow, sprinkling fine flurries of dust that seemed to hang gold and heavy in the air before diffusing over the landscape of her dressing table, settling on vials, jars, bracelets, peacock feathers, bottles of half-used perfume and petrified nail polish, stones, seashells, photographs, lacquered boxes tumbled with jewellery, all of it already coated with the dust of years. The light reflected off the bronze embroidered chrysanthemums on the shattered silk of her Chinese robe. She caught my gaze and her reflection smiled back at mine. An artist's model/whore from Montmartre, one hundred years ago.

'I'm looking forward to this, Rilke. Thanks for inviting me.' I grunted like a ten-year-married husband and lifted a magazine that had been making its way across the floor to that stoorie netherworld beneath Rose's bed, where tissues, lost wine glasses, forgotten paperbacks and other things best forgot reigned. 'It'll be fun. It's good for us to go out occasionally away from work. We don't do it often enough.' I flicked through the glossed pages watching half-naked, skinny girls pass by, a starved parade.

'At the risk of sounding ungentlemanly, I didn't invite you, Rose.'

She lit a cigarette. Two red tips glowed a crimson warning, as she and the woman in the mirror inhaled. She narrowed her eyes and squinted at me through the smoke.

'You think Les and me don't get on and it's true, we don't always see eye to eye, but you know, deep down, I admire Leslie. He's true to himself. Even if his taste isn't quite what I would choose.' She selected a small cut-glass pot and smoothed balm round her eyes. 'I mean,' she shut her left eye, 'the last time I saw him,' and began applying a slate-grey tint, 'he was way overdressed.' She turned round to face me, checking for offence.

'You look a bit peculiar yourself right now,' I said.

She fluttered her eyes comically and returned to her mirror; balancing her eye-shadow, lining her lids with soft, dark kohl, curling her lashes, then coating them with thick, black mascara; concentrating on her art, but concentrating on the words she was saying to me as well.

'I'm never sure if he's just making fun of women.' She sucked in her cheeks and applied her blush; for a second I could see the skull beneath her skin. 'For all that Leslie dresses like a woman, I don't know that he likes them.'

'If you don't like him, don't come.'

She retrieved a slim brush with a long tapered handle that had fallen behind a line of perfume bottles. A dark shadow danced across the wall.

'There's no need to be like that. I'm just trying to explain why I never feel comfortable with Les.' She began to load the brush with lipstick. 'It's nothing to do with the way he dresses, although obviously I think he could do better,' and began to paint on her trademark scarlet mouth. 'It's more the way he looks at me sometimes, as if I've stolen something that should be his.' She blotted her lips with a scrap of tissue, then scrutinised her reflection one last time. Satisfied, she stood up, dropping her robe, revealing black lace-topped stockings, black silk cami-knickers and

black underwired brassiere, and began to flick through the
dresses in her wardrobe.

'Rose.'

'What?'

'Have you no modesty?'

'What's it to you?'

The taxi driver kept sneaking looks at Rose in his rear-view
mirror. I turned and looked at her myself. Sure enough, she
had crossed her legs high on the thigh, showing a glimpse of
white flesh at the top of her lacy hold-ups.

'You're distracting that man from his job.'

She leaned conspiratorially against me. I smelt her perfume, Chanel No. 5 laced with cigarettes and red wine.

'Stop being such a spoilsport. It's the only fun taxi drivers
get, looking up women's skirts – well, that and couples having it
off in the back of their cabs.' I gave her a sideways look and she
winked at me. I wondered how many glasses of wine she had
drunk before I'd arrived. 'They're all voyeurs. It warps you
driving a cab, boredom and depravity, nothing in between.
They end up like Travis Bickle.' She leaned forward again and
started to talk to the driver, asking him if he had seen the movie
Taxi Driver. I knew where this was leading. The taxi driver
game, invented by Rose, the object of which is to coax the driver
into repeating lines from the film, specifically 'You looking at
me? You looking at me?' 'Well, I don't see anybody else here,
do you?'

We slipped through a fluorescent white tunnel, then
climbed high over the city on the curving expressway; the
River Clyde oil-black and still beneath us, a backdrop to the
reflected lights of the city; the white squares of late-night office
work; traffic signals drifting red, amber, green, necklaces of car

headlamps halting then moving in their sway; the Renfrew Ferry illuminated at its permanent mooring; scarlet neon sign of the *Daily Record* offices suspended in the dark sky to our right. The driver was repeating his lines as if they were something clever. He had diverted his gaze towards Rose's bosoms, which quivered gently with the motion of the cab. On the radio a Marilyn Monroe sound-alike whispered an invitation to an Indian restaurant, where, her voice intimated, she would fuck and then feed you.

> Why not make your way
> To our buffet?
> Take your feet
> To the end of Argyle Street

I stretched back into the shadows and watched the driver watching Rose, his eyes glancing between her reflection in the rear-view mirror and the heavy city traffic. Willing to risk a crash, blood and carnage and the death of us all, for a glimpse of her trembling cleavage.

The Chelsea Lounge looks like a club for dubious gentlemen, designed by a Georgian poof with a Homeric bent. The walls are lined with mauve and cream striped wallpaper, the floor tiled, with a sober brown/beige compass at its centre. Chaises longues and high-backed sofas, upholstered in wine velvet, group round tables. Corinthian columns flower into the fondant cornicing of the high ceiling. The effect is expensive, somewhat austere, and spoilt by the sheer twenty-first-centuryness of its clientele.

Some people hold that ancient Greece was a golden age for inverts. Old men and boys walked hand in hand through Elysian fields, and Sapphic love flourished in an island paradise. Personally, I see many reasons youth should be attracted to old age; all of them can be folded and put in your wallet. I also know that there are not a few who would happily transport all the dykes to some Hebridean colony. So, unlike Mr Wilde, I am cynical about Greek motifs. Still, I cannot walk into the Chelsea Lounge without feeling that the look of the place would be enhanced by a toga-only dress code, some laurel leaves and a few naked, curly-haired youths in the mould of Caravaggio's young Bacchus. As it was, two bouncers in anonymous dark suits nodded us through.

'Do you think they thought I was a lady-boy?' asked Rose.

'Always possible.'

I was scanning the room looking for a familiar face.

'They are beautiful aren't they?'

'Who? The bouncers?'

'Stop being annoying. Thai lady-boys.'

'Not my thing, Rose.'

'I know, but you can appreciate that they're lovely.'

I could see my quarry on the mezzanine above the bar. 'Do you want to look like a lady-boy?'

'I can think of worse things.'

'Rose, they all want to look like you.'

She edged through the crowd to the bar, cutting in front of young, fresh-shaven office types, clearing her way with a smile, a turn of the hips and an elbow. These are the men your mother should have warned you about. The look these days is smart-casual, a sporty James Dean meets a corporate Rock. The cowpoke is back on the range and the leather queen has hung up his handcuffs. No more kerchiefs of many colours flouncing from back pockets. It's got so that my anonymous charcoal is in fashion. But make no mistake. Everyone is here for the same reason.

'Honestly,' Rose turned to me, 'some of these men are so arrogant you have to push them out of the way to get by.'

The barman moved towards her, compelled by the strength of her stare. Rose beamed at me. 'It's half-price cocktails. Let me buy you a drink.'

While my employer instructed the barman to make our pink gins with double gin – 'Pub measures are a waste of time' – I stepped backwards and stared towards the mezzanine.

This is a good trick. Try it if you don't believe me. Stare at someone for long enough and I guarantee they will turn and look at you. Leslie twisted in his chair, peered through the wrought-iron banister, frowned, then smiled and waved me up.

'Rilke, and you've brought Rose with you.' Leslie shook my hand and stretched towards Rose, air-kissing her like an LA star. 'What brings you to this den of iniquity? Does he need you along for bait these days, Rose?'

'Don't be crude, Les. I was looking for you.'

'And you remembered it was my group night, I didn't know you cared.'

He shifted along the settee and we slid in beside him.

On the third Wednesday of every month those transvestites who desire like-minded company convene in the Gay and Lesbian Centre, a dreary meeting house with the air of a jaded youth club. They sit under fluorescent lights in a spartan classroom, discuss matters of style, swap fashion tips, debate the desirability of 'passing' and generally relax, unmolested. Copies of *The Tartan Skirt*, the TV fanzine, featuring a fresh, kilted cover-girl every issue, are distributed. Perhaps there will be a guest speaker, or one of the ranks will give a talk of TV interest. The meeting closes at nine and those who wish to prolong the ecstasy retire to the Chelsea Lounge.

It is a sober grouping. Its manner at odds with the party frocks. They sip ladylike drinks, a single G & T, or perhaps a spritzer, followed by sparkling mineral waters. They will leave early, long before raucous drunks stream from pubs, walk briskly to nearby parked cars then drive home, within the speed limit, uncomfortable at those long red-light pauses. Somewhere on the journey, they may pull into a lay-by, or perhaps a deserted alleyway, remove their wig, ease out of their carefully selected frock, the satin slip, so nice to the touch, the constricting nylons, brassiere swollen with silicone mounds and bought mail order, the package collected from a PO box hired for the purpose and opened with quick anticipation; they strip themselves of the tight knickers that squeeze their genitals so pleasantly, and resume the rough fabric of their man-clothes. Last of all, they open the glove compartment, remove a moist wipe and, in the dim glow of the car's interior light, clean away the face they put on for a night. But while they are in the Chelsea Lounge, dressed with care, they are the girls.

Most of the girls are not gay. They are part of what we call the transgender community, and good luck to them. Dressing up never hurt anyone, except perhaps Gianni Versace, and according to Les he was asking for it.

Rose was talking to the girl next to her. They looked like they were having a good time, Rose fingering the fabric of her new friend's skirt admiringly, knocking back the gin. Any minute now they would be visiting the powder room to-gether.

'So what do you think?'

Les raised his hands in a *ta da!* showgirl gesture, giving me a full-toothed smile, opening his eyes wide as Josephine Baker. His white-blond wig was layered into soft ringlets which sprawled in artful disarray across his shoulders. His red dress had a 1940s feel, broad shoulders tapering into an alarmingly tight waist, cinched by a black patent belt, a plunging neckline with the illusion of a significant bust. No one would mistake him for a woman, but, for a man in a dress, the effect was pretty smooth.

'Aye, very nice. Are you on the hormones?'

'No, dinnae be daft. I'm dedicated but I'm not ready to die for the cause yet. Anyway, what's all this about? You needing to score? You know I never carry any when I'm out dressed. Can you imagine getting busted and thrown in the cells in this get-up? Some six-foot shirt-lifter trying to shove it up my arse? No thank you.'

'You flatter yourself sometimes.'

'Ach, don't be so touchy. I'm just having a laugh, you know that. So twice in one week, eh? And you don't want to score. Let me guess, it has something to do with the introduction I gave you.'

'Bright boy.'

'Girl.'

'Okay, then, clever girl.'

'Well, I'm not interested. You wanted an intro. I gave you an intro. This is R & R time, Rilke. Have a few drinks and forget about it.'

'I'll buy you a drink. I just wanted to know a wee bit about the set-up.'

'How old do you think I am?'

'I know better than to answer a question like that.' I knew Les was ages with me.

'Come on, how old?'

'Twenty-nine.'

'Aye, very good, nice to see you settling into the spirit of things for once. I'm a wee bit beyond twenty-nine.' He smiled. 'No that much, mind. But I think I look okay for my age, don't you?'

'I already said.'

He lit a cigarette and drew hard; razor cheekbones sharp against hollow cheeks.

'And, at the risk of flattering myself, as you would put it, I'd say I looked not bad for someone heading towards their mid-thirties.' He broke into a hacking cough. I sipped my drink and rolled my eyes at him. 'None of your cheek. I've kept my girlish figure.' He smoothed his hands down his curves. 'That comes from watching what I eat. I've got a lovely head of hair.' He toyed playfully with his curls. 'That's due to never scrimping on stylists or hair-care products. And, best of all, I have a lovely, unlined complexion.' He zigzagged his index fingers down his face, over the tributaries of laughter lines and wrinkles. 'Specifically, no scars. I owe that to maintaining a regular skin-care regime and knowing when to zip the lip.'

'So they're a heavy mob.'

'You don't give up, do you? I must have been high as a kite to give you his number in the first place. Let's just leave it at that. No harm done, eh? Sometimes Rilke, it's best not to know.'

'They didn't look that heavy to me.'

'What do you want? A sign above the door?' He put a hand on my wrist; his nails were painted the same shade of red as his dress. 'Listen to Aunty Les and drop the Philip Marlowe impersonation. Okay, so you may not carry your age as well as I do, but there's no need to make it worse.' He laughed. 'This is getting a bit heavy. Where's that drink you promised me?'

Downstairs I ordered a swift Jack Daniel's and knocked it back while the barman made up a jug of the gin fizz everyone seemed to be drinking. The staff were easy on the eye. They swift-stepped behind the cramped bar, avoiding collision like a long-rehearsed variety act. The preparation of cocktails involved a lot of shaking and stirring. In the charged atmosphere of the lounge every action had a sexual gravity. I watched while a bar girl dipped the dampened rim of a glass in salt. A punter leant towards me, his leg pressed against mine. I turned and met his gaze. Broad black pupils, hazel irises, heavy lids fringed with dark lashes.

I gestured towards the frosted glass. 'That looks like it might sting the lips.'

He smiled. 'It might prick a little, but you know, it can be a lovely sensation, a prickling against the lips.'

His name was Ross and he worked with computers. Who cared? I told him that a prickling sounded too small and he said that he preferred full size himself. I delivered the tray of drinks, then met him down in the basement toilets.

We stood close. Our alcohol breath merged, hot and heavy in the sanitised cubicle. I held him with both hands, kneading his balls, warm and moist, with my left, while I pulled at his prick with my right. He felt me gently, then hard, easing my foreskin to and fro, up and down, our fists keeping time with each other and the music from the bar above. He came first, spurting against the cistern, cream spunk on white porcelain. I cradled his wilting penis in my hand until I climaxed, sperm fountaining from me in quick muscle pulses; then dripping, slow and viscous, onto his black trousers. There was no toilet paper, so I handed him my cotton handkerchief. He swore softly, then laughed at the albumen stains silvering the fabric.

'Never mind, they were due for the wash anyway.' The

material rasped as he tried to clean it. I could smell the piss
and spunk beneath the mask of disinfectant and suddenly the
cubicle seemed too small, the music from the bar above too
loud. The bright light stung my eyes. I rubbed my temple and
he touched my arm.

'You all right?'

'Aye, fine.'

'Takes it out of you a wee bit these days?'

'Perhaps.'

I'd done with him. The only cheeky banter I engage in
comes before the act. I gave him a chill smile, then followed
him up the stairs to the bar, noting the marks on his trousers:
drink and spunk and sweat.

'You took your time.'

'D'you think so?'

'Not if it annoys you. Here, get some of this down you.'
Les poured a tumbler of cocktail and pushed it towards me.

'I thought these were meant to be sipped elegantly from
champagne flutes.'

'They're meant to get you pissed.'

Les is an exception to the sobriety of the other TVs. For
some, living life to the full involves hill walking, poetry
readings, bungee jumping in the interest of charitable causes.
For Les it means dressing as he likes and a regular high.

I looked around, taking in the crowd on the mezzanine.
There were about fifteen of them grouped round a large table.
Some would do fine, at certain angles, in sympathetic lighting.
A couple of the girls could pass you by on the street and you'd
be none the wiser. One could take a man home, blow him and
he'd be thankful. Others could pass for large matrons,
accepting that no one really looks at large matrons anyway.

But some were fooling nobody. There are things that cannot be hidden; the forty-inch barrel chest, the large hands, size-eleven feet. They could stare at fashion plates, visit the beauty salon, buff their body bare of hair, but they would never be anything but a man in a dress. Poor Cinderellas, never to be transformed. It was enough to make you weep. I refilled my glass.

The company had splintered into small groups, like with like. There appeared to be a hierarchy, with those who could pass for women at the top. Leslie could pass at a distance – a hundred yards, say – and he had a confidence, a certain toughness, which counted almost as much as a pretty face. He crossed his legs and his dress rode up, high black boots and sheer stockings.

For people who weren't drinking much, the girls certainly had a buzz on. There was an air of anticipation, a first-night atmosphere. A haggard redhead clicked open her handbag mirror and sighed at her reflection. She stretched her mouth out in a long ghastly grin and freshened her lipstick. She passed the mirror to the girl next to her, who grimaced, then repainted her own lips a dark shade of magenta.

Someone settled another cocktail in front of me. It tasted fine, pleasantly palatable. I wondered why I didn't drink them more often. From now on my tipple would be pink and fizzy and made with double measures of gin. I raised my glass and saluted the company. A few of the girls raised theirs in response.

Everyone was in women's clothes apart from me and a portly middle-aged man in a terrible jumper, talking intently to two of the more exotically dressed girls. The jumper was orange, a red cartoon cat leered toothily across it. It looked like a stand-in for a personality and had probably cost more than my suit. *Trust me*, the jumper said, *I'm made of wool. Look, I have a sense of humour, I'm not afraid of making fun of myself. No one who wore me could ever be a threat.*

A large girl in a red velvet dress who looked as if she might spend the daylight hours cementing bricks sat beside me. Her wig was a chestnut helmet of curls.

'So, is this your first time?'

I told her it was.

She opened her handbag and removed a small tub.

'I remember the first time I came.' She unscrewed the lid, took out a moistened pad and started stroking it across her nails. Pink polish streaked away. 'I was terrified.' She raised her eyes from her task. 'I came dressed, though.' She gave my knee a protective pat. 'When you feel ready, just you come along. You know how it is, things are never as bad as you think they're going to be.'

I told her I'd often found that.

'There you are then, and you know' – she smiled kindly – 'I really hope you don't mind me saying this, but you would look a lot better with some make-up on.'

I said I'd give it some thought and asked why she was removing her nail polish.

She sighed. 'My wife hates it. She says that she used to worry I might run off with another woman, but she never thought the other woman would be me.'

Rose was talking to a tall girl, almost as tall as me. The girl's long legs were encased in skin-tight, black spandex trousers. She wore an off-the-shoulder black top and a pink satin bomber jacket. The ensemble was completed by a blonde-bombshell bobbed wig.

Rose waved me over. 'This is Sandy.' Sandy and I shook hands. 'Sandy's a pink lady from *Grease*.'

I began talking to her about Piraeus harbour in Athens.

'No.' Rose interrupted me. 'Not Greece. *Grease*, the musical. Sandy's an Olivia Newton-John look-alike. Excuse him, he's got no culture.'

I wasn't interested in talking to anyone apart from Les and he was holding court, pointedly not catching my eye. I fetched another jug of cocktail and sat beside him.

'These slip down pretty good, eh?'

He turned away from his entourage. 'They hit the spot. Cheers.' We touched glasses. Les knocked half of his back with one tilt. I followed suit. 'So what were you at earlier? Did you pull?'

'And you call me nosy.'

'You are nosy, Rilke. A nosy cunt.'

'Aye, well, I'm nosy for a reason.'

'So you say, but see, I still can't work out what your reason is. We swapped favours the other day, that's fair enough. What you get up to is none of my business. But now you want something for nothing and I want to know what it's all about before you go sticking your neb in where it doesn't belong.'

'I told you what it was about.'

'You're losing it. Look at yourself. You're cracking up, man. Is that it? They photos?'

I nodded.

'Pure loco. What have they got to do with anything?' He finished his drink and gestured for more. 'Jesus, that's no his game.' I refilled his glass. He took a sip and looked me in the eye, grave as a bank manager refusing a loan. 'I think you're getting things out of proportion here. Maybe it's not this girl that's upsetting you. Have you thought of that? There's people you can talk to nowadays, you know, counsellors and the like. There's no shame in it.'

I shook his suggestions away. 'I found out McKindless was a regular there.'

'Sweet Jesus, there's no stopping you. So what? What does that prove that you didnae know already? He bought his porn from the same place I sent you. Big deal. It's a small world. I bet you know every antique dealer in Glasgow and beyond. It's the same with crime – there's only so many of us. You tend to run into the same faces.'

'He never mentioned seeing McKindless when I showed him the photographs.'

'Why would he? His type work on a strictly need-to-know basis. He decided you didnae need to know. Be grateful.' He turned a glazed stare on me. 'He's not a nice man, Rilke. Now piss off, you're bringing me down.'

'Ach don't be like that, Les. Come on, tell me why he's not a nice man.'

'Jesus Christ.' He shook his head in silent exasperation. 'If I tell you, do you promise to leave me alone for the rest of the night?' I promised. 'And do you promise to show a bit of discretion?'

'When have I never?'

'When you were fucking that guy in the toilets. We could hear the grunting up here. Christ, the whole bloody balcony was shaking.'

'Very funny. I'll be discreet.'

'Okay, remember I'm telling you this for your own good. I trust you, we go back a long way, but this is serious. It's not a subject for gossip.'

'I get the message.'

'Just see that you do.' He took a long drag on his cigarette. 'Trapp's a ponce. Appeared a few years ago, I don't know where from. I don't know the scale of his operation, don't want to know. *Sirens* is just the tip of the iceberg. He's also involved in several massage parlours cum brothels – no pun intended – and he has a couple of amusement arcades.'

'Amusement arcades? Money laundering?'

'Possibly. That and boys.'

I must have looked bewildered.

'Oh come on, you're not going to tell me you don't know. You walk past these wee grocer's shops converted into amusement arcades. Nothing in them but fruit machines and half a dozen young kids.'

I shook my head.

'You mean to tell me that you've never clicked what they are?'

'I've never really noticed them.'

'Well you will now.'

'And that's what he does?'

'One of his sidelines. You go in, buy a boy a shot on one of the machines, except you're not buying a shot on the machine. See what I mean? Not a nice man. A corrupter of youth and God only knows what else. But he's into enough dodgy dealings and he's making big money. He's nothing to do with your photos. Why would he be? So he knew your guy. Hardly surprising, is it?'

'McKindless wasn't into boys.'

'Aye, but he was into porn. Christ, you're hard work sometimes. Anyway, this guy doesn't confine his business to boys – he's an equal opportunities exploiter.'

'How did you meet him?'

'Not through choice. Ponces are always big into drugs. Good means of control. He wanted a supplier, some cunt gave him my name. I didn't deal in the kind of thing he wanted but I put him in touch with someone who did. To be honest, I would have bumped him anyway. Glasgow likes to think it's a hard city but compared to London or New York, fucking Paris probably, we're a peaceful wee haven. Our career criminals are junkies and third-generation unemployed. Trapp, well, he's something else. Fucking international flesh bandit. The sooner he moves on the better.'

'He offered me a lot of money for those photographs.'

'Do you want my advice?'

'Not really.'

'Take it. This is turning into an unhealthy obsession. Take the money and forget all about it. Give it to charity if that makes you feel better. The society for buggered orphans. Bad things happen. You're not responsible.'

'I found them.'

'So what? You think you're streetwise, Rilke, and so you are, for your own scene, but you know nothing about this. Shall I tell you the truth? I was glad to get rid of the favour he owed me. It made me uncomfortable, him being in my debt. You want as little to do with his like as you can. That's my last word on it. Change the subject or bugger off.'

'He was desperate to get the photos off me.'

'Bugger off.'

I poured us both another drink. 'I have a feeling about it.'

Leslie lifted his glass. 'Cheers. Now bugger off.'

He turned from me, back into conversation with the girls next to him. I sat quietly, nursing my drink, sulking.

The bricklayer girl with the chestnut hair leaned towards me. 'Now's your chance to become famous.'

I looked up, confused. 'Pardon?'

She gestured across the balcony. The jumper man had moved. He was talking to Rose's Pink Lady now, nodding, giving her his full attention. They sat alone in a pool of white light. Sandy looked happy. She was talking, smiling, moving her hands gracefully in the air. The man said something and she threw back her head and laughed. It was a Hollywood gesture, Joan Crawford might have brought it off, but Sandy didn't quite make it. Jumper made a swift signal with his right hand and for the first time I noticed his companion. A blue-jeaned, paunchy man, kneeling on the floor before them, his face concealed by a video camera. It was pointed at Sandy. I watched him focus in on her face, saw the repeated image on the tiny video screen.

In the cruel fluorescence Sandy's magic was gone. She laughed, head thrown back, Adam's apple revealed, laughter lines creasing and the camera man captured the shot. The line where the thick Max Factor *Make-up Artists to the Stars* foundation ended and the gooseflesh neck began. He broke the illusion, took her carefully constructed beauty and turned it into a clownish mask. Fast words tripped from her, desperate to tell her story before they tired and left. She gestured to her pink satin jacket, opening it, revealing the lining, pointing to her name, chain-embroidered, *Sandy*, to the right of her lapel. She slipped it off and exposed her black top. Her eyes glittered with excitement. Jumper nodded, asking her questions, leading her on. She laughed again, bending towards the camera. Too close the lens zoomed in, roving over the pits and craters of a lunar landscape. She smiled and the camera focused on her mouth. Seeing beyond the full painted bow to the thin lips, the receding gums and nicotine teeth of the man Sandy wanted to forget.

A wave hit me and I was on my feet. I heard a voice shouting, 'So you think it's funny, do you? You think this is all a big laugh?'

The voice was familiar. I ignored it. I had problems of my own. The floor of the balcony was unsteady and I needed to get to those men. Someone caught my arm. I shook them free against a shatter of breaking glass. Other voices were raised. Somewhere in the distance Rose called my name. The cameraman was still squatting on one knee. He turned, taking in the company in one seamless cut, aiming the lens at me. I gave him a swift kick, catching him off centre, wresting the camera from him as he toppled. I was going to smash it in the smug face of the man with the deceiving jumper. He was dangerous. He took people and killed them with a lens. I saw Sandy's face, her fear. Tears trembled in her eyes. It's okay, I wanted to tell her. I won't let them hurt you any more. The camera slipped from my grasp and I fought to gain purchase on the pitching floor. Strong arms caught me from behind. I bucked against them, then others joined in the restraint, pinning me until I moved no more.

Darkness.

Darkness.

I wanted to die. My throat was dry and my heart barren. A pulse throbbed a slow heartbeat on my temple, pounding tarry blood through my aching head. I massaged the hard bones around my eyes, feeling the tight skin move, slick against the planes of my skull. Small sparkles of light glittered for an instant in my blind eyes. I opened them again.

Darkness.

I remembered a time when I was afraid of the dark. Some of the fear returned with the memory.

Slowly, I raised myself on one arm. It wasn't my bed. The throw was patched; heavy, soft velvets mixed with cool cottons, ridged corduroy bordering decaying satin. There was a smell of face powder. The musky odour of old clothes and unwashed sheets. I ran my hand across the quilt, feeling the rents, the half-finished embroideries. Something was digging sharp into the soft flesh at the small of my back. I shifted a little. A hairpin.

The evening came back to me, as evenings do, in the darkness of the night. I hoped I'd managed to hit the jumper man just once before they pinned me down. But my memory of his face was unbloodied, my knuckles free of grazes. I continued running my hands across the landscape of the quilt, over the mound of another body beside me in the bed.

There was a groan. 'Jesus.'

The voice came from far away. It was a hundred years old. The voice of a dying ancient muttering a last prayer. I nudged the body and the covers moved.

'Jesus Christ.'

'Rose?'

'Leave me alone, Rilke, I feel terrible.'

'Rose, I need to talk to you.'

'In the morning.'

She moved across the vast bed, away from me, but she lifted her pillow and pounded it, once, twice, three times, before settling down again.

'Rosie.'

'Don't.'

'Come on, Rosie.'

Under the covers a cold foot connected with my shin.

'Call me that again and you're on the floor where you belong.' Rose wriggled, pulling the quilt further over her head, trying to regain the comfort of a moment before. It was no good. She moaned, beat her legs hard against the mattress, then rolled over and clicked on the bedside lamp. 'I would have thought you were in enough bloody trouble without annoying me.' Her hair was still half up, traces of the make-up applied so carefully the evening before still around her eyes. She started to cough. 'Pass me a cigarette.'

Rose sat for a moment with the cigarette in her mouth, then shook her head slightly and lit up. I helped myself from her packet and tore away the filter.

'Oh, very macho.'

'I suppose so.'

'Quite the macho guy all round, aren't we?'

'If you say so.'

'What on earth were you thinking of? Les and I had to huckle you out of there. We were lucky to get a taxi, the state you were in. He's furious.'

'I'll make it okay with Leslie.'

'You'll have some job.'

We sat for a while, smoking in silence. There was a bottle of painkillers by the bed. I dry-swallowed three and passed them to Rose.

'You're only meant to take two.

'I'm a big boy.'

'And nothing exceeds like excess?

I ignored her.

'So are you going to tell me what that was all about?'

'Oh, I don't know, Rose.'

'I think you owe Leslie and me some explanation. Not to mention Leslie's chums. Jesus, you were like a man possessed. I've never seen you like that before. You frightened me Rilke.' She regarded me, eyes narrowed, through the wispy spirals of smoke. Suddenly she smiled, clasping her arms round her knees. 'It did have its comical aspect, though. All those squint wigs. Oh my God, the screams.' She started to laugh.

'Don't. I feel bad enough. Don't make it worse. They were making a fool out of that girl. I couldn't stand it any longer.'

'Rilke, she was the centre of attention and loving it. It was probably one of the best nights of her life and you ruined it with your carry-on.'

'Aye, but she couldn't see what they were doing to her.'

'So you decided to be the knight in shining armour.'

'Something like that.'

'Well, that was a good idea, wasn't it?'

'You've made your point.'

I opened the cabinet next to the bed and felt around a jumble of bottles and tissues. For a second my fingers rested on the cold, ridged torpedo of a vibrator. They recoiled and found their prey. A cool, dimpled half-bottle of whisky slipped behind a pile of paperback thrillers. I unscrewed the lid and took a sip. It burnt. For a second I thought I might throw up, then it was down and I was feeling better.

'Oh, just help yourself. You shouldn't go rooting around in people's cupboards, you might find more than you bargained for.'

'Rose, you don't know the half of it.'

She frowned, then held out her hand for the bottle and raised it to her lips, screwing her face up as she swallowed.

'Euch. Kill or cure, right enough.' She replaced the cap and shoved the bottle under the bed. I knew I'd not see it again. 'I wonder about you sometimes. What's it to you if they were making fun of her? You think she's not used to that? Any man who goes out dressed as a woman must be able to handle himself. Things aren't always as they appear, Rilke, you should know that.'

I leant back in the bed. I wanted to ask Rose to hold me. Just take me in her arms and keep me safe until night was over. She stubbed out her cigarette.

'Well, you've given them something to talk about at their next meeting. Christ, can you imagine? They'll be talking about that one for the next ten years.'

'Rose, I'm sorry.'

She touched my hand gently, then turned and switched off the light.

'Never mind. You didn't hurt anyone. Go to sleep. Things are always better in the morning. Anyway, there's a busy day ahead of us.'

I sat listening to her breathing grow slow and regular, watching the orange tip of my cigarette, until the glow faded and there was nothing left but darkness.

9

Caveat Emptor

THERE WAS ACTIVITY AROUND the lift, antique dealers and West End trendies crushing together, pushing it close to capacity. I slipped through to the back stairs and began to climb the three storeys to the saleroom, my leather soles silent against the glittered concrete. Grumbled negotiations drifted down the stairwell. I leant back against the half-blue, half-white wall and peered through the curving, cobwebbed banister to the floor above. Four men hunched together on the dimly lit middle landing. I could make out two of them, one a bowed back in a black Crombie, the second short denimed legs, worn fabric concertinaed at the knees. A protracted division. Biros denting the catalogue in frustration. The pre-sale conference of Jenson's ring.

'Ach, no,' a voice said, 'how come I always get the fuzzy end of the lollipop? Yous are doing what yous always do, you've been shafting me for years.'

'And you've been moaning for years.'

'C'mon.' A nasal whine not calculated to inspire sympathy, though you might give in just to get the noise out of your head. 'I can sell that bookcase.'

'We can all sell that bookcase. I could sell a hundred plain bookcases. You got they three fireplaces last week. I had a boy desperate for a fireplace. An easy score, two hundred, no problem, but it was your shot. Did you hear me moaning?'

'Aye, cut it out. This takes longer every week. That bookcase has got yuppie written all over it, anyway. We'll run them up to two hundred more than we could sell it for and they'll walk away thinking they've got a bargain. We'll all lose out and Rose Bowery gets double commission. I tell you, she should put us on a retainer.'

'Interesting idea that, Jenson.' The man in the Crombie turned towards me, mushroom face blanching. 'Something I should know about?'

A ring is an illegal and ancient association of dealers who trade in the same class of goods. Its one objective is to keep prices low. The ring gathers before the sale, forming a circle. Each individual takes a turn of standing to the left of the ring's chief, in this case Jenson. They declare which lots they are interested in and the price they are willing to pay. After the sale the ring meet again for their own auction, the knock. Here the difference between the estimated and realised price is divvied up. Each man declaring what cut of the difference he will take, then being reimbursed by the purchaser. In theory, a member of the ring could make money by simply turning up and declaring an interest, though I wouldn't advise it. The ring also discourages newcomers, banding together, bidding them up, making sure those outside the brotherhood pay top price and beyond.

Jenson's ring had run for years. A sour and unlawful guild, organising who got what, uniting against outsiders. They held us to ransom. If we exposed them, they might boycott us, stop buying and more importantly stop running things through the auction house. We couldn't afford to lose them. I loathed them, needed them and took every opportunity to needle them.

Jenson was looking down the stairs towards me. Short in his long coat, white hair trimmed, neat, well-shaven, the midget undertaker. He was tough but I'd made sure he never knew how we stood. All queers are unstable – who knows when I might turn?

He blustered, 'Mr Rilke. We were just discussing the amount of furniture we put through Bowery. You should put us on commission.'

'Do you think so, Mr Jenson? Perhaps I'll look into that. It's been a while since I went over the furniture records, took a note of who bought what.'

'Just a joke, Rilke. A wee gag. Time hangs heavy after you've viewed.'

The others were moving away from him, their main business done, anyway. I gave them the professional smile.

'Well, gents, the sale will be starting soon. I'm sure we must be in breach of some regulation all gathered together on this wee landing. There's wine and sandwiches in the saleroom. Go on through and help yourselves.'

They went ahead of me, the dark hallway illuminated for a moment as they opened the door to the sales floor. Warm wine at eleven thirty in the morning. I made a note to myself to run the bookcase sky-high against the chandelier.

In the saleroom viewing was in its closing stages. I made my way towards the rostrum, nodding at those I recognised, but not stopping to talk, making a mental note of who was in the room, marrying them to lots I thought they might chase.

There is no dress code in the salerooms. Here the rich mix with the poor, and who can tell them apart? The man checking pictures, one by one, against the scribbles in his notebook. The jacket of his grey polyester suit bears the brown-edged melts of fag burns. His trousers droop at the hem. A grubby soul, not worth a second glance, but he may reach into his inside pocket and draw out a thousand in cash. *A hundred pounds for a new suit — you could buy a decent painting for that, reframe and sell it on for three more.* The guy in the tweed jacket, smart as paint, leaning against the pillar, talking on his mobile, who is he talking to? A contact in the States? *Hank, I've got something here you're going to cream over.* Or his bank manager? *Mr Menzies, I know I've been sailing close to the wind, but if you could see your way to honouring these three cheques I'll ensure the funds are with you by the end of the week.*

Empty this crowd into the street and no one would guess what they're about — a large chapter of Alcoholics Anonymous is the closest you might get. They jostle between the trestle tables and furniture, marking their catalogues with codes of their own devising, scribbled hieroglyphs, top-secret formulae to wealth.

Over every auction house doorway should be placed the legend *Buyer, Beware.* You can lose your redundancy in the salerooms as sure as you can lose it in the bookies. Over on the love seat, a new recruit, fresh into early retirement with his *Miller's Guides* around him, his new chums, so friendly, solicitous. In all his years in the office he never met such nice men. Clever, too: they know a lot, and are generous with it. They tip him on what to buy. Scene one in the aged rake's progress: *The Rake comes into his inheritance.* And I do nothing to stop the fleecing of this good man straight, straight from his

everyday job, salaried security and into the hands of the
players. Should I lean over the podium and whisper,

> Run, sir,
> Run for the hills.
> You are fair game to us,
> And we will take you,
> And shake you,
> Till the last penny has
> Rolled
> From your pockets.

Why? Sitting there tipsy on early-morning wine, his
catalogue conscientiously marked. The blind man at the card
game. Ready to buy, to pit himself against the rag-taggle
gypsy crowd that we are, and we, the seasoned crew, ready to
take him. Him thinking he's found Easy Street.

If you are old enough to sign a cheque, you are old
enough to bid. Mad? Never mind, you and your money will
find a welcome here. Drunk? Ach, aren't we all at some
time? Have another glass and let me steady your hand while
you sign. We are not prejudiced. Whatever your creed,
whatever your affliction, roll up, roll up and buy.

The furniture ring had congregated by the door, a nonchalant
knot. But the runes had fallen wrong for Jenson's men. At the
other side of the room, poised like the visiting team they
were, the Irish boyos. Fresh over on the Cat with their empty
Lutons, ready and waiting. The Irish band with their harsh
voices, their humourless wit and thin, veiled hints of the 'RA.
Big men, farmers' sons, fed yellow bile in place of milk.
Jenson could ring all he liked. Their loot could breach any

corral of his making. The best was going back to the Old Country with them.

Rose settled at my right side, watching the room. Her eyes scanned the crowd, looking for ticks and trades ready to tally the bids. When it comes to money, Rose's mental arithmetic is spot-on every time. The evening may see her prone before midnight, but while the sale is on she will ride the crowd.

She leant towards me. 'See who's here?' I nodded without looking at her. 'I love those Irish bastards.'

'You love their money.'

'I love their money. But I'll tell you what I love almost as much, they fuck that cunt Jenson. Tell you, Rilke, one day I'm going to expose Jenson's ring.'

She caught my eye and we laughed. Sometimes I could almost like Rose. I gave her a pre-performance smile and she straightened up to me. Shimmying her shoulders in the excitement of the joke and the money to be won. For an instant I glimpsed, beyond the open V of her jacket, the demanding breasts, black lace trim of brassiere. Her throat white, soft, perfectly indented. I looked away.

As I climb onto the podium I shrug off myself and don a lean hard-to-pleaseness. I'm dressed for the part, costumed as the Auctioneer. Put me on a dais. Raise me on a pedestal and watch me roll. A navy suit with a silver pinstripe that echoes the gleam in my slicked-back, sleek black hair. Al Capone jacket, double-breasted and wide-lapelled. I wear my mirrored aviator's shades. The black of the lenses is like the eyehole gaps in a skull. Instead of my eyes, a mineral reflection of the crowd. A scented red rose in my buttonhole, the shade of a vamp's velvet gown; its petals will drop, one by one, as the day goes on. I ascend the rostrum, rest my weight against the lectern and take the gavel in my right hand. There's a buzz in the air, a low drone that descends to a whisper. Three sharp beats of the hammer and . . . silence.

'Welcome to Bowery Auctions, for our monthly special sail of fine art and collectables. Viewing is now over. I'd like to remind those intending to bid to register for a paddle number at the front desk. There will be no viewing during the sale . . .'

Eyes glaze as I give my spiel. I scan the room mapping who stands where.

I closed my introduction and started the bidding.

'Lot number one, an etching in the style of Muirhead Bone.'

Jimmy James hunched by the picture wall, an ancient troll, morose in his khaki dust coat. He was at his worst, Smike-like, hangover biting, beaky nose red and dewdrop-tipped. He scowled at the assemblage, raised his pointer slowly, as if it was made of lead rather than balsam, and indicated, way up in the corner, a small, dark etching.

'This one here.'

'Thirty pounds? Thirty? Who'll start me at thirty? Twenty-five? Twenty? Come on, ladies and gents. You've been and viewed. Unsigned. A very fine etching, in the style of Muirhead Bone.'

I dropped to ten and suddenly they moved. A catalogue snapped and we climbed, three of us, in jerky bids of five, until we were back at thirty. Below me a mob who would spend an hour for fear of losing a fiver.

At its best you soar. When the mood is right and the chase is on we can fly through the figures and the crowd stands silent in admiration of the gall, the sheer strong-livered ballsyness of the bidders, pursuing each other through the hundreds, while I beat out the rhythm. The corpse dancing on the scaffold.

One twenty
One forty

One sixty
One eighty
TWO HUNDRED

Two twenty
Jenson versus a private, an

Two forty
all-week-in-the-office boy,

Two sixty
smart in his smart-casuals.

Two eighty
My gaze slipped from one to the

THREE HUNDRED
other, conducting the scores.

Three hundred and twenty
The Auctioneer,

Three forty
impartial in the pulpit.

Three sixty
My loyalty is with the loot.

At every third bid

Three eighty
Jenson's head twisted

FOUR HUNDRED
towards his rival,

Four hundred and twenty
face harsh,

Four hundred and twenty
giving him the evil eye.

Four twenty
◉

Four twenty
Maleko!

The private faltered,

hesitated,

shook his head.

I could have been a contender!

Four twenty
I let the hammer hover,

Four hundred
lingering over the last bid,

and twenty
suspending Jenson's triumph in

pounds,
the air, no sale until I say so.

Going once,
slow,

Going twice,
but slow,

Last bid,
my arm, descended.

Going,
On the far side of the room,

Going,
one of the Irish,

That's four hundred and
looked me in the eye

twenty pounds,
and tupped his head,

Ladies and gents,
as I knew he would,

For this rather fine . . .
I stayed the hammer,

flashed a grin and . . .

Fresh Bidder!

'Bastard.'

Their gazes linked, the bids went on, but the battle was decided.

'Why don't you boys just tell us what you've got written down in your notebooks there?' A Belfast accent cut through the crowd. 'Come on, tell us how far you'll go so we can top it right now. Get it over with and save us all a lot of time.'

A woman laughed. Jenson held his head high, but defeat brought colour to his cheeks.

'Remember where you are, gentlemen. I'll have order on the floor.' Inside I didn't give a damn if they fought. 'This is an auction house and we are bound by certain rules.'

I resumed the sale but there was something out of kilter, a tremble in the crowd, a drift towards the centre of the room. Then I saw him. Standing by the entrance, taking in the view, Inspector Anderson. He caught my eye and gave me a nod. The bid was standing high and for a second I thought of counting him in, but friend or foe he was police. I gestured towards the open office door and he took the hint. I could see him through the window, sitting himself at my desk, glancing at the impatient invoices, the red reminders and black final demands splayed across its surface, selecting a back copy of *The Antique Dealer*, settling down to a long wait.

'Good sale?' Anderson put down the magazine and turned towards me.

'Fine. Average.' My mind was fast-tracking to Les and the drugs. 'Developing an interest in antiques?'

'Perhaps. You're busy.' He looked towards the crowd paying Rose at the cash desk, showing their receipts to Jimmy James, removing what lots they could carry, arranging terms with carriers. 'A few familiar faces, too.'

'No doubt. I trust you'll leave them alone while they're on the premises.'

'Nothing that can't wait.' He leant back in my chair and placed his hands, palm up, on the desk. 'I'm off duty, anyway.'

'I wouldn't have thought that would stop you if you had a mind. So is this in the way of a social call?'

I climbed onto a chair, stretched up to the top shelf and toppled a small box into my arms. The bottle of malt was still there, hidden under a gross of manila envelopes.

'Drink?'

'Why not. I take it alcohol has a habit of evaporating around here.'

'Positively vaporises.' I poured out two measures and we touched glasses, 'Slàinte.'

'Yes, good health.' He took a sip. 'Nice. Very nice.'

'So what can I do for you?'

'I'm not sure. I was intrigued by that wee ornament you showed me the other night.'

'The netsuke.'

'Aye, that's it. Horrible thing. The name you mentioned, McKindless, I told you it rang a few bells.'

'Yes?'

'Well, I got one of the constables to have a root around and see if we had anything on him.'

'And?'

'And he came up with a file. It made interesting reading, so I thought I'd pop round here and see if you knew anything else about this guy. He's dead, you say?'

'Three weeks since. We're in there clearing the house right now.'

'Find anything I might be interested in?'

'Like what? Japanese erotic art?'

'Anything of a dubious nature that might interest me in my professional capacity?'

'Nothing.' I lied, not sure why or where we were going. 'To be honest, I've been leaving it to Jimmy James and the rest of the boys. I've been on a bit of a skive.'

'I remember. Nocturnal wanderings.'

'Yes, well, thanks for the other night.'

'I wouldn't want anyone to overhear you saying that to me.' He shook his head. 'No, it's no problem. Forget it. I can't do it again, though. Get caught a second time and you're on your own. You should really watch yourself. Man of your age wandering about the park at night. It's not exactly safe.'

'What did the file say?'

'Classified.'

'The man's dead.'

'Aye, so you said. I spoke to the officer in charge. He was delighted at the news.' He finished his drink.

'The officer in charge of what?'

I lifted the bottle to pour him another, but he put his hand over the glass and shook his head. 'No, thanks. I'd better get going. Tell you what, if you find something, anything, let me know and then, maybe, I'll share what was in the file with you, a trade. How does that sound?'

'Sounds like my life.'

He slipped a card with his telephone number on it across the desk and I added it to the stack in my wallet.

The door opened and in came Rose. She was flushed, eyes wide, hair half tumbled from its knot, but I noticed she had freshened her lipstick. She gave us a smile, the full hundred watts.

'Well, that's another sale over. I just thought I'd say cheerio.'

Anderson removed his hand from the glass. 'Ach, you twisted my arm. Just a small one, then.'

I freshened his drink and did the introductions.

'Rose Bowery, my employer. Rose, this is Inspector Anderson, an old schoolfriend who joined the other side.'

She leaned over the table and shook Anderson's hand. I wondered who had the firmer grip.

'He's an awful man isn't he, Inspector?'

'Call me Jim, please.'

'Jim. Was he as bad at school?'

'Worse.'

'Would you care for a drink, Rose?' I held the bottle of malt in the air.

'No, thanks.' She turned to Anderson. 'I'm not much of a one for the hard stuff. No, I'll have some of my own, if you don't mind me joining you.' She fished her Dunhill, a bottle of Rioja and a corkscrew from her bag, then set to pouring herself a drink. 'Bottoms up!' Half the glass disappeared with her first swallow. 'Anyone mind if I smoke?'

'Not at all.' Anderson took his Players from his pocket. 'I was going to have one myself, but I thought it might be against fire regulations.'

'Well, not if we're careful!' Rose laughed, placed a cigarette between her lips and leaned towards Anderson's proffered lighter. B-movie as ever, a flash of cleavage in return for his flame. We talked and drank for a while, but I could tell my presence had become superfluous.

It was a relief when Rose turned to me and said, 'Is this not your night for going on the randan?'

'Are we keeping you back, Rilke?' Anderson poured himself a shot and offered Rose one of his Players.

'No I'll stick with these, if you don't mind. You get away if you want, Rilke. Me and Jim'll lock up.'

'Why not?' I shrugged on my jacket. 'I'll see you both later.'

Rose winked. 'Be good.'

Anderson loosened his tie. 'Be careful.'

I closed the door behind me.

10

Gilmartin's

I LEFT THEM TO it and headed towards Gilmartin's. I wanted
to punt the McKindless sale and I wanted to feel myself in the
real world. The world of objects and people. The black and
white basement where the dead girl lay was in the past. I
could see her eyes, her torn throat, but I couldn't reach
through the celluloid and touch her. If I thought too long
about Anderson's proposition I might accept. I was too late to
save her, too late to avenge her. If she was murdered it was
sad. Meaningless, like most deaths. I had found her but that
was no obligation. Les was right: I should leave well alone and
get on with life.

These were the thoughts spinning through my head, all
caught up with calculations from the sale. I was beginning to
roast beneath my dark suit. The warmth made me conscious
of my own body, the white shirt brushing against the hairs on
my chest. The weight of the black jacket on my shoulders, a

roughness across the back of my neck where the collar rubbed. Beneath these clothes I am completely naked. Awareness of my body made me think of other bodies, and I knew I didn't want to be alone that night. I pushed open the swing door into the bar-room and I was out of the sunshine and into the familiar, anytime world of smoke and drink.

Gilmartin's is a quarter-gill shop three blocks away from the saleroom. Victor Gilmartin bought it twenty years ago when he decided to retire from the building trade, a decision which coincided with reforms in planning-application law and the resignation of a number of city councillors. The genesis of Gilmartin's is a story Victor loves to tell.

'I'd made my money, but you can't sit still, boy. When I bought this place, it was a dump, nothing like it is now, a real working man's pub, you ken the like, sawdust on the floors, no decor at all, just a dump. I gutted it. Pulled out the insides and redid it, top to bottom. When it was finished you wouldn't recognise the place. The old regulars wandered back, but I let them know they weren't welcome. I started to attract the university crowd, a better class of drunk. On the surface things were going well, but it still wasn't right, there was something missing. Don't get me wrong, it looked good, oh aye, compared to what it'd been it was a palace, but it just wasn't there, know what I mean?' This is the cue for a dramatic pause. The listener realises he is meant to nod sagely, as if he really can see Victor Gilmartin's gleaming, new pub, fresh from its makeover, but mysteriously incomplete. 'That's when I met this boy,' and he'll wave his hand at Ferrie, grey and grizzled, on his usual high stool by the bar, 'and it all fell into place. ''What you need, Mr Gilmartin, is a few antiques, something to add a bit of class, some old-world

charm,'' and he showed me this, this masterpiece,' Victor
indicates a huge oil hung to the right of the gantry, an addled
stag at bay leering lopsidedly from the peak of a peppermint
mountain (here the listener might have to struggle with his
expression), 'and a whole new world opened up to me.'

Victor Gilmartin is the antique dealer's angel. A hard man,
responsible for the expressway that slices through the city and
the consequent eradication of some of the finest Victorian
architecture in Britain. A man under whose tarmacadamed
roads are reputed to lie not a few bodies. In the rolling eyes of
a frightened stag Victor Gilmartin discovered a love for
antiques, and in Victor Gilmartin's enthusiasm for a dreadful
daub he had spent a day hauling from pub to pub, Ferrie
discovered a mark.

Ferrie is close. He worked Victor slowly, testing him,
pushing a little further with every deal, but careful not to kill
the goose. The day he scored fifty pounds for a white
porcelain po he knew he would never go thirsty again.
Ferrie's dealing days are over. He is now the unofficial
curator of Victor's collection. Installed by the bar from
2 p.m. till closing time every day, he gives Victor the nod
on when to buy. Slip the Ferrie a bung and he'll give your
goods a boost.

'Lovely that, nice piece of carnival glass,' he might say
about some ugly dish confined to the hall cupboard since
Granddad won it at the shows. 'Don't see much of that
nowadays.'

And Victor's hand goes into his pocket. Ferrie guards
Victor, treats him gently. A greedier man would have blown
it, but Ferrie allows three scores a week. He keeps a rota of
whose turn is when and charges only 10 per cent commission plus a courtesy pint. Views on Ferrie are divided. Some

think he lacks ambition, others that he is playing a long game, working up to an audacious deal that will see him comfortable, somewhere far away, where it would be difficult for Victor Gilmartin to put his hands round Ferrie's neck and squeeze.

The gantry in Gilmartin's is twelve feet long, amber-stocked and glowing. Patrons gather round long wooden tables on pews and prayer seats. Oak, culled from churches Victor demolished in his previous incarnation, lines the walls. Barmen, in swinging kilts of mismatched tartan, glide from table to bar, floating silver trays of drinks above the heads of the crowd, without spilling a drop. If it were not for the girning faces in the portraits that line the walls, the illuminated, chipped porcelain and flawed glass, it would be a pleasant place. As things are, it is an aesthete's nightmare.

There was a buffalo head mounted at eye level on the far wall. A young girl stroked the sparse hair on its nose sadly.

Time.

A hundred years ago this strange-looking beast had run across a green grass plain in a herd that shook the ground with the weight of their hooves. Alongside comes a train. Red cattle-guard pointing the way, grey smoke trailing behind. The stoker shovels coal into the boiler, the driver pulls the whistle from the sheer excitement of the chase. Midway, in the third carriage down, a man lifts his rifle to the open window, levels his sights, focuses, squeezes the trigger and bam, one buffalo to be sawed, scooped, stuffed and preserved.

Victor was behind the bar, avuncular as ever.

'What do you think, Rilke? I just bought it this afternoon. It took three thirsty men forty minutes to get it up there. I'm going to have a competition to see who comes up with the best name.'

'It's great, Victor.' I moved the girl's hand from its melancholy caress. 'But maybe you should hang it a wee bitty higher. Victorian taxidermists used arsenic as a preservative. That stuff's got a long shelf-life – you don't want to poison the customers.'

Victor's expression hardened; the friendly uncle was gone and for a second I glimpsed the other side: a look caught in the brief sway of a car's headlights, a man watching silently from the verge of a half-laid road.

'Bobby! Give Mr Rilke a drink on the house, then get that bloody buffalo up somewhere high.' He turned to Ferrie. 'That's your job, telling me things like that.'

The Ferryman took a deep drag from his cigarette then placed it in the ashtray beside the cremated remains of a dozen others. He lifted his face into the light. Thin weaves of new lines ran into deep tributaries of established wrinkles. A wise old Galápagos tortoise. He affected a slow response, the better to think of a reply, then feinted it back to me.

'Ask him how he knows.'

I am not in Ferrie's sway. But it does no good to make enemies.

'It's not well known yet, Victor,' I lied. 'There was a circular sent round the auction houses last week, otherwise I wouldn't know myself.'

'Aye, well, much obliged to you. Amazing, eh?' The enthusiasm was back. 'The world of antiques. You never know what you'll find next. Bobby, fill the Ferrie's glass while you're at it.'

There was a congregation of dealers in the centre of the room. I picked up my drink and joined them.

Edinburgh Iain was passing round the jewellery. A simple silver bracelet set with one blue-green stone. 'What do you think that is?'

'Navajo Indian.'

'Right enough. What do you think it's worth?'

'Fifty quid.'

'More or less. What about this?' holding up a single green-flecked, turquoise stone set in simple silver bracelet. 'What do you think this is worth?'

'The same,' guessing a gag but going along with it anyway.

'No.' Edinburgh Iain holds the bracelets side by side across the table in the midst of the shorts and the beers and the half-finished glasses; the blue of the stones catches the lace frill of dried, snowflake frost on drained tumblers. 'No. Bugger all. And do you know why that is?'

A shake of the head.

'Racism. This is Navajo Indian and this is Indian. Racism. Indian silver, the kiss of death.'

Dodgy Steve has to be seen to be believed. A soiled yellow cravat fails to conceal that beneath his fawn Abercrombie he wears no shirt. His hair is thick and dark and parted on the left. He has a new Zapata moustache.

'Hi, Stevie. You in disguise?'

'Very funny.'

He turns to a woman sitting beside him. Right now she is not drunk enough to go home with him, Steve waits. He has the patience of a sinner.

Arthur has a book. 'What do you think this's worth?'

The wrapper is clean, bright, with a small chip in its lower front corner. I wonder if that chip was there this morning and what new flaws will be added before Arthur hits the sack. I peel the wrapper away and examine the boards. Fine, no bumps or cocking, spine straight and true. First edition, Eric Ambler, *The Mask of Medusa*.

I pass it back to him. 'Nice. Good condition.'

'Oh it's fabulous, fabulous. Out of this world.' He's on his third red wine. 'Come on, what price do you think I'm asking?'

'Ach, you've got me, Arthur.'

'Guess. Go on, have a guess.'

'Well, it's in good condition and that's everything with books.' I'm hoping this will filter through and Arthur's prize will not be taken out, displayed, fingered, jacket rent, spine snapped, lain in slops and eventually left under a stool in some bar between here and Yoker. 'Detective fiction, first edition, 1943, good condition, say a ton?' I'm flattering him. I think fifty would be nearer the mark.

'No that's where you're wrong.' Arthur's face is flushed, little red veins stand out on his cheeks, blossom across his nose. He is the happiest-looking drunk I've ever seen. 'The warehouse was bombed during the war, went up like a rocket. Only a handful of these ever got distributed. A grand and a half!' He slams the table with the book, the force of the slam goes through the company. 'A grand and a half, Rilke. Christ, you can say what you like about Adolf but he done me a favour that night.'

An old soak by the bar spots his chance. 'Hi, my faither was killt in the war.'

'Nae offence, man, nae offence. I'm a silly cunt on the drink sometimes, just ignore me. What're you drinking?'

The soak motions to his glass, still keeping the righteous indignation, but indicating a pint of heavy will be reparation enough. 'Just watch what you say about Hitler. He was a bad bastard.'

'True enough, true enough.' Arthur isn't bothered, he wants to get back to his book. If Hitler was here he would probably show it to him. 'Max, give him a pint when you're ready.'

'He killt my daddy.'

'Aye, a bad bastard, right enough,' says Arthur, turning away from the soak. 'Mind, say what you like about the Nazis,' he stage-whispers in the direction of the main company, 'they did the booksellers a fair few favours.'

We laugh. We are wicked men.

'Give us a look at it, Arthur.'

'Jesus, the brothers Grimm, Don Juan and Holy Joe,' Arthur stage-whispers to me as John the book dealer stretches across the table. John's brother Steenie sits, a morose, silent shadow, behind him. Never a word passes between the brothers.

'It's a beauty, right enough,' John holds the book in his hands, milking the moment, 'but what about this wee embellishment?' The cover shows a primitive drawing of a man's face. With a gentle finger John traces an outline of moustache, glasses and goatee beard. 'It isn't part of the design, Arthur.' John builds to his punchline. 'It's done in ink.'

Steve's quarry is on her sixth G & T. No one knows who she is or where he found her but she looks good. Short blonde hair streaked white round the crown and fringe, artful tendrils feathered around her face, forty-plus but neat behind and thighs tucked into tight black trousers, a scoop-necked top which shows just enough cleavage.

Just as I'm wondering why she's with Steve, Arthur leans over and says, 'What's she doing with that manky bastard?'

'The female mind remains a mystery to me.'

'Aye, sorry, I forgot you were a poofter. No offence, like.'

'None taken.'

'I mean I've been married twenty years now and the female mind remains a mystery to me, too.'

'Try going home now and again,' shouts Moira across the table. There's laughter from the women, then a lull in the conversation while they recover from their hilarity and the men re-summon their dignity.

Into the hush breaks Dodgy Steve's voice, soft, seductive and slurred with booze. 'You're gorgeous. I'd like to fuck your brains out.'

The table explodes into mirth again. The woman stands and pushes Steve from his bar stool onto the floor. It's a short drop and he does it easy, hitting the deck in a low roll. We get a glimpse of twin holes, one on the sole of each shoe, the size and shape of thrupney bits. It should be poignant but it isn't and I laugh with the rest of them.

'Good on you, doll.'

'Away over here and sit with us – he's nothing but a wee sleaze.'

The women pull her to them.

'You here on your own?'

'Ach sit with us.'

'What're you doing with him, anyway?'

Their concern is drink-fuelled and inquisitive.

Moira's talking now, holding the table. They listen in silence, reaching for their drinks every now and then but pacing themselves, No one moves for the bar before she has finished. She's in her early fifties. A dealer in whites. Moira can turn a piss-stained sheet from Paddy's into a thirty-pound object of aspirant desire. She shifts the stains of decades with potions and patter.

'My mother and father never had a shop. I don't know why, maybe they just started on that way of doing things and it worked fine, so why go to the extra expense? Oh, and they loved the stuff. My mother liked nice things around her, so whenever my father bought something good he'd bring it home and the house became their shop. It's all the rage now, your house as a showcase, but I never heard of anyone doing it before them. Trouble was, as a child you never knew where you were. You'd be having your tea and someone would come in and buy the table from underneath you. It'd be "Just mind a wee minute, Moira, Mister so and so just wants a look at the table. Take your plate away through to the front room beside Gran the now." And all the while the newspaper would be getting taken off the table and you'd be huckled out of the kitchen.' The company like this, they're laughing along. 'It did have its funny side. I remember my granny, my mother's mother – she lived with us for a long time – I mind her sitting on a chair in front of the fire, comfy as a queen, just beginning to doze off, when there was a ring at the door. My father went to answer it and next thing you know he's shifting her. "Come on then, Mum," he's saying, "you'll be as comfortable on this chair as that and there's a chap willing to pay five shillings for your move." Oh, she never let him forget that one. Still, as a child it was unsettling. They'd bring in this cabinet or something, they'd be saying how it was the nicest thing, the best of its kind they'd ever seen, next thing you know this gem was gone.'

'But that's the name of the game, Moira,' cuts in Arthur. 'You've got to buy to sell and you'll buy what you like.'

'I know that now, but I was just a wee girl. The thing was, they were always saying how lovely I was, how I was their best girl and there was no one as pretty as me in the whole world. The same time they were polishing and repairing the stock, they were brushing my hair, feeding me up, putting me in nice frocks. I thought they might sell me. I mean, I wasn't sure where I'd come from but they obviously thought a lot of me and I reckoned I would get a good price. Every time the door went I thought my time was up.'

The company laugh again.

'He maybe would have, Moira,' shouts a voice, 'just never got a good enough offer.'

'Aye, maybe so,' says Moira, 'maybe so.' And she sounds sad.

The company moves on, rounds bought. I move closer and ask, 'So you realised, Moira, that they loved you and wouldn't sell you like a tallboy or a coat stand?'

'Not for a long time. My mother had another bairn, see, a wee boy; they called him Charles and you can imagine the fuss they made – oh, they loved that baby. There'd been five years between me and him and I can only think they thought their family was complete. It was Charles this and Charles that, but I never felt jealous, I thought he might be more liable to sell. It made me feel that bit safer.'

'Poor you.'

'No, there was worse. Thing was, Charles died. A cot death, I suppose, but it fuelled all my suspicions. In those days no one spoke to children about that kind of thing. It was their way of protecting you, but all that happened was you made up your own reason, which was usually worse. I thought they'd sold Charles and I was next. My mother cried every day for a year and I hated my father for selling him. Hated him for years, until hating him became a habit. I don't think he ever knew what he'd done wrong. He was a good man, my father.'

She looks upset so I pat her arm and buy her another whisky and ginger.

Iain's watching us. He thinks Moira is maudlin, bringing

down the mood. He holds out his wrist to Steve, pulling up his shirt cuff.

'New watch, Iain?'

'Aye, genuine imitation Rolex.'

The game has started. An illustration of the dealer's ethos. Everything is for sale. Walk into my house, appraise my person. These are the men who embarrass their wives by examining the underside of crockery in the neighbour's house. Who offer to buy the furniture in the B & B. Take them out for dinner and their eyes rove the restaurant.

'You like?' He undoes the buckle and passes it across the table to Steve.

Steve turns it over in his hand. 'Nice, really nice.' Steve knows nothing about watches. He's a swag man, purely cash & carry and end-of-lines.

'Tell you what, I could let you have it for fifty.'

Steve pretends impressed. 'Sounds like a good deal. I just bought this the other week otherwise I'd've been interested.' He raises a lean wrist, displaying his own watch.

'Let's have a look.' And Steve has no choice but to hand it over. 'Och aye, it's nice enough, fine for every day, not as good as the one you have there, though. Tell you what, I'll do you a special deal. I'll give you thirty for this, then that's just twenty you owe me.'

Anyone else would tell him to get stuffed, but Steve reaches into his pocket and takes out his roll, surprisingly big, and hands over the twenty.

Arthur gets into the act. 'That's a bonny tie, Iain.'

'Do you like it? My mother gave it to me just before she died. "Iain," she said, "this tie was your daddy's. Before that it was his daddy's and his daddy's before him. Where *he* got it from I'm not sure. Won it in a game of cards, likely. It's our

only heirloom. Treasure it, son.'' And then she passed away.
Do you really like it?'

'It's a cracker. I've never seen such a smart item.'

'Yours for a fiver, then.'

The fiver is delivered, the tie uncoiled and handed over.
Iain slings it round his own neck, then leans across the table.
'Arthur, that really is a smart shirt.'

The women start to object.

'No, Iain, leave him his shirt.'

'Come on, son.'

But they're laughing as well.

'Calm down, ladies, it's only his shirt. It could be his
trousers I was admiring,' Moira clutches her face in embarrassment at her own mirth, 'or his underpants.' They are
beyond themselves now, holding each other and wiping their
eyes. 'But it's only his shirt, and you must admit it's a pretty
fine example of the tailor's art. Tell me, Arthur, would that
fine shirt be for sale?'

Arthur is boozed to the eyeballs but he's still in tune with
the game. 'Of course it is, Iain. Everything is for sale, even
the shirt off my back.' He pulls off his jacket, opens his arms
and displays the shirt in question to the world. It's lawn
cotton, slightly yellowed, with a faint textured stripe.
Arthur's nipples, pink, trimmed with hair, show through
the thin weave. There is a stain the colour of weak tea
under each arm. 'For you a special price, today only, five
pounds.'

'A bargain indeed.'

Arthur unbuttons his shirt, exposing his fish-white chest, a
sparse scattering of dark hair, his drinker's belly.

'Ach, put it away man, put it away.'

'A deal's a deal.' Arthur laughs, unembarrassed, taking the

folded blue note from Iain's outstretched hand, bundling the shirt up and throwing it across the table at him.

'Hey, Rilke man, that's some jacket.'

They're teasing me, testing me out. I shake my head, but there's no getting away from it. I'm part of the game.

'Christ it's flattering. You look a hundred dollars in that. What would a jacket like that go for?'

'Well, Arthur,' I say, 'it's been good to me this jacket. In fact, I call it my lucky pulling jacket' – they *Oooh* at me from across the table – 'but I like you and I think perhaps it would help you out, so to you, ten pounds.'

'Does it work on lassies as well?' asks Arthur.

'Now that, my son, is something you'll have to find out for yourself.' I am as drunk as they are.

'You know it's been so long I think I might turn queer. A ten spot it is.'

He gives me the note and I empty my pockets, laying my wallet, keys, the netsuke still wrapped in my handerkchief on the table. Quick as a flash Arthur is onto the netsuke. Sober or drunk he has an eye.

'It'll be in the next sale. I should have left it up at Bowery.'

'You just don't see these any more. This is museum quality. Christ, I've drunk more than I thought if I'm telling you that. Steenie, you sell enough dirty books, what do you make of this wee grotesquerie?'

Arthur threw the netsuke in the air and caught it, pretending to launch it across the table towards the solemn brother, but retaining it in his grasp.

Steenie wasn't smiling. He looked at the clock above the bar, downed the dregs of his pint, then grimaced, as if it had tasted bitter. 'That's me away.'

His brother reached out as if to restrain him.

Iain chipped in,

'It's hours to last orders. Hang on and I'll get you another.'

'No. I'm fu' enough.' Steenie rose from his seat, he looked at me, hesitated, then shook his head as if he wanted to rid it of something. 'Early start tomorrow. I'll see yous all later.' He made his way towards the door.

'Ach, Arthur,' chided Moira, 'you shouldn't tease Steenie. You know he's religious.'

'Aye, one of the righteous. He gets on my tits.' Arthur remembered John's presence and nodded towards him. 'Sorry, no offence, I ken he's your brother.'

'None taken. Just be thankful you don't have to live with him.'

Laughter returned to the company, a Saturday-night fracas avoided. Without thinking I picked up my belongings, making sure of the netsuke, and started after Steenie.

'Hey, Rilke, hold on, you'll catch your death.' Arthur shoved a jacket at me. I struggled to put it on as I went, drink making me awkward. In the hours we'd been there the bar had grown busy, and now it was standing room only. I eased my way through the press of bodies, trying to keep Steenie in sight, almost closing in on him as he reached the exit, slipping my left arm into its sleeve, reaching to catch the door before it slammed. My elbow knocked against a tray of drinks being ferried across the room sending them into the air. 'For Christ's sake!' Tumblers, pint glasses and shorts hit the floor together in an almighty smash. A cheer went up from the drinkers and Victor Gilmartin came towards me with his hand out.

By the time I'd settled with Victor for the drinks Steenie

was nowhere to be seen. Half a mile from the pub I realised that instead of my sober black jacket I was wearing Arthur's dogtooth check.

11

The Worm on the Bud

Dark and wrinkled like a violet carnation
Humbly crouching amid the moss, it breathes,
Still moist with love that descends the gentle slope
Of white buttocks to its embroidered edge.

Rimbaud and Verlaine,
'The Arsehole Sonnet'

IT WAS TOO EARLY to go home. I found myself heading towards Usher's. Once there I knew I had made a mistake: there was nothing in the throng of well-dressed men that drew me. They were too clean, too well disposed.

I took my drink and sat in a corner by the window. In the street opposite, a young man leaned out of a third-floor tenement, taking the air. He stretched his body, then, in a single move, discarded his white T-shirt, pulling it over his head, tossing it behind him, somewhere into the dark recesses of the room. A shaft of light cut across the building, illuminating his torso, silver-white in the black of the window. He reached up and pulled the blind half down, leaving his body on view, concealing his face.

I sipped my beer, looked at the bustle of men in the bar around me, then returned my gaze to the boy, wondering if he could see me watching him. He was sitting on a chair now, his arm resting on the sill, swinging to and fro, marking time to a beat I couldn't hear. I watched the shadows creep across the orange sandstone, reaching towards him. When the light was gone, and I could see him no more, I left the bar, crossed the street and pressed the third-floor buzzer. The intercom hummed in response. I let myself in and climbed the stairs.

The door to the apartment was open. I pushed it wide and glanced down the dark, narrow hallway. The place looked derelict. Paper peeled from the walls in jagged tongues, exposing the dark treacle of Victorian varnish on the plaster beneath. The floor was bare, untreated boards. I walked towards a light at the end of the corridor, ready for anything, ready to run if need be. I hesitated, listening for a moment, then, hearing nothing, stepped into a long sitting room.

The light came from two tall picture windows which let in the glow of the street lamps; the only furniture was a wooden table and two upright chairs. The boy still sat by the window. He turned towards me, tousled blond hair, dreamy face, lids drooping as if in an opium trance. I judged him to be about twenty, slighter than me, good muscle tone, but I knew I could take him in an unarmed fight. He smiled a lazy smile, rose slowly, and came towards me.

When he was close enough for our breath to merge he

stopped, passive, waiting. I could feel the heat of him, sense his quickening heartbeat. The blood moved faster through my veins, breath shortened, balls tightened. I stood still, playing master, forcing him to make the first move. He tilted his head, glazed blue eyes met mine, then he put a warm, lazy hand inside my jacket, smooth fingers running a light touch up and down my torso, unbuttoning my white shirt, licking his tongue through the dark hair on my chest, tasting the salt sweat on my body, flicking against my nipples hard and strong. I put a gentle hand on his shoulder, tightened my grip slowly, then took him by the hair at the nape of his neck and forced his head back. The boy's body tautened, panic welling with the change of tempo. His fear gave me an infusion of power. He trembled in my grasp and my cock hardened. I forced his head back further, until he was looking me straight in the eye, then put my mouth to his and kissed him. I felt his young boy skin, soft against my bristles, and our tongues met. I loosened my grip and ran a hand across his hairless chest, feeling him relax, tracing the faint swell of his pectorals, glancing over the pebble-hard nipples, trailing my index finger down to his navel, undoing his fly button, feeling his cock, as hard as mine, straining against his jeans. I rubbed him through the denim and he whispered, 'I want you to fuck me.' An American accent.

I released him and he led the way. Once more the room was sparse, empty save for a mattress in the centre of the floor, raised slightly on wooden pallets.

'You like fucking young boys?'

Running his hands down his groin, showing me the bulge beneath, turning himself on. I didn't want him to talk.

'Seem to.' Turning macho. 'Get undressed.'

He unzipped and pulled down his jeans; white skivvies

tented towards me; he discarded them and his cock raised itself almost to his belly, an exclamation to his navel. I started to undress, folding my clothes as I went.

He watched from the bed, playing gently with his erection, teasing me. 'You're not in a hurry?'

'Some things are better slow.'

A man of the world. My cock felt like it might explode with his first touch. I put myself on the bed beside him, ran my hands over his chest again, then took his hard, medium-thick cock in my hands, feeling its strength, moving the foreskin up and down until he groaned at me to—

'Stop! I'll come too soon if you keep that up.'

'I'm concerned to keep something up.'

'No problems there, my man.'

He laughed, flipped over onto his belly, head level with my groin and took my erection into his mouth. I let him blow me, his mouth working its way up and down the shaft, paying special attention to the head, then moving down to engulf each of my balls, gently, probing his tongue to rim me until the feeling became so intense I pulled away.

The boy gazed up at me, pupils dilated, lips glossed with a sheen of pre-cum. His voice was soft, insistent. 'C'mon, fuck me.'

I didn't need to be asked a third time. 'Got any lubrication?'

He reached beneath the pillow and pulled out a tube of lube and a couple of condoms. 'I like to keep it handy.'

The boy tore at the silver package with his teeth, his eagerness giving my balls another twist, then he placed the unwrapped condom in his mouth, leant over, took my cock in his hand and unfurled the condom over my erection, giving it a few hard flicks with his tongue for good measure. He rolled flat onto his belly, wriggling to get comfortable, arranging a couple of pillows to raise himself slightly, positioning his rear. Tight buttocks more square than round, hairless except for a few blond tendrils creeping from the cleft between his cheeks. I started to grease him, smoothing the lube up towards his asshole, then gently inside, rubbing tenderly round the sensitive ring of his sphincter, hearing him moan, '. . . you've no idea how much I need this . . .', nudged his legs far apart with my knee and set to work.

In anal sex it is of great importance that your partner is relaxed. Too much resistance can lead to tearing of the anal sphincter, resulting in infection, or a loss of muscle tension, leading to leakage of the back passage – unpleasant. Other possible side effects include a split condom – which may result in the contraction of HIV or several other harmful infections – piles, and a punch in the face for inflicting too much pain. All this aside, I like my sexual partners to have as good a time as I can give them. I find it stimulating.

I massaged his ring gently for a while, slipping a finger inside to open him up. He responded, moving towards me, then whispered, 'Do it.' I added a glob of lube to the tip of my cock then moved hard, pressing against him, forcing my way in, paying no mind to his moan of discomfort. I grasped him round his chest, holding him to me, working slow to build up a rhythm, gentle, insistent against the resistant muscle, forcing myself forward, deeper, hearing him say, 'That's it . . . yes . . . like that . . . Yes . . .' Then putting my finger in his mouth, allowing him to bite it hard, to help him respond to the pleasure/pain I was giving him and because I didn't want to hear any talking now, just to see the images flashing in my head.

Memories of encounters honed into fuck-triggers. I imagined myself in a movie I'd seen . . . raping this boy . . . taking him against his will . . . forcing him into liking a big cock up his arse . . . I was in a tunnel way beneath the city . . . the smell of ordure in my lungs . . . the scuttle of rats around me . . . fucking a stranger against the rough brick of a wall . . . The shuffle of footsteps coming closer . . . My climax was building, balls slapping against his buttocks, spunk swelling. The images scrolled on. It was coming now . . . getting close . . . blood-red vision of the orgasm blackout . . . Here it came . . . a wound, red and deep and longing . . . the dark basement . . . the slash of blood across her throat . . . the reflection imposed on the inside of my retina as true as if I was looking at the photograph . . . the girl, used and bound, lying dead on her pallet. I came, spurting into him, grasping his buttocks for support, rocking with the force of my orgasm.

'You're squashing me.' For an instant I couldn't make out what he was saying. His words a jumble of noise intruding on my thoughts. 'Hey, buddy, you can get off now.'

I rolled over and pulled at the condom. It came away with a snap, and my member lolled out, tired, flaccid already. You and me both, pal, I thought. There was a smear of spunk across his belly where he had come while I was fucking him. Thank Christ. Depression was creeping in, 'the after dream of the reveller on opium – the bitter lapse into every day life – the hideous dropping off of the veil', and I had no stomach for tender mercies. I wiped myself on the sheets, got up and started to dress.

'That was neat. Say, I like your jacket.'

I could feel his relief at my leaving, and for the first time gave him a smile. 'Any time, son.'

I let myself out of the apartment and began the long walk home.

Sunlight and birdsong woke me at 4 a.m. The light hurt my eyes and the birdsong disagreed with my hangover. I willed myself back to sleep. Then I thought about buying a rifle, nothing fancy, just long-range enough to shoot a few birds. I lay prone on my mattress, dimly aware of flaked paint and fine cracks etching a fantasy landscape across the yellowed ceiling, then propped myself up on a couple of pillows, rolled a joint and lit it. I held the smoke down in my chest until my lungs creaked, then exhaled slowly. Slender arabesques crept upwards and settled in a haze below the ceiling. Prisms of cut glass swayed gently from the window lintel. Refracted light – red, indigo, yellow, green – floated around the room. I watched silently, rolling and smoking. My body seemed the repository of a dead man. I could think and smoke but all feeling was gone. Inside was nothing. Beneath my slack skin was a skeleton framed by blood and gore. I possessed the required internal organs but the soul was missing. I felt like taking the lit end of the joint and placing it against my arm, cauterising despair in one definite act of pain.

I lifted a paperback from the floor and tried to read. It was a tale of adventurers in the desert, but the distant smell of the river drifted across me, the smell of John and Steenie's bookshop. I coughed and turned a damp page. My mind went back to the girl, her riven throat, the eye behind the lens. Steenie knew something. He'd left the bar like a man pursued. Yesterday, I had decided to drop the investigation. Today, it seemed I had no choice but to go on.

Coloured light danced across yellowed walls. The birdsong faded. I lay back and closed my eyes.

12

Making Up is Hard to Do

When I am dead, my dearest,
Sing no sad songs for me;
Plant thou no roses at my head
Nor shady cypress tree:
Be the green grass above me
With showers and dewdrops wet:
And if thou wilt, remember,
And if thou wilt, forget.

Christina Rossetti, 'Song'

PERHAPS IT WAS A public holiday. Les's street was full of children. Three wee girls were practising a dance routine they'd seen on the television, singing and stepping in quick time. A couple of admiring toddlers formed their audience. One tried to join in and was shushed back to the role of fan. A football match was taking place in the middle of the road. The ball scuffed around half a dozen boys, bouncing occasionally onto the pavement. A Sikh shopkeeper scattered fragments of stale morning rolls in front of a commotion of pigeons. Someone headed the ball across the road. A tackle became a scuffle and it slipped from between the players' feet, ricocheting with a bang against the side of a parked car. The pigeons flapped into the air, wearily circled the rooftops once and returned.

The shopkeeper muttered, 'I wish they'd never bloody traffic-calmed this street. I'd take cars over they boys any day.'

A man, stripped to the waist, leant from his tenement window and shouted directions to the players. A couple of middle-aged corner-boys stood outside the pub, smoking, watching the game. You have to learn to pace yourself when you have all the time in the world.

I'd told Rose that I would put things straight with Les, but now I was on my way to see him I wasn't so sure he would let me. The problem lay in that blanked-out space. The forgotten part of the evening where, instead of a memory, there was an empty feeling of shame.

A young girl crossed the street and made towards me. Once upon a long time ago she'd been pretty. You could see it in the length of her leg, the turn of her cheek. The corner-boys' gaze followed her, checked out the taut thighs, the neat rear, then turned away, pitched downwards on the seesaw of desire, as they caught sight of her gaunt face, the creased, dark hollows of her eyes. She hurried through the football match in a jerky puppet dance, avoiding the ball without looking. Her thin frame crackled. Mercury in her veins. A girl living on borrowed time.

She fell into pace beside me. 'I need to talk to you.'

I kept walking, but put my hand in my pocket and rooted around for small change. 'Sure you do, but it's fine.'

She stepped into my path, holding me there, dark eyes sunk deep in her skull, looking at me from somewhere far away. She'd cut her hair herself. It hung in ragged tufts about her face.

'You're a friend o' that guy Les, eh?'

She pulled her lips back in a smile. Her teeth were the colour of old ivory, a tainted, canine yellow. Tiny flecks of grey foam gathered at the corners of her mouth.

'I'm in a hurry.'

'Aye he's a nice guy, Les.' I tried to side-step her but she met my manoeuvre with a neat block. She'd be some dancer if she could find her way to the floor. 'You away up to see him the now?'

'I'm out for a walk.'

It was as if I hadn't spoken.

'Tell him Rita was asking after him. That's my name, Rita. Short for Marguerita. He'll ken who you mean. He's a nice guy, Les. Some folk round here haven't got time for him, but he's all right. Do you know if he's holding?'

She ground her teeth from side to side. The sound made my own teeth ache.

'I don't know what you're on about, Rita.'

The men outside the pub had turned their attention from the football match and were watching us. Perhaps they were having a bet on how long she could keep me there.

'Aye ye do.' That smile again. 'But it's all right.'

I found three pound coins and gave them to her. 'Away and get yourself something to eat.'

'I'm not hungry.'

'Aye, well it's yours now, do what you want with it.'

'Three quid goes nowhere for me.'

'Fucking junky,' muttered one of the corner-boys, and I made to move.

Rita reached out and took my hand. Her distant gaze slipped further, eyes dark tunnels I didn't want to travel. Strung-out sibyl, amphetamine seer.

'You're looking for something. You'll no find it. But dinnae mind, you'll find something else along the way.'

I reached into my pocket and handed her another coin. 'We're all looking for something, even you.'

'What I'm looking for has to find me. It'll no be long now. I never ever got the photographs.' My stomach did a quick flip. She held me with an iron grip and leaned forward, just the two of us now, no street, no noise, only Rita's pisshole-in-the-snow pupils piercing me. 'Keep looking. Go on with your quest. Seek and who knows what you might find?' Her eyes refocused and she let go of my hand. 'Mind and tell Les that Rita was asking after him.'

I stepped forward. 'Wait, we need to talk.'

She gave me a last smile, then slipped through the tall shadows between the tenements without a backward glance.

Leslie opened the door and let me in without a word. I followed him through the dim lobby, into the cluttered living room. He stood facing me, with his back to the gas fire. There wasn't enough room for both of us to stand, so I shifted a pile of newspapers and took a seat on the couch. The Mexican portrait grinned at me. From where I was sitting, it was all skull.

'I take it you've come to apologise?'

He was in mufti today, jeans and a blue shirt. I cleared my throat. The encounter with Rita had almost put the reason for my visit to Les out of my mind.

'I did, yes. I don't know what got into me.'

'Half a gallon of cocktail would be my bet.'

'You might have a point.'

'Go on, then.' He put his hands behind his back, Prince Philip-style, looking down at me.

'Leslie, I'm sorry for embarrassing you the other night. I lost the head. I promise it won't happen again.'

He opened a press to the right of the fireplace and started to root around inside.

'You chose your company well.' He pulled out a box of papers and looked through them roughly. 'You gave me a right showing up, but I'm no so bothered in front of that bunch of jessies. Now if it was somewhere else' – he shoved the box back into the cupboard and started on the shelf above, swearing softly under his breath – 'certain circles, then it would have been another thing. I might have found it harder to forgive and forget.' He turned and gave me a warning stare to show that he meant it. 'No matter how much I wanted to. But as things are' – he lifted a pile of magazines, looked behind, then replaced them – 'let's just call it quits.' He tumbled a box of video tapes from the top shelf. 'Jesus Christ, how come I can never find any bloody thing? Do you want to tell me what it was all about?'

I looked at the floor. The carpet needed a hoover: there were thin threads of Rizla papers and ooze caught in its pile.

'No. It was just stupid.'

'Fair enough. I tell you who was a real revelation. Rose. She might be a bit of a slapper, but be glad she's for and no agin you. I'm not sure I would've managed to get you out of there in one piece if it wasn't for her.' He shook his head admiringly. 'No offence to Rose. I'm a bit of a slapper myself. D'you fancy a coffee?'

'That would be good.'

'Make me one while you're at it, then.'

I went through to the kitchen, relieved to be let off the hook so easily. I should have known better. Call it karma, call it sod's law, the world has a way of extracting revenge. I filled the kettle, switched it on and began to get the makings together for coffee.

I shouted through to the lounge, 'I met a friend of yours outside.'

There was half a jar of instant on the kitchen shelf. I spooned some into two mugs.

Leslie joined me. 'Oh aye, and which member of the exclusive club was that?'

He took a carton of milk from the fridge, sniffed it, wrinkled his nose quizzically, sniffed again, then passed it to me. I poured a measure into his mug. I could take mine black. Les opened the kitchen cabinet and started to empty it.

'Rita. Marguerita, she asked to be remembered to you.'

He looked up. 'Aye. Looking for a lay-on more like. Telling your fortune, was she?'

'She did, yes.'

'Freaks me out when she does that. Good idea, though. Ye ken what they're like round here. Stupid. No one touches her because they think there might be something in it. They probably think she's going to put the evil eye on them. Ignoramuses. Still, it gives me the creeps.'

'Why should anyone bother about her? Surely she's just a wee speed freak. There's no shortage of them round here.'

'Can you not guess?' He looked up from his task. 'HIV.'

I shook my head. 'I didn't realise. She said something about not getting any photographs.'

He laughed. 'She got you, didn't she? You thought it was

something to do with they photos you showed me the other day.'

'No . . .'

He hooted and slapped his thigh. 'I tell you, Rilke, you crack me up. I look at you sometimes and I still see that wee snotnose in the school playground. The little boy that Santa Claus forgot, right enough.' He put on a falsetto. 'I feel sorry for that laddie, he didnae have a daddy . . .'

'Nor a mammy, either, for very long.'

'Aye, that's right, just go and make me feel rotten, why don't you?' He shook his head. 'Sorry, I get beyond myself at times. I guess that's us quits, right enough. Rita's nothing to do with your pics, but it's a sad story if you're in the mood for one, a real tear-jerker. I'm not sure I should tell you, though. You're too sentimental. You'll away and marry her or something.'

The kettle came to the boil. I pushed away the memories, poured the water into two mugs, stirred and handed one to Leslie. He cupped both hands round it and breathed in the coffee scent.

'Come on let's sit at the table. Fuck it. I'm getting fed up with this.'

He pulled a pack of cigarettes from his pocket and offered me one. We lit up and he began his story.

'There's no much to tell, really. You know how it is. A pretty face can be a help or a hindrance. I guess it didn't do Rita any favours. She was fun, liked a good time, liked a drink, liked her drugs. A walking Merks manual at one time, our Rita.' He smiled wistfully. 'I had more than a wee fancy for her myself. Anyway, it wasn't to be. She hooked up with a bad lad. Now, you and me, we're no angels, but why Rita stayed with this bloke is beyond me. Nancy and

Bill Sykes. D'you remember that song? "As Long as He Needs Me". That should have been Rita's signature tune.' He took a long drag on his cigarette. 'I would have given evens on him killing her. Made everyone sick. A lovely lassie like that. But there was no telling her, and by that time the folk she was mixing with weren't in much of a state to tell anyone anything.' He mimed the press of a plunger against his arm. 'Aye, well, it was everywhere then. Even had a wee dabble myself.'

I nodded. Les's wee dabble had lasted five years. I wasn't sure he didn't still dabble occasionally.

'Then against the odds Rita got a break. It didn't look like a break at first, but it was. She fell pregnant. She cleaned herself up and surprised everybody by having a healthy baby. A bonny wee girl. Spitting image of Rita. A touch of that bastard she lived with around the eyes, but no so much you couldn't ignore it. He'd been in the habit of lifting his hand to her, but as soon as the baby came along, that was it, Rita was off. Got herself a housing association flat. Seemed sorted. Aye, well, this is the sad bit.' He took a sip of his coffee.

'HIV.'

'If it was just that it would be bad enough. But Rita was a fighter. She kept the wee one until she was three or there-abouts, then she realised it wasn't going to work. You remember how it was. Back then AIDS was a death sentence. People dropping like flies.'

I nodded to show I knew what he was talking about.

'Aye, well, Rita loved her kid. The wean wasn't infected and Rita wanted what was best for her, so she made the ultimate sacrifice. She put her up for adoption. Rita reckoned it was best to make the break while the wee one was young enough to bond with someone else. She knew she was going to die, and she certainly didn't want that bastard of a father getting a look in. She only set one condition.'

He paused for another drag on his cigarette.

'What was that?'

'She wanted photographs, twice a year, birthday and Christmas, until she died, which she reckoned probably wouldn't be that long. Aye, well, you ken what happened.'

'No photographs.'

'Not a single, solitary one. Of course, when she was giving them the baby they promised her the world, but as soon as they got their hands on the kid that was the end of that. Who wants some junky Mum in the background? I don't know, maybe they were right, but it seemed all wrong to me. Rita took it hard and, to make things worse, along came combination therapy. With bad luck she could live as long as you or me. She's trying to do herself in with speed now.'

'And you're helping her along?'

He drained the last of his coffee. 'You know me. I like to be helpful.'

I felt sick.

Les got up and resumed his search. 'Fuck, I'm going to have a real clear-out. This is ridiculous.'

He left the kitchen and started on the hall cupboard.

I was stupid. I had to ask. 'What are you looking for?'

'My baseball bat.' There was a clatter as something tumbled. 'You know, Glasgow imports more baseball bats than any city in Britain and there's not a single baseball team in town.' He laughed. 'Maybe all the drug dealers should get together and make up a squad. Help improve our swing.'

I followed him through to the dimly lit hallway. Les was half inside the lobby cupboard.

'Bingo!' He straightened up, brandishing his bat. Liberty with her torch. 'At bloody last.'

I wished I had never called round.

'Leslie, what are you planning to do with that?'

'I told you. I'm starting a new hobby.'

'Seriously.'

'Par for the course, amigo. Some wee nyaff owes me. I've warned him three times. That's the rule — three strikes and you're out.' He took a measured stroke with the bat, swinging it like a golf club.

'You're not going to hit him with that. You could kill him.'

'Give me some credit. I do know what I'm doing. Left leg and the telly. If he doesn't come up with the dosh after that, then it's right leg and the stereo.'

'What if he doesn't have it?'

'I'll break his fingers and smash his guitar. What can I do, Rilke?' He looked genuinely perplexed. 'Call the police and tell them I've been robbed? No, of course not. I've got to go and teach him a valuable lesson. Do you think I'm going to enjoy it?'

I looked at him. He was already psyching himself up. Once the adrenalin got into his veins I wasn't so sure.

'Jesus' — he laughed his phlegmy laugh — 'you're all the same, you sensitive souls. You like a wee smoke of the ganj, but you don't want to know where it came from. Face facts, old chum.' He took a sports bag from the cupboard and stowed the bat inside it. 'Someone has to suffer for your pleasure.' He pulled on his jacket and patted the pockets, looking for his keys. 'Tell you what, if it makes you feel any better, I'll not rape his girlfriend.'

I turned and grabbed him by his jumper pushing him up against the wall, bringing my other hand up to his neck, pressing against his Adam's apple, crushing the breath out of him. I could hear the struggle for air in his throat. The creak of his last gasp.

I hit him, for selling Rita speed that might kill her, for threatening rape, for reminding me of the past and because I didn't know who the real abusers were.

Les tensed against me, then turned his head to the side, freeing his windpipe, gulping for oxygen. His foot twisted round my ankle, levering me off balance and a fist hit me in the stomach, forcing the wind from my lungs. I fell back against the door and he hit me twice. There was blood in my mouth. I raised my hands to show I was finished and he hit me once more.

'Jesus, Rilke! Jesus.' We stood there panting in the small corridor. 'Christ, do you not know when I'm joking?'

'It wasn't much of a joke.'

'So what will you do if you run into Fred McAulay? Batter the shite out of him?'

I turned and opened the door. His voice followed me as I ran down the close.

'You're a nutter, Rilke. A fucking nut.'

13

Steenie

*Hence it came about that I concealed my pleasures; and that when I
reached years of reflection, and began to look round me, and take
stock of my progress and position in the world, I stood already
committed to a profound duplicity of life.*

Robert Louis Stevenson,
The Strange Case of Dr Jekyll and Mr Hyde

ELEVEN A.M. SAW ME turning into the cobbled lane that led to
Steenie and John's bookshop. As the van swayed over the
uneven surface, I caught a glimpse in the rear-view mirror of
the eyes of a stranger. I parked, adjusted the glass and
examined my reflection. The man of three days ago was
gone, in his place a troubled spectre. The broken nights and
drunkenness had taken their toll: every debauch was etched
on my face. Perhaps Les or Rose had something among their
cosmetics that might help. I smoothed back my hair, put on

my shades and practised smiling, one, two, three times. I was scaring myself.

Steenie Stevenson's bookshop was once an arrangement of stables and outhouses. Steenie and John acquired the buildings twenty years or so ago and bashed them into a maze of windowless rooms, some open to the public, others locked chambers, unopened for years, where spiders rule and paper moulders in dungeon darkness.

There was the usual fine drizzle. A bookcase half filled with rotting paperbacks sat by the door. A couple of cats meandered among damp cardboard cartons of books dumped in the lane for sorting. I fished into a tumbled box and retrieved a discarded household Bible. The title page bore a family tree, births, marriages, deaths, all carefully entered in curving copperplate. I read through the names: *Death Comes for us All*, *Please Remember Me*; then let it fall. A large ginger tom brushed against my leg. I reached down and stroked him, rubbing hard behind his ears. He purred, responding to my touch, rolling onto his back, snaking his spine in exaggerated ecstasy. I tickled the soft hair of his tummy and he grabbed my hand, claws out, scoring deep, red rents across my skin.

'Ye wee bugger!'

The cat got to its feet. It walked away leisurely, tail erect, displaying its rear. Would I never learn?

A bell rang as I entered the gloomy, toadstool dampness of the shop. John was on desk duty, his bald head barely visible behind an uneven wall of books reminiscent of the Manhattan skyline. A burning cigarette rested in an ashtray, next to a bottle of cherry cough linctus. An elderly customer got up from the chair next to John and walked slowly out of the shop. His hand brushed against mine as he passed, a low voice whispered, 'Excuse me,' and I turned away without seeing his face.

'Hi, John, how's tricks?'

'Fine.'

A black cat leapt onto the desk and fixed its green gaze upon me.

'Steenie around?'

'No. He had an idea you might come by.' John's lazy voice seemed unnaturally loud. He scrawled on a jotter as he talked. 'He gave me a note to say he'd catch up with you.'

What Steenie and John fell out about had never been established. Though, as Steenie was a stalwart elder of the Free Kirk and John conducted a thriving under-the-counter trade in red-hot smut, religious differences seemed a safe bet. No one had ever seen them converse. Their business was conducted via scraps of paper, sentences that began, '*Tell my brother . . .*' entrusted to intermediaries. John tore the page from the book and passed it to me. '*He's at the back, behind the travel section.*' I nodded my thanks.

'Ach, well, tell him I dropped by. I'll catch him later.'

I opened the door and let it swing to, jangling the bell, then walked, as stealthily as I could, round the high bookcase that divides the shop. A solitary customer lifted his head from an open volume and followed me with his eyes. I found Steenie sitting on a low ladder, hunched over a copy of Sir Richard Burton's memoirs, a pile of red *Baedekers* at his feet.

'Steenie.' I whispered his name and Sir Richard hit the floor.

'Rilke.' He tried to cover his confusion, retrieving the book. 'Long time no see.'

The *Baedekers* slumped softly, maps slipping from between their covers.

'Not since last night.'

Steenie swore, hunkering down, reforming the pile. He

attempted a laugh, but it died, half formed. 'Aye, right enough.'

'You didn't seem yourself when you left. I thought I'd pop in and see how you were doing.'

'Doing fine, Rilke, you know. Pretty busy as per. A lot of stuff coming in, no much going out. The usual. Hard to turn a coin these days. Not like when we started, eh?' He was talking double speed.

'Aye, well, things change. I was hoping you'd have a wee minute for a chat.'

He stood up, tried to look me in the eye, then settled for some point to the right of me.

'Ach, I'd love to, but I've to be away to a valuation in a minute. Stay and talk to John, though, he's aye been a gabby so and so.' He lowered his voice. 'Never able to keep his mouth shut that one.'

'It was about something in particular.'

He turned to go. 'Aye, well, as I said, maybe some other time.'

'I'm in clearing the McKindless house.'

'Whose house?'

'Never kid a kidder, Steenie.'

He looked me in the eye. 'You're clearing a house. So what?'

'I'm finding some funny things.'

'What's that to do with me?'

I bluffed him. 'I think you know.'

Steenie leant back against the ladder and closed his eyes. 'The evil that men do lives on.'

He stood there for a moment, then took out his keys. 'Come on.'

The key tumbled the oiled lock easily. I followed him

through a half-concealed door at the back of the shop, and waited while he secured it behind us. For a second all was darkness. I put out my hand to steady myself, then Steenie hit a switch and a dusty fluorescent strip batted awake. We were at the top of a narrow stone staircase.

'Come on.'

Three curved flights of bevelled steps led down to a musty basement storeroom. It was cold. A damp cold that rose from the hard packed earth beneath the concrete floor crept through my boots and settled like fear in my belly.

I said, 'Why don't we go and sit in the van? We'll get privacy there. I'll put the heater on and you can tell me all about it in comfort.'

'No. I've something to show you.'

I followed him past metal racks of books to a second locked chamber. The smell of the river was stronger here. The light flickered on and off like an impatient wrecker's signal. At first I thought this must be the end of our journey. It was so full I couldn't see how we could go further. But Steenie went on, leading me along thin paths, walled either side by books and boxes, sometimes having to turn sideways to squeeze through, sometimes having to haul ourselves over tumbled avalanches of splayed volumes. We travelled through rooms each less finished than the last, until they were no longer graced with doors and locks, just simple rough-hewn openings in the basement's stone walls. We seemed to be descending; there was a methane taint to the air and I wondered if we were beneath the river. At last the light faded and I thought, once more, that we must be at journey's end, but Steenie lifted a torch from a shelf, clicked on its wide beam and whispered, 'This way.'

I brushed away the lingering touch of soft, stroking

cobwebs and followed him. Christ only knew what state my suit was getting into down here.

'Steenie, man, do you remember what they used to say in the war? Is your journey really necessary? What do you think? Maybe I could come over tomorrow after you've searched this thing out. I'll meet you at the Orlando and we can discuss it over a bacon roll and a cappuccino. What do you say?'

'It's not much further.'

In a distant corner something rustled and I remembered why Steenie had so many cats. Then the torch picked out a tall structure at the end of the room. A shadow among shadows. I peered hard, trying to make out what it was; a wooden rake . . . a scaffold . . . a steep, wooden staircase.

'Jesus.' My battered morale took another dip. 'Steenie, you know I'm not so good on heights.'

'No, I didn't know that.'

'Aye, you did. I told you that time we went to thon country house sale out Bowling way. Do you not mind you brought those boxes down from the attic for me?'

'Ach, that was years ago. Have you not got over that yet?'

'No, not really. I find myself getting dizzy at altitude. That and a poor head for drink's my only weakness.'

'Just brace yourself, trust in the Lord and you'll be fine. Look' – he cast the beam up to a dizzying crow's nest three storeys above – 'the stairs are steep but they're solid enough. Just don't look down. I'll go ahead. If you need a rest, give me a shout and we'll stop.'

'Steenie.' I rested my hand on his arm. 'I've followed you through this rat-infested basement. I've not questioned you beyond what was said in the shop. So come on, give me a break. Will you not bring it down here?'

He turned to face me. 'Can't you guess?'

He was turning my trick against me, calling my bluff as I had called his.

'Aye, I can guess.' I tried to put some conviction into my voice. 'And I don't see why I have to go up there.'

Steenie's smile looked grim in the dark. We were bartering men, used to bluffs and bids. We gambled for a living and neither of us was willing to show his hand yet.

'Aye, well, it's a matter of bulk. I'm afraid it's the stairs or nothing.'

I hesitated, wanting to know what he had but not sure if I could manage the climb. I looked upwards, rocking gently on the balls of my feet. There was a familiar ringing in my ears. How badly did I want to know?

Perhaps, if Steenie had kept his mouth shut, everything would have been avoided. Perhaps we would simply have stood together for a minute, in the dark and the cobwebs, then I'd have slapped him on the back and asked if he wanted to go for a pint. Maybe I'd have told him, over a jar or two, the wonders of the McKindless library, and he'd have nodded sagely. Perhaps. He spoke and I was decided.

'I mean, it's not like it's any of your business. Why don't you just leave well alone what doesn't concern you? Least said, soonest mended.'

I lowered my voice an octave. 'Lead on, Macduff. What doesn't kill us makes us strong.'

Steenie turned abruptly, put his foot on the bottom rung, grasped the banister and began the ascent.

I once read the memoirs of an astronaut. As a young boy, he watched the first moon launch, cross-legged in front of a flickering black-and-white TV set. Neil Armstrong uttered the words 'Houston: Tranquillity base here. The eagle has landed,' and our hero was captivated. From that moment he dedicated himself to space exploration. Instead of fading, as youthful fascinations often do, this enchantment grew stronger. At the age of eighteen he joined the navy as an aviator. In the air he soared and swooped, cutting a swathe through the skies, always wishing, *Higher, higher*. It seemed that he could land on a dime. Aboard ship, life was cramped. The men rotated bunks. At the end of each shift, our man slept between sheets which smelt of the sweat of a greasy lieutenant. But in the air he was free. While fellow seafarers played chequers and cards in the noisy mess room, this paragon trained his 20:20 vision on science texts. During night watches he prowled the deck, looking at the stars. At the end of his tour he entered the University of California, graduating with a Master of Science in aeronautical engineering. He became a test pilot, hurtling across the desert with a supersonic growl, face pulled back in a rictus mask, a hand on his chest that was G-force. Eventually, twenty years after that giant step, he was selected as an astronaut by NASA. At last, sealed into a spacesuit, helmet tucked under his arm, waving to the assembled crowd, he climbed into a rocket, ready to journey to the stars. Fifteen minutes beyond Earth's atmosphere he was gripped by a creeping nausea. Within the hour, he lay immobilised and vomiting. Unpleasant at any time, but at zero gravity . . . Still our man was not to be defeated. Like that seasick mariner Nelson, he turned a blind eye to adversity and flew mission after mission vomiting all the way. Hundreds of his hermetically sealed sick bags still orbit the moon. I tried to summon the courage of that astronaut, rubbed my damp palms against my trousers and followed Steenie.

The staircase was practically perpendicular. As I climbed, gravity seemed to increase, pressing firm and insistent against the lid of my skull. With every step, the pressure grew. And it seemed that the rungs beneath my feet began to take on an elastic quality, shifting with my tread. As the ground moved further away, my body began to sway. It started with my head and shoulders. They listed gently, this way, then that. It was an elegant motion. The kind some sweet, old lady might make on hearing a forgotten love song on the radio. Soon my chest was getting in on the act, and before I knew it my waist had joined the waltz. A milky film swam across my vision and I felt that I might float. I held on to the ladder, shook my head and forced my sight on the rung in front. That was what had been wrong with the astronaut. He had no horizon to focus on. There were no fixed objects, out there, hurtling through space – no, mustn't think of that – I had a horizon. These ladder rungs were as stable and as fixed as the coast of Fife. I held fast to the banister, eyes level with the bevelled heels of Steenie's boots. The weaving sensation passed, the chimes in my head faded. The air below had been dank and sparse. Now I could feel it lifting. I was going to make it. My tread got surer, my grip firmer. Was there nothing this boy couldn't do? I coughed as the fresher air hit my lungs. I'd roll a smoke when we got to the top.

The ladder ended in a trapdoor. Steenie pushed it open, hauled himself up, then reached towards me. I was weary. There was an ache at the back of my calves and I was glad to be done with the climb. I grasped his outstretched hand, but instead of the boost I anticipated he slipped my grip and hit a sharp jolt to my shoulder, pushing quick and sudden.

I felt the atmosphere rush by, my hair fanned out, stomach leapt with the shock of the fall. I braced myself for impact, but it was all panic. My reflexes were faster than his. I caught my weight against the stair, holding the ladder with my left hand, catching Steenie's wrist with my right, pulling him towards me. There was terror in his rolling eyes. I tilted his balance until he gave a gasp, teetering on the final edge of gravity, then, brought his face to mine, feeling the warmth of his onion breath, and dashed my forehead against his nose, hearing the crunch as cartilage crumbled, taking a step upwards and pushing him into an attic room.

'Jesus Christ, Steenie, Jesus fucking Christ.' I was on a loop, it had to stop. 'Jesus, man.' It wasn't so easy – 'Fuck me. Fuck man' – but I could do it; I'd always prided myself on my vocabulary. 'What the . . . fuck? What the . . . fuck? What the fuck was that all about?'

If you know how to give one, a Glesgae kiss hurts the recipient more than the giver, but it had been a while for me and my vision went red. Still, I was doing better than Steenie. He lay on his side, blood streaming from his nose. I went to pass him my hanky, then remembered he could have killed me and gave him two swift kicks in the side instead. His body convulsed with sobs. I paced the room, fighting the pain in my head, shaking it like a boxer, slapping my hand against my forehead, attempting to shift the red, unable to take in what had just happened. Then I remembered something, returned to the trembling body and rolled him over. Steenie whimpered. I kicked him again, said 'Shut the fuck up or you'll get a fucking doing,' reached into his pocket and retrieved his keys.

We sat facing each other propped against opposite walls of the attic. Steenie had removed his jumper and held it against his face, stanching the flow. His eyes shone. I'd broken his nose. Right now he was in agony, but soon that would deaden to a dull ache. Too soon. I looked down at my suit. It was covered in grime, the jacket decorated by a diagonal smear of blood from lapel to hem.

'Jesus fucking Christ. You fucking cunt.'

I issued another kick. He whimpered and edged beyond my reach. I rolled two smokes and passed one to him.

We sat for a moment, smoking in silence. Somewhere, far away, the wind moaned in the trees, but not a hint of it entered the room where we two sat. Take deep breaths, that's what they say after a shock. It's good advice. I inhaled the smoke all the way down, deep into my lungs, deeper. I felt a little light-headed; my vision settled and I wished I had a drink.

'Anything to drink up here?'

Steenie shook his head, silent, the jumper fastened to his face, expression hidden.

'Are you going to tell me what that was all about?'

He sat unmoving.

'Fuck's sake, Steenie. Jesus. I tell you, I could kill you right now and no court in the land would convict me.'

He spoke for the first time since the assault, in a voice made thick by tears and blood. 'It would be your word against mine.'

'No. You don't seem to understand. You would be a broken thing at the bottom of the stair, you'd be saying nothing.'

Steenie returned the jumper to his face, clutching it to himself. He started to rock, gently, to and fro.

'Jesus.' I stood up. 'Fuck you,' and started to pace. The room was empty of furniture but strewn with papers. I bent over and absently lifted a sheet from the dusty floor.

Christ Jesus when on earth saw the streets of Jerusalem
  filled with decay. Male queers holding hands, kissing, &
   swaying about publicly, some in the dress of women.
  Also groups of shorn lesbians, dressed in men's apparel,
    openly fondling each other sexually.

What a filthy disgrace.

Young children & others were participating, or made to watch these unnatural & sick

PERVERSIONS

Because of this queer disgrace, God was compelled by his love for mankind, to instruct the righteous to drive the homosexual from their cities, to kill & destroy them by any means.

LESBIANS are females determined to hate & undermine all male authority.

Given the opportunity, will urge decent women to explore sex in their evil ways.

Lesbians seduce wives, daughters, infants & beasts for their unnatural dog-like sex acts.

Lesbians are consumed with the lust of the flesh, but are unable to love, they are without any feelings of guilt.

Other ungodly titles lesbian are known by:

Dyke, Bull dyke, Butch, Sapphic primates, Menstruating cross dressers, Split muffins, Bitchy bitches, Hags S.F., Riot grrrls, Handsome homegirls, Homeric tomboys, Hard & soft ballers, Rugby widows, Corporate nuns in sensible shoes, Bike messengers from hell, Power femmes with Tourette's Syndrome, Carpet munchers, Backyard bitches & their dogs, Balloon smugglers, Funpigs, Menopause babes, Baby daddies, Pussy suckers, Cunt lickers, Pubic hair spitters.

It is acceptable for the righteous to heap words of filth upon the obscene lesbian & homosexual.

DESTROY their warped, obscene, filthy, VD infected, drug dependent lifestyles.

Only DEATH will rid man of their plague.

I dropped the paper and turned towards Steenie. He gave me a small smile. I lifted the next page.

Homosexuals fellate almost 100% of their sexual contacts & drink their semen. Semen contains every germ carried in the blood stream, it is the same as drinking raw human blood
VAMPIRES!
Sperm penetrates the anal wall & dilutes the blood stream, making their urge for semen ever stronger.
50% of male syphilis is carried by homosexuals.
Around 67–80% of homosexuals lick &/or insert their tongues into the anuses of other men rimming, anilingus, faecal sex they eat faeces. This is called the prime taste treat in sex. 33% of homosexuals admit to FISTING inserting the hand, sometimes a whole arm, into the rectum of another man Urinating on each other GOLDEN SHOWERS & torture has doubled among homosexuals since the 1940s, & fisting has increased astronomically.
17% of homosexuals eat &/or rub the faeces of other men on themselves.
12% of homosexuals give/receive enemas.
The average homosexual has fellated between 20 & 106 men, swallowed 50 seminal discharges, had 72 penile penetrations of the anus & eaten the faeces of 23 men EVERY YEAR
Most homosexual sexual encounters occur while drunk, high on drugs AT ORGIES.
Activities of homosexuals involve rimming (anilingus), golden showers & fisting.
Homosexuals account for 3–4% of all gonorrhoea cases,

> 60% of all syphilis cases, & 17% of all hospital
> admissions. They make up only 1–2% of the population.
> 25–33% of homosexuals are alcoholics.

I kicked through the pages. Hate leapt out in jagged words.

Steenie was lying on the floor, smiling like a victor.

I found myself whispering, 'You're mad.'

He looked weary. 'No, not mad.' His voice became heavy and pedantic as it took on the cadence of a sermon. 'Even as Sodom and Gomorrah, and the cities about them in like manner, giving themselves over to fornication, and going after strange flesh, are set forth for an example, suffering the vengeance of eternal fire. You should repent, Rilke. It is too late for you to enter the Kingdom of Heaven and sit at God's right hand, but if you were to repent His wrath might be tempered. Otherwise you will surely burn in eternal Hell.'

'Thanks for the tip.'

I was familiar with the unloving Presbyterian god of Steenie's faith. I had never lost a minute's sleep over his opinion, but then I'd never suspected one of his disciples would come gunning for me. Caught at last in a faggot fatwa.

Steenie rambled on. 'Vengeance is mine, sayeth the Lord.' The cruelty of the Old Testament complemented the harsh West Coast accent we shared. 'The Bible tells us, if a man also lie with mankind, as he lieth with a woman, both of them have committed an abomination!' *A-bomb-in-ashun!* 'They shall surely be put to death; their blood shall be upon them. They committed all these things, and therefore I abhorred them. Fall on your knees and beg for God's mercy.'

'You said that you brought me up here because you had something to show me about McKindless.'

Steenie gazed wordlessly at a point high on the wall.

I put all the menace I could muster into my voice. 'Are you aiming to join the ranks of the martyrs?'

He shook his head. 'You talk like a papist, Rilke. John was brought up, as I was, to fear God, but while I chose to follow the path of the righteous John allied himself with the forces of evil.'

'What do you mean?'

'He's obsessed with Mammon and the sins of the flesh.'

'I hate to break it to you, but that goes for most of the world. What do you know about McKindless?'

'He was a sinner.'

'Steenie, tell me you didn't . . .?'

'The Lord came for him. He rots at the bottom of the fiery lake.'

'Thank Christ for that. You recognised the netsuke last night. What did it mean to you?'

'I saw it at his house. He was a pervert, a filthy degenerate. Know ye not that the unrighteous shall not inherit the kingdom of God? Be not deceived: neither fornicators, nor idolaters, nor adulterers, nor effeminate, nor abusers of themselves with mankind, nor thieves, nor covetous, nor drunkards, nor revellers, nor extortioners, shall inherit the kingdom of God.'

'Plenty of room, then. Other than that, what did you have against him?'

'Did you see his library?'

'Aye, I did. A fine collection.'

'That's what you would say. It was a disgrace, an offence to God.'

'Stick to the point.'

I moved towards him and he cringed.

'John helped McKindless acquire much of that library. I was against it. I handle only righteous books. John is a sinner. Only once did I deliver a book to him. It was expensive, and greed overcame me. I, too, am a sinner. But not as big a one as John. McKindless came to the door playing with that ornament.'

'The netsuke?'

'Yes, rolling it around in his hands as if it was the most natural thing in the world. He unwrapped the book in front of me. Opened the pages, flicking through the filth as if there was no shame in it. He examined every illustration, checked every plate, while I stood there.'

'That's it? You sold him a book once?'

'John sold it to him. I delivered it, against my principles. I, too, am a sinner in the eyes of the Lord, but I am a repentant sinner, I get down on my knees and beg for mercy.'

'Are you telling me you know nothing about McKindless?'

Steenie looked suddenly old and tired. 'I know enough. My brother was always of the world. He paid too much attention to the temporal and not enough to the spiritual, but he was never bad, never evil until he met that man.'

'McKindless?'

'He was one of John's customers. They were as thick as thieves. Had been for years.'

'So why did you bring me up here?'

'I was glad when I heard McKindless had died. I hoped John would renounce his past and choose salvation. Then you came to the bar and I realised you were one of them. I left last night because I knew you were there to corrupt my brother and I wished you harm. When you came here today, to persecute me, I knew that it was a sign. The Lord wanted me at His right hand.'

'Well, it looks like the lord is going to keep me around for a while.'

Steenie rubbed the jumper across his face. 'He surely moves in mysterious ways.'

14

The Imp of the Perverse

I SAT IN THE van, outside Steenie's shop, thinking about what I should do. It was obvious. Give up. I took my mobile out of the glove compartment and switched it on. An electronic bugle beeped and a megaphone flashed in the corner of the display. Someone always felt the urge to talk. They could wait. I peeled back the thick elastic band that held my wallet together and began sorting through scraps of paper, disappointing bank statements, troubling invoices, scribbled telephone numbers, business cards, unfiled receipts, three pink parking tickets. Anderson's thin card with its blue badge crest was still there. Perhaps I had intended to phone him all along. I propped the card against the dashboard and looked at it. That was the only option. Call Anderson, tell him about the photographs. I lifted the card and tapped its edge against the bridge of my nose. What had Les said? These were bad men. Master of the overstatement, Les, until it came to the real thing. Yes. That was what to do. Hand the whole mess over to Anderson. I was doing no good chasing clues by myself. They only led to blind alleys and madness.

Steenie and I had made the return journey through the subterranean passages in silence.

At the final room he turned to me and hissed, 'Will you renounce your sins and accept the Lord Jesus Christ as your one true Saviour who died on the cross for you?'

I told him I'd think about it. Then he stumbled. I moved forward to brace him and he wound his arms around my neck, catching me in an unexpected embrace, putting his face to mine in a blood and snot kiss that appalled me. I pushed him away roughly, then we climbed the stairs together, my soles scuffing a defeated rhythm against the concrete.

The soft, dancing mote-light of the shop seemed bright after the gloom of the storerooms. It had been all but deserted when we left, now it was lunchtime. Half a dozen browsers were ranged round the shelves. At first no one noticed our presence. There was a pause, a minute's delay. Enough time for me to take in the state of us. Steenie's flattened nose, the blood and stoor smeared across us, his tears and ruined jumper. The browsers browsed on, some-one turned a page, a student undid the intricate, origami folds of his reading list, an elderly man bent creaking knees and eased himself gently towards a neglected volume, a soft fart escaped him. Radio Three played a choral song. The black cat settled on the easy chair reserved for customers, and blinked. Then John, perhaps feeling a draught from the open basement door, looked up from the book he was wrapping. His eyes met his brother's, took in his wrecked clothes and damaged countenance. He sat for a full minute looking at us, then gently placed the half-finished parcel on the desk, got to his feet, toppling a listing tower of books, and strode the length of the shop. He hesitated, then placed a hand against Steenie's bloodstained cheek.

'Steven, what happened?' Panic quivered his voice. He looked into Steenie's face, trying to gauge the hurt. 'Did you take a fall?' Steenie shook his head, tearful again. John hesitated, then embraced him, looking over Steenie's shoulder at me, asking once more, 'What happened?' Never suspecting me the agent of injury.

'He's flipped.'

The browsers had lifted their eyes from the books, silently reviewing the scene. I made a token attempt at dusting myself down, and stared them out. Their gaze shifted away.

'Loco, pure loco.'

John rubbed his brother's back, bewildered, looking at me as if I was some dangerous stranger. 'Rilke, what on earth went on through there?'

'What do you know about a party name of McKindless?'

John hesitated. 'Nothing. Why? What's he done?'

I leant in and whispered, 'I know you two were in cahoots. Now, if you don't want your clandestine trade becoming public knowledge I suggest you tell me as much as you can.'

John patted Steenie's back. 'Why don't you away and clean yourself up, Steven. I'll talk to Rilke the now, then we'll close and I'll drive you home.'

Steenie started to protest. His brother gave him a gentle push. 'Away, Steven.'

John and I retired to the shelter of his desk. He opened a drawer and lifted out a bottle of malt.

'I guess we could both do with one of these.' He poured a measure into two mugs. 'He was a client and a book collector. He died recently. That's all there is to it.'

'What kind of books did he collect?'

'He had specialist tastes. I was happy to cater for them.'

'Lawful tastes?'

'Lawful!' John laughed. 'What's the law? A series of changing conventions. What's lawful today might be a crime tomorrow. You should know that. Wasn't so long ago your type were being thrown into jail or shipped off to the gas chambers. McKindless's tastes were at least consistent.'

'So what were they?'

'Have you looked at his library?'

'Not in detail.'

'Have a look.' He laughed again. 'Take a browse, old boy. I guarantee you'll be left in no doubt.' He wiped his eyes. 'And as for spilling the beans on my specialist trade, as you so delicately put it, there won't be much of a trade now McKindless is gone.'

'I don't get you.'

'He was my main supplier. He acquired stock for me, and in exchange got first refusal on anything antiquarian or out of print I thought might take his fancy. I'm going to miss the old reprobate.' His laughter grew louder. 'And so are quite a few folk in this city.'

I turned and left the shop, the untouched malt, the reconciled brothers, the bemused browsers keeping watch from the shelter of trembling, open volumes.

I gave Anderson's card a last look, then replaced it in my wallet. I would go and see him. But not yet. The engine caught on the first turn of the ignition. It was a good sign.

Everything was going to be all right, and even if it wasn't the world would go on. I backed slowly out of the lane, then turned in the direction of Hyndland and the McKindless house.

15

Abandon Hope

Some Wretched creature, saviour take
Who would exult to die
And leave for thy sweet mercy's sake
Another hour to me.

Emily Dickinson, *c.* 1867

IT SEEMED AN AGE since I had walked into the bookshop, but a glance at my watch showed that it was only one o'clock. The drizzle was heavier; raindrops clung to the windscreen, rolling down the glass, the same trajectory as Steenie's tears.

I stopped on the red, at the junction of Byres Road and University Avenue and waited for the parade of lunchtime shoppers to pass. I wondered if any suicides were buried beneath these crossroads. They'd have trouble enough rising now, under the weight of tarmac, traffic and crossing pedestrians. I tried to conjure them in my mind's eye.

The waltzing host of the dead meeting the afternoon passers-by. Then the lights changed and I hauled the van over the hill. The grey of the morning was slipping into black. The rain grew more urgent. Water streaked across the glass, warping my vision, forcing me to slow to a crawl. I switched the wipers up a gauge, and the rubber sawed back and forth at a quickened tempo. *She's dead, she's dead, she's dead*, they seemed to sing in off-base harmony.

John had told me what I should have known. I had been avoiding the house, avoiding the truth. Looking under stones while the facts were waiting for me in black and white in the attic library.

I saw the house from the bottom of the street. Every window illuminated against the slate of the sky. It should have been welcoming, but it wasn't. A strange face with too many eyes and a door for a mouth that could swallow you up.

'Welcome to Bates Motel,' I said out loud. 'En suite bathroom as standard.'

I pulled up the collar of my jacket and ran the length of the drive. Jimmy James answered the door on the first ring of the bell,

'You made it, then.'

'It would seem so.'

This was the skeleton of the house I had entered three days ago. The thinning Bokhara rugs and fine hall table were gone.

'You got my message.' Too late I remembered the flashing light on my phone. 'Some bloody morning we've had here.'

'What's happened?'

'What's no happened?'

There was no point in rushing him. Jimmy James lived all of life at the same slow, sour pace. Disasters were of equal scale, the assassination of a president equivalent to that of a sparrow.

They merely confirmed his view of the world as a bad place where the devil concealed himself in any good fortune. Only the power of drink could move him, and that rarely. He was too old for portering, too poor to retire.

He shivered and wiped his nose. 'You've brought the cold in with you. I've had a job keeping warm with all the comings and goings. Doors opening, doors closing. It's no the weather for comings and goings.'

There was a whisky odour to his breath and a whine to his voice. I reminded myself he was an old man and asked gently, 'What's been going on?'

'It's done. The place is clear.'

He turned and began to climb the stairs. I followed, slowing my pace to his, knowing from the echo of our footsteps that the task was complete. Bright shadows shone from dulled wallpaper, where pictures had once hung. Was that what photographs were? Shadows, X-rays of the past, ghosts that could do you no harm?

He led me into what had once been the music room. Remnants of the squad lounged listlessly around the walls. The sale was a wrap, but there was none of the usual last-day banter. Ennui seemed to have settled early. All eyes were on me, the backslider. I took out my wallet, removed a fold of notes and handed it to Jimmy without counting. I knew exactly how much was there. My emergency roll, three hundred in tens.

'Is that the place empty?'

'Aye.'

'Well done.'

He felt the bundle, weighing it in his hand, assessing the amount.

'That's just for now.' I'd settle his own whack with

him later. 'Once you've unloaded, take the boys for a good drink on me.'

'Will you be coming by?'

'I expect so.'

He nodded to the team and they made for the door, keen to get the last load into the salerooms and be away to the pub.

Jimmy James waited beside me until they had left. 'I left a message on your phone.'

'I didn't get it.'

'Aye, you never do.'

He stood still, rheumy eyes downcast, taciturn, miserable as a wet terrier. I'd known Jimmy for twenty years. He'd been no more cheerful at fifty than he was at seventy. I'd have to drag everything from him. That was my punishment.

'Well, I'm here now.'

'Aye, we wondered where you'd got to. Not like you to lead from behind.'

I glanced at him, searching for intent in the double entendre, finding none. 'There's been things going on.'

'Aye.'

'So what was your message?'

'She was taken no well.'

'Who? Rose?'

I was surprised by a surge of panic from my groin to my chest. He shook his head impatiently.

'No. The auld wife. She took bad this afternoon. It was as well we were here.'

There was a lodestone in my stomach. A weight of misfortune drawing disaster towards me.

'What happened? Was it serious?'

'We called an ambulance. I tried phoning you, but you never answered.'

Guilt made me impatient.

'We've established that. I'm here now. Tell me from the beginning. Where was she taken ill?'

'If you're going to interrogate me, let's have a seat. Even the bloody Gestapo let people have a seat when they were under interrogation.'

He wandered over to a window seat and eased himself onto it groaning. Seventy. Probably not that much older than Cliff Richard. I sat, in awkward proximity, beside him on the bench.

'I'm sure you all dealt well with the situation. I'm sorry I wasn't here to deal with it myself. It couldn't be avoided.'

'Aye.' His tone told me he doubted it.

'I'm just trying to establish the facts.'

He sighed wearily. 'She came out of that office on the ground floor, eleven o'clock or thereabouts. Maybe she felt no well and wanted to get help, I don't know.'

Jimmy James's hands were linked together on his lap. I looked at them as he talked. Their skin was too loose. Waxy folds and puckers, criss-crossed by vulnerable, raised veins. Some other, larger man's hands, stolen, husked, wrinkled on like ill-fitting gloves and topped by chipped, nicotined nails. When he died I could polish those nails and pass them as tortoiseshell.

'She had a funny turn in the hallway. Luckily a couple of the boys were shifting some stuff out the front door. They put a rug over her and called the hospital.'

'She collapsed?'

'It'd be no surprise if she came back in a box.'

'That's right, Jimmy, look on the bright side.'

'You didn't see her. I did. She wasn't an advertisement for health.'

He took a soiled hanky from his pocket and blew his nose. I wondered if he was thinking of his own mortality.

He looked up at me. 'What'll this do to the sale?'

'I don't know. It could blow it.' I banged the heel of my palm against the seat in frustration, thinking of more than the sale. An opportunity lost. 'It depends how bad she is. If she comes to and still wants to go ahead, there's no reason why not. She's of sound mind. If not, I suppose we have to wait and see. Find out who the next of kin are. Take it from there. I should have known it was too bloody good to be true. What hospital is she in?'

'The Infirmary. The ambulance fella said you could phone later if you want to see how she's getting on.'

'I'll do that.'

He shifted from the seat, rubbing his back with his hands as he stood.

'Aye, well, it comes to us all. Anyway, I've done my bit. You coming with us or are you stopping?'

'I'll stay a while.'

'Please yourself.' He gave the room one last look. 'I dinnae envy you, though. This place gives me the creeps.'

I stood for a moment by the window. Jimmy tottered down the front steps, ejected Niggle from the passenger seat of the Luton and hauled himself in. I watched as the van drove on, leaving Niggle on the pavement. The boy ran after it, shouting, catching up, banging on the doors as it slowed, then shouting again as it picked up speed. I could imagine Jimmy James inside, moaning at the driver. Finally the boys tired of their sport and the van reversed, back doors opening. Niggle's laughing mates dragged him in and it disappeared over the hill.

*   *   *

I inspected the first floor. My boots echoed from room to room, along the hallway, then back again. I fingered the key to the attic, walked to the window and looked out at the approaching night. Nothing there, just the accusing fingers of branches pitching in the wind, pointing towards the house, towards the man at the window, me.

Silence.

I wished that I had resealed the envelope and put it back in the box where I had found it. Let some other sod worry about it. Or not worry at all, light a match, touch flame to paper, watch it curl, the image brown, flake into cold ash. I wondered at my obsession, thought about the girl lying dead on her pallet and another woman, dead long ago, who I had tried to help without hope of success. I thought about people I knew. Strange to feel more for the dead than for the living. But then the dead stayed the same, the dead didn't judge. They loved you through eternity, even though they couldn't put their arms round you and heaven didn't exist.

When the inspection was complete, I sat on the floor of the empty bedroom, smoking, looking up at the attic.

I wondered vaguely about calling Derek and inviting him for a drink. If I did, would he come? If he came, would it be anything more than a drink?

After a while there were no more cigarette papers. I turned off the lights and walked from the darkness of the house into the dark of the night.

16

In the Shadow of the Necropolis

A SHADOW HORIZON OF half-tumbled monuments and mau-
soleums formed the backdrop to the Royal Infirmary. The
Necropolis. Glasgow's first 'hygienic cemetery', established
in the early nineteenth century, designed to avoid the spread
of cholera and a slippage of corpses from ill-dug graves, which
had become a city scandal. A convenient stroll across the
Bridge of Sighs from the hospital. John Knox pointed down at
us sinners from his vantage point high on the hill, 'next only to
God'. I gave him a V sign and steered the van into the hospital
courtyard.

The Royal Infirmary is a typical Victorian hospital. Seven
glowering, soot-blasted storeys, criss-crossed by perilous fire
escapes. Up on the high balconies silhouettes shifted. One
pinpoint red glow, followed by another. Patients, shrouded in
dressing gowns, smoking, watching my progress, cursing my
health.

I went into a public toilet and attempted to clean myself up. A man in a suit lingered at the urinal. He turned before zipping himself away, giving me a could-possibly-be-mistaken-for-carelessness glimpse of his member. I nodded towards the large vanity mirror covering the wall of the attendant's booth. A lot of vanity for one small toilet. Two-way glass, erected for the benefit of a wanking attendant, or idle police. I blotted what dust I could from my suit, washed my face and left.

I had bought a bunch of cellophaned chrysanthemums in the hospital shop, but wasn't sure how appropriate they were. An efficient voice, crackling of starched linen, had asked over the telephone if I was a relative. When I confirmed that, yes, I was a nephew, it had told me that Miss McKindless was 'comfortable, but very poorly'.

The voice had told me visiting times, then curtly excused itself, replacing the receiver before I could inquire what 'comfortable, but poorly' meant.

Attempts had been made to make the interior of the hospital look cheerful. The walls of the public area were lined with bright wallpaper, floral patterns; yellow daisies on blue stripes, blue irises against yellow gingham, topped, tailed and bisected by decorative borders. The paper wasn't bearing up well: it edged away from the walls, curling in the heat. The old hospital was breaking through. Asserting its dark self, pushing away this unsuccessful graft. I joined a tired queue of visitors waiting for the elevator. A jumble of no particular age or class, brought together by disease. We shuffled into the confinement of the lift, coats and hands brushing, touching for an instant, so close we could smell each other; a taint of sweat, a sweet whisper of scent. An old man backed onto my

foot and murmured, 'Sorry, son.' He had just visited a
barber. White hairs speckled the back of his collar. Trying
to look smart, to reassure someone – himself? – that he could
cope alone. I watched an orange light edge across a row of
numbers. There was a percussive ping and the doors breathed
open. Caught in the frame, a porter and a man in a wheel-
chair. The man looked like death. He looked like me.

He smiled and said, 'Don't worry, I'm not in a hurry,' then
laughed.

The porter laughed with him and doors hissed to. A girl's
long hair brushed against my lips. People shuffled out in dribs
and drabs, at different landings, eyes lowered, afraid that in
this building of hard truths and fluorescence too much might
be revealed.

I reached the ward and held the door open for a departing
visitor. The shambling figure was vaguely familiar. A shrun-
ken old man, shabby cap pulled low, dark suit that had seen
better days – some time around the 1940s, judging from the
cut. He was struggling with an old-fashioned cardboard case.
It took me a second to place him, then I recognised the
gardener glimpsed at the McKindless house on my first visit.

I introduced myself. 'Hello. I think we're visiting the same
person. I'm Rilke, the auctioneer handling Mr McKindless's
estate.'

He looked confused and I felt sorry for him, wondered how
many friends he had visited in hospital, how many funerals he
had attended, each one bringing his own closer. I held out my
hand. He gave it a weak shake.

'Grieve, Mr Grieve. I did the garden.'

'How is she?'

'Poorly. Sleeping now.'

His accent came from another era. A less complicated

time. He waved his hand in dismissal and lifted the case with effort. I wondered what was in it.

'Hang on.' I followed him. 'Here, let me give you a hand with that.'

'It's no bother.'

He struggled on towards the lift.

'Honestly, if Miss McKindless is asleep there's no rush. I'll get this to a taxi for you.'

The lift arrived and I took the case from him, ending the argument. The visiting-time crowds were cloistered in the wards. We descended down the floors alone.

'So did you know Mr McKindless long?'

'A fair time.'

I thought I saw the ghost of a smile.

'How was he to work for?'

'He could be very demanding at times. But that's all in the past for me.'

'Retirement at last?'

He looked well past retirement. Withered and benevolent, almost as old as Miss McKindless.

'Aye, though to be honest it's not entirely voluntary.'

His tenacity was admirable.

'Time to concentrate on your own garden, perhaps?'

'My gardening days are over. I'm retiring in style. There's a wee nest egg coming to me, then I'm away to the sun. This climate's no good for old bones.'

'Good for you.'

I helped him to a taxi, admiring his strength of character, hoping his nest egg would come through, wondering if I would ever make old bones.

Back at the ward the duty sister eyed me with suspicion. If she had been a maître d' she would have given me a thin smile and sent me on my way. I could see her point. The bloodstain had faded to black, but it was a stain nevertheless. Stubborn smudges of dust and stoor still clung to my suit, and my cowboy boots bore the mud of Steenie's lane. Add to that the mad look I seemed to be developing around the eyes and I didn't blame her one bit.

I identified myself as Miss McKindless's visiting nephew and inquired about her health. Sister still looked like she would prefer me fumigated, stripped and on the operating table, but she pursed her lips and resisted the temptation.

'She's not well at all, I'm afraid. A heart attack's no joke at her age.' Then, as if she suddenly doubted me. 'You are the next of kin?'

I faltered, afraid of giving myself away. 'Yes. I suppose I am. My uncle died recently. Prior to that it would have been him.'

'I see.' She made an attempt at a sympathetic expression, then gave up. 'Well, I'll need you to sign some forms before you go. Just a formality. We have to know who to contact should there be any need.'

'Do you anticipate need?'

The nurse spoke with self-conscious patience. 'Your aunt is a very old lady. She's had a heart attack, and one is often followed soon after by a second, so we'll be keeping a good eye on her. She's had a major shock to her system, so don't be surprised if she rambles a bit. Bear with her and don't let her see you upset. She's been sleeping a lot, which is good. Gives the body time to heal itself. If you find her asleep just sit quietly for a while. She'll no doubt be glad to see you when she wakes up.'

Miss McKindless lay dormant. A negative of the woman I had met three days ago. Her lips were bloodless; pale and vanishing. Skin bleached powdery white, except for around her eyes where a waxy indigo smeared the lids above and below. A Kabuki player interrupted at make-up. Clear solution meandered through plastic tubing and into her arm. An inch of tannin-coloured urine gathered in a transparent pouch hanging beneath the bed. The thin body lay still beneath the sheets. The coffin-shaped hump of a neglected grave mound. Her hands rested on top of the covers. Purple bruises spread beneath the knuckles where someone had tried for blood. She looked vulnerable, almost transparent. If her cotton nightdress were opened at the breast, her red heart might just be visible, a dark, bloody jewel, still trembling from shock, beating back in time beneath flaking, translucent skin.

The same scene repeated itself around the ward, a timeless image, recurring over like a distorted mirror-carousel, a family grouped round a bed. Nativity or death? From a distance it was hard to tell. I watched them. Normal-looking people. Punters, we called them, thinking ourselves different, better. I tried to imagine myself working in an office, travelling home to a warm hearth, children, a salary at the end of the month, pension for old age. It was too difficult; the image refused to appear.

I took a seat and placed the flowers on the cabinet beside her. It felt strange watching her asleep, intrusive. A lot had happened since the day we met. My last sane day. I wondered if she was dying. Victorians believed the sick must never sleep in a room with cut flowers, lest they choke the oxygen from the patient. I pushed the bouquet away, just in case, and turned to leave. The body in the bed moved.

'Mr Rilke.' Those blue eyes still had the power to hold me, but her voice didn't sound young any more. 'You find me at a disadvantage.'

'Miss McKindless, I hope I didn't wake you. I was just going to creep away. How are you?'

She smiled weakly, her head remained on the pillow. 'You thought you would see if I was going to kick the bucket.'

The truth brought a flush to my face. 'Not at all.'

'Don't be coy.'

She closed her eyes for a second, then motioned for me to come closer. Ill as she was, it was an imperious gesture. I sat on the chair and leaned forward. Beneath the smell of disinfectant was a stale scent of disease. The hairs on the back of my neck tingled as they rose. I breathed in and smiled like the trooper I was. When my time came I'd shoot myself.

'It is imperative that the sale goes ahead.'

I kept my tone professional. 'Is there anyone that you would like to appoint as your agent, somebody you might like me to act through while you're in here?'

'Not unless you can get help from the dead. There's nobody left except me.' There was a hint of a laugh behind her rusty whisper. 'Let the sale go ahead. The moneys can go into my account as arranged.'

'I give you my word on that. The auction will take place, as agreed, on Saturday.'

She gave a shallow nod. 'You gave me your word on something else. Has it been done?'

'We finished clearing the house today. I'll dispose of the contents of the attic myself tomorrow.'

Miss McKindless shifted a little beneath the covers. For the first time she looked agitated.

'Mr Rilke, we made an agreement. The attic is the main reason I employed you and not a larger firm.'

I wanted to take out the photographs, lay them on the bedspread in front of her and ask if these were the reason for her anxiety, or if worse awaited me. My right hand drifted towards the pocket where they rested but her condition stayed me.

'It was impossible to dispose of the material while the rest of the house contents were being removed and catalogued. It would have taken too much explaining.'

She closed her eyes again. 'Yes, I can understand that. When will it be done?'

'By the end of tomorrow the attic will be cleared and its contents destroyed.'

'Mr Rilke.' Her eyes opened. 'I am relying on you. For your own sake I advise you not to let me down.'

'Miss McKindless –' I couldn't stop myself – 'there are some disturbing things in that attic.'

'I don't doubt it' – she didn't blink – 'and I want them destroyed. My brother would have done it himself before he died if he had been able, but old age creeps up on you, Mr Rilke, time is a cheat and before you know it there's no strength left for climbing ladders or lighting bonfires.'

I couldn't let it rest. 'I'm concerned about what I might inadvertently destroy. I think your brother may have been involved with some questionable people.'

'Mr Rilke,' her voice was mocking, 'my brother was always involved with questionable people. It enabled him to avoid having to do anything too questionable himself. He died three weeks ago. His life is an episode closed. Whatever he did, it is in the past. It cannot be altered or redeemed. What is the point now in worrying about what you destroy? I'm an old lady. Allow me some peace.'

'You're very loyal. My brother, right or wrong.'

She gave a long sigh. 'Do you have any brothers or sisters?'

'No, I was always alone.'

'Then perhaps it's hard for you to understand. When you have known someone as a child, you can always see the child they once were. My brother grew up to be . . .' she hesitated, 'an unfortunate adult. But he was a lovely child. A clever, beautiful boy who could have been anything he wanted. When we were growing up and he was naughty I tried to protect him from punishment — and it was harsh punishment. As he grew older his misdemeanours became more complex, but I continued to do my best to shelter him from their consequences. Perhaps I shielded him too much. I'm willing to take my share of the blame. Somewhere something went wrong. But I could always see the child in him. Remember, there were just the two of us. He was my only family. How could I abandon that child?'

'And you'll protect him after death.'

'After his death. After mine I suspect there will be little I can do.'

The short speech had taken it out of her.

Will you at least look at what I found?'

'Mr Rilke, if you present me with anything from the attic I'll call a nurse and have her eject you from the hospital, then I will call your employer and remove the goods from sale.'

'Okay.' I put my hand gently over hers, mindful of the bruising. 'The contents of the attic will be destroyed by the end of tomorrow.'

She smiled faintly, laid her head back on the pillows and closed her eyes. Through the window the outline of John Knox raised his hand in malediction.

Rose was trying to look concerned. 'Poor woman. Do you think it's serious?'

'She's over eighty. Sneeze and it's serious at that age.'

We were sitting in the office. Rose had taken one look at my ruined suit, shaken her head and poured me a glass of wine.

'It's sad. A brother and sister dead so soon after each other. You hear of it in marriages, don't you? One can't live without the other. Old-fashioned devotion. Does she have much other family?'

'No, not so far as I could make out. No one, in fact.'

'Poor soul. Still, at least she still wants to go ahead with Saturday.'

'She was insistent.'

I looked up and caught Rose's expression. She wore her Mona Lisa smile, cryptic, mischievous.

'Okay, what is it?'

She shook her head, lowering her eyes in case I read their secret intent.

'Tell me.'

'What if we kept the money?'

'Rose, she's not dead. I just took instructions from her at the hospital.'

'I know that.' Rose's tone was hurt. 'That's why I said it. Christ, it would be a terrible thing to say if she was dead. Then you might have taken me seriously.' She topped up my glass. 'Still, if she was . . .'

'We would contact her bank and let them do the rest.'

'You, you're always so moral. *We can't do that, it's wrong.* You arenae always so particular though, are you?'

'Maybe not, but I've never fucked a policeman.'

Her mouth opened in feigned outrage. 'Neither have I!' She laughed. 'But it'll not be long now. I've been trying to be gentle with him. Seriously, Rilke, what harm would it do? If she was dead and didn't have anybody, the money would just go to the Crown. What's the point in that? The Crown has enough. They'd only waste it. Come on.' She sat on the desk and crossed her legs, her shoe dangled off the tip of her toe. 'Wouldn't it be nice to have a wee bit more than not-quite-enough, just for once? I'm sick of worrying constantly about money. It's all right being poor when you're young, you're strong, the future's ahead of you. But recently I've been thinking about what it must be like to be poor and old.'

'Come on, Rose, it's not as bad as that.'

'Oh no? How's your pension plan? Non-existent like mine. What are you going to do when you can't cut it in the auction trade any more? Shuffle round the salerooms every week, hoping you'll find something you can turn a coin on. Still working when you're seventy? Eighty? This could be our chance.'

'Rose, you're talking about robbing an old woman. We don't do that. We're the good guys. We leave the stealing and coffin-chasing to others.'

'I'm not talking about robbing an old woman. I'm talking about robbing the Crown. I'm just saying that if she does die, God forbid' – she crossed herself, stumbling over the gesture midway – 'why don't we keep the money and bugger the Crown? We could spend it better than them.'

'And what would your friend Inspector Anderson make of this plan?'

'Jim?' Her face softened. 'Jim wouldn't know and what he didn't know wouldn't hurt him.'

'It might do when he's in the visiting line at Cornton Vale.'

'Ach.' She batted my words away.

'It's the truth, Rose. I've managed to get to this age

without ever going to jail. I'd like to see if I can avoid it a while longer.'

She sipped her wine. 'You'll not go to jail. Anyway, she'll hopefully make a full recovery. It was just idle speculation.' She turned and looked me straight in the eyes, always a bad sign with Rose. 'A nest egg doesn't land in your lap every day, though. Worth thinking about, I would say.'

The telephone started to ring. Rose held my gaze a little longer, then swivelled round and lifted the receiver.

'Good evening, Bowery Auctions.' She raised her eyebrows. 'For you, *Mr Rilke*, a girl.' She lowered her voice in mock wonder. 'A young girl.'

17

Inside the Frame

Sweet is the lore which Nature brings;
Our meddling intellect
Mis-shapes the beauteous forms of things:
We murder to dissect.
Wordsworth, 'The Tables Turned'

ANNE-MARIE OPENED THE door wearing her black tracksuit.
She smiled. I liked her smile.

'Hi, come on through and I'll make us a cup of tea.'

I followed her into the kitchen, wondering if they ever
drank anything stronger in this house.

'It was good of you to come.'

'No problem.'

I asked about her acting, while we waited for the kettle to
boil, hoping to put her at ease. She related a couple of
anecdotes about working with Derek on his gorefests, as she

called them, but they were polite routines, worn from retelling. We didn't discuss why she had invited me there until we were settled in the lounge.

It was a pleasant room, furnished in a mismatch of periods. A glass kidney-shaped table circa '54, 1930s semi-deco, brown bouclé couch, '40s standard lamp with tasselled floral shade. The lamp illuminated a silver '60s cocktail bar. I gazed at the bar. It *twinkled* back.

Anne-Marie placed the tea things on the table and shifted a pile of fashion magazines, creating space for us on the settee. The room was no longer dominated by the harsh lights and small stage, but traces of the camera club were still there. They lingered around the walls in framed black-and-white prints: Man Ray's desert curves of girls; Louise Brooks's backward gaze; the even invite of Brassaï's hoors.

I am used to sipping tea in stranger's homes, appraising their belongings. Anne-Marie had taste but, for a girl who regularly took her clothes off in front of strange men, her fixtures and fittings wouldn't fetch much. She curled beside me, cradled her mug in both hands and raised it shakily to her lips. I realised she was trembling.

'Are you all right?'

'Fine, yes. It was good of you to come.'

'You've said that already.'

'Have I? Sorry.'

She got up and switched on an ancient record player. It hummed and a green glow illuminated:

Third, Light, London

Munich, Moscow, Motola

Hilversum, Paris, Budapest

Long-gone channels. Stations of the dead.

'Stations of the dead,' I said and Anne-Marie looked up.

'Pardon?'

I shook my head and she turned away, lifted the arm and let the needle descend. Janis sang, '*Ohhh, I need a man to love me* . . .'

Anne-Marie re-joined me on the settee. 'Before we begin I've got to swear you to secrecy.'

I promised to keep whatever she told me to myself.

'Is that your solemn bond?'

'I'd offer to swear on the Bible but I'm not a believer. I'll swear on a bottle of malt if you've got one.'

She smiled politely, humouring me. 'No, that won't be necessary. I've wanted to speak to you since you showed us those photographs. I can't get them out of my head. You see' – she looked away – 'I took him up on his offer. I let that man come back and photograph me.'

'By yourself?'

'By myself.'

I walked to the window. Over on the expressway the early-evening gridlock was beginning to clear. Amber headlights snaked in slow procession along criss-crossing bridges, beads of light suspended in the night sky. A helicopter hovered over them for a while, then rose high into the air, gusting off centre for a second, then flying beyond the frame of the window. I turned back towards her and took my seat on the couch.

'What happened?'

'Just what he said, he photographed me.' She lifted a hand to her eyes. 'Sorry. It wasn't that bad, I suppose. I mean, he didn't hurt me or rape me or anything.' I felt in my pocket for a handkerchief, but I'd given the last one to Steenie. She fished a tissue from up her sleeve, blew her nose, then made an attempt at a smile. 'But he unsettled me. I was scared and when you showed us those pictures' – she started to sob – 'I began to think what might have happened . . . Oh God, don't tell Christian. He'd go ape if he found out.'

Perhaps making tea is more of a cure for those ministering to the distressed than for the distressed themselves. I went through to the kitchen and brewed another pot. It made me feel better.

Back in the sitting room, Anne-Marie took her cup.

'I'm sorry. I'm hardly ever like that.'

'No, don't worry about it. We all need a good cry sometimes.' The friendly uncle was an awkward fit, but I did my best. 'Are you happy with tea or do you think something stronger might help?'

'You're really kind, but tea's fine, thanks. The cup that cheers but doesn't intoxicate.'

I didn't feel cheered. 'What was it that frightened you so much?'

'Perhaps it would just be easier if I tell you from the beginning. Do you know what makes me most angry about all of this, though?'

I shook my head. 'No.'

'That I was such a fool. Christian's right. He's told me over and over not to get into situations like this, but I did it anyway. It's my own fault.'

'We've all done things we regret.'

'I suppose. But I did it for money, pure greed, and that's crap. It makes me feel ashamed. Maybe that's why I asked you here. I want to help you find out about the photographs, of course I do, but it's not just that. I needed to tell somebody.'

'Go on, then, tell me.'

She pulled her knees up to her chest and wrapped her arms round them. Her feet were bare, her toenails painted Marian blue.

'Christian told me some old guy wanted to photograph me alone. Unfortunately, he also told me how much he was willing to pay for the privilege. It was a lot of money and I was tempted, stupid bitch that I am.' She hugged her knees tighter. 'I wanted Christian to work out a compromise, but he wouldn't even try. He reckoned the guy was a nut and there'd be no compromising with him. He'd wanted to ban him from the club just for asking. Maybe it wasn't just for asking, though. Maybe Christian sensed something. I don't know. Anyway, my brother may be a black belt, but he's a big softie. Him and me, well.' She made a rueful face and twirled her index finger around her pinkie. 'I've always been able to twist him around my little finger, ever since we were kids. I persuaded him not to ban the guy as long as he behaved. The following week I passed over a note with my mobile number on it. He phoned the next day and we set up a session, simple as that.'

'Weren't you afraid he would get the wrong idea, I mean, paying over the odds like that, didn't you think he might want you to do more than just pose for him?'

Her voice hardened. 'Obviously not or I wouldn't have allowed him to come here.'

'Okay, I take your point.'

'No.' She touched my arm apologetically. 'You're right, sorry. That's what I should have thought, but the money seemed to affect my brain. He was very smooth, gentlemanly. What was it he said? He appreciated that I was conferring a rare privilege and he gave me his word he wouldn't step beyond the boundaries I placed upon him. *The boundaries I placed upon him.* So of course, after that, I set out my boundaries, quite the thing. I told him he could stay for forty minutes, we could go straight to swimwear or nude if he wanted.' She gave an embarrassed smile. 'I thought he should get something for his money; and I said I would only do the same kind of poses you saw me doing. Tasteful.'

'And he agreed?'

'Positively delighted. Asked if I would mind including a couple of summer dresses. I thought he admired the whole act.'

McKindless had read her well, anticipated her concerns, played to her weak spot, money, and flattered her with an interest in her costumes.

'And was it like that?'

'Of course not or I wouldn't be sitting here crying my eyes out. At first I thought he wasn't coming. He was five minutes late. I'd reckoned with only forty minutes, and the meter running, he'd be there on the dot. It turned out it was the day of the Old Firm game. He'd got caught up in traffic. When he did arrive he seemed flustered and that made me more confident. Even the way he rang the doorbell was tentative. I opened the door and there was this pensioner almost hidden behind a big bunch of flowers, white lilies. I was actually touched. I decided he was just a lonely old man with a kink. Harmless.'

'What did he look like?'

'Very smart, quite dapper, really, but old, really old.'

'How old? Sixty? Seventy? Eighty?'

'I don't know. Past a certain age I find it hard to tell. Old, older than you, maybe seventy. He didn't seem ill, though. In fact, I would have said the opposite.'

'What happened?'

'I'd got myself up really nicely. I've got this lovely nineteen-fifties day dress. I imagine it as a picnic dress. It's blue with white polka dots, a touch of the ''New Look'', a lovely full skirt with frothy petticoats . . .'

I danced with a man who danced with a girl who danced with the Prince of Wales.

I was fascinated. For days I had been carrying McKindless's photographs in my pocket, trying to reach past the two dimensions of the image, to peer round corners that weren't there. Anne-Marie had got closer than me. She had been inside the frame. I let her go through the description of the dress, sensing it would calm her.

'. . . a white shawl collar, cut low at the front and a white rose just here.' She indicated the centre of her cleavage. 'And I did my make-up to match. Typical fifties, you know, a bit of a doll face, lots of red lipstick, roses in my cheeks. As I said, when he first came in he was shy, deferential almost, but as soon as we came in here he changed.' She faltered. 'I can't believe how stupid I am. It's not as if I'm a wee lassie, I'm old enough to know better.'

'Anne-Marie' — I touched her arm — 'I'm older than you and I've lost count of the stupid things I've done. If this man abused your trust, it's him to blame and not you, no matter how unwise you think you've been.'

'I suppose you're right, but I'm right, too. You know, I go to Christian's club, I know about self-defence and I know the best defence is not to get yourself into stupid situations, don't make yourself vulnerable. I know that and yet I still went ahead and put myself in harm's way. I don't mind being wrong, but I mind being a fool. I'd like to get revenge.'

'Tell me what happened.'

'When he first arrived he was pleasant, nervous even. He apologised for being late and gave me the flowers. He seemed a bit flustered so I offered to get him a glass of water. He asked if he could use the bathroom. I showed him where it was and then went to get his drink and put the flowers in a vase.'

'How many rooms are there in the flat?'

'Four, kitchen, living room, toilet and bedroom.'

'Did he look into the bedroom?'

'I don't know. I showed him where the bathroom was and then went through to the kitchen to pour him a glass of water. He was only gone for a minute, then he joined me, collected his water and we went through to the lounge.'

'Where's the bedroom?'

'Opposite the bathroom.'

'My guess is he peeked in. He wanted to make sure you were alone.'

'Could be. All of a sudden he was different, kind of cocky, more confident, as if this was his gig and he was in charge. He asked me to bring the lilies through. I did and he took them out of their vase, dripping water all over the floor. I was put out, but didn't say anything. I suppose I thought he hadn't noticed. I gave him a Polaroid camera and a new packet of film. He laughed and said he would rather use his own. Maybe that was when I knew I'd made a mistake. I insist on Polaroids because then there's no negatives. I control the image. But there was something in his laugh that made me give way. Somehow I couldn't insist.'

'Anne-Marie, I'm not criticising you, but why didn't you just order him out, or, if he wouldn't go, walk away?'

'I don't know.' The tears were back, shimmering above her lashes. 'At that point I didn't feel frightened, he hadn't done anything for me to be frightened of, I was just a little . . .' she hesitated, 'uneasy. He was still polite, over-polite, if anything. And it wasn't as if I had expected to like him. Okay, things weren't going the way I'd expected, but he was paying a lot of money. I didn't want to blow it.'

'What happened next?'

She sighed. 'He asked me to take off my make-up. He used a funny phrase. "Could you remove your face, please." Of course I knew what he meant, but for a second I had a vision of myself with no face. Now's where it starts to get freaky.' She stood up, 'Fuck it,' and walked across the room to the bar. 'If I'm going to go through all of this again, I think I'm going to need a drink. How about you?'

'Why not?'

'There's not much of a choice; vodka and orange?'

'Perfect.'

Anne-Marie mixed the drinks in a cocktail shaker then brought it and two tumblers to the table. She handed me a loaded glass and settled back on the couch with hers.

'Tell me if it's too weak. There's almost a full bottle, so don't be shy.'

I took a sip. For a second I couldn't speak, then it came out with a high cough. 'No, that'll be fine.'

She sipped hers coolly.

'You were about to tell me the freaky part.'

'Yes.' She rolled her eyes. 'I suppose the trouble is, I don't have anything to compare it to. I'm an actress and artist's model. The whole situation was freaky. It was just afterwards, when you showed us those horrible pictures, that I really started to put things into context.' She took another sip of her drink and grimaced. 'I cleansed my face. All this had taken about fifteen minutes, so I was beginning to feel better again. Less than half an hour to go. He had his camera loaded and I expected him to ask me to get undressed, but he didn't.'

She paused.

'What did he ask you to do?'

'He asked me to sit next to him and look at his album.' She

laughed, embarrassed, and raised her drink to her lips. 'He wanted me to look at his dirty photographs. So of course I did.' She emptied her glass, refilled it from the shaker, topping me up at the same time. 'I mean, anything to waste time.'

She shook her head and took a drink.

'What were they like?'

'Freaky. Of course I realised he was getting a kick out of showing them to me, but I was relieved. Like I said, the longer I avoided stripping off, the happier I was.' She blushed. 'I couldn't think of anything to say. I mean, should I admire the girls or the camera angles? So I just kept quiet. At one point he smiled and said, "You're not enjoying this, are you?" Like he got a kick out of that too.'

She went over to the bar and began to put together another batch of drinks.

'What were the photographs like?'

'Pretty horrible. They were black-and-white, which surprised me, kind of old-looking. I commented on it and he said something about the older one got the more one looked back to the boldness of one's youth.'

She returned with the freshened shaker and refilled our glasses. I sipped mine. The strength seemed about right now.

'Tell me more about the photographs.'

She took a deep breath.

'In a couple of them, the worse ones, the women looked like they might have been whipped. There was one, the woman, you could see her clothes dumped any which way on the floor. She was lying face down on an unmade bed with marks across her back. Straight lines like prison bars.' She shivered and took another drink. 'It was in black-and-white, so I told myself it was just make-up. Chocolate sauce.' She made an attempt at a laugh. 'She was still wearing her shoes. I remember thinking I'd like a pair the same.' She looked at me. 'Shallow, eh?'

I shook my head. 'You can't help what you see.'

'That was it, though. He never laid a hand on me, but he got inside me anyhow.'

'Were they all like that?'

'No. For the most part they were just naked, or half-naked women looking' — she missed a beat — 'languid.'

'Languid?'

A deep intake of breath. 'They were posed like corpses.'

I kept my voice calm, but inside I felt like committing murder. 'Posed?'

'Unfocused eyes, limp limbs, slack mouths, but I didn't think for a second that they weren't posed.'

'And now?'

'In the photograph you showed us, the one from the other night, that woman looked dead. And well, I'm still here, aren't I?'

'What do you mean?'

'He posed me in the same way.'

I looked at Anne-Marie: her clear skin flushed from drink; dark hair slightly dishevelled; eyes red-rimmed from crying, and reached across, taking her hand in mine. She moved closer, our shoulders touching, I felt the quickness of her breath. A faint smell of oranges. She squeezed my fingers.

'We finished looking through the album. I arranged the room the way he wanted. The couch draped with throws, the screen behind it as a backdrop. Then it was show time. He asked me to get undressed. I went behind the screen and stripped. I don't like them seeing me taking my clothes off, that's private.' She looked away from me, towards the window, out into the night sky. 'It was warm in the room but, as soon as I took off my clothes, I felt cold, really cold. Goose bumps rose on my arms and across the back of my neck. He asked me to lie on the couch, then described the positions he wanted. I'm good at taking direction, but I guess I already knew the kind of pose he wanted from his album. He arranged the lilies around me like some kind of funeral decoration. Sap leaked from their stems onto my skin. When he'd first brought them I thought they smelt lovely, but now it was as if they'd been standing in dirty water for too long. A rank scent, like a dead pond when there's been no rain.' She shivered and squeezed my hand tightly. 'I'd expected the session to be awkward, but I felt' – she took a sip of her drink – 'I felt strange. Charged. As if I was hyper-sensitive. The colours in the room seemed brighter. The ticking of the clock, the click of the camera shutter, sounded like slamming doors. But the worst was my skin. I could feel everything, the cool of the air, the pile of the fabric beneath me. The old man moved and a breeze brushed my body like a caress. He said nothing, but his gaze pierced me. His eyes bored through the lens, deep into me. And I began to feel . . .' she hesitated again, 'aroused. For a second I felt that if he touched me, old as he was, much as he disgusted me, I wouldn't resist. Christ.' She groaned and downed the last of her drink. 'I didn't mean to tell you that.' A tear rolled gently down her cheek. She had beautiful skin. 'Now I've disgusted you.'

'No, not at all.'

I hesitated, unsure of what to do, how best to reassure her. A sob shuddered her body, breath whooped as she tried, and failed, to stop it escaping. I put an arm tentatively round her shoulders and she leaned into me. The strangeness of holding a woman, delicate, fragile, a hollow-boned bird. I stroked her hair; it smelt of vanilla.

'Tell me.'

'I'd put the clock where I could see it. As soon as his time was up I jumped off the couch and threw on my robe.' She stopped.

'Was that the end of it?'

'Not quite, no.' She drew a hand across her face and sighed. 'I was the one who was flustered now, embarrassed. I felt he knew. He started to pack away his equipment, then said, ''How much to cut you?'' I asked him, ''Pardon?'' even though I'd heard him the first time and he repeated it. ''How much to cut you?'' I was tempted.' She started to cry again. 'It was almost as if he had hypnotised me. I was disgusted with myself. I get like that sometimes. The posing, the way it makes me feel. It was almost as if I wanted some kind of punishment. A physical hurt to take away the hurt inside. I got a tingling feeling at the top of my arms where I felt he might begin. I remember every word. ''A small cut, hardly a scar. Let the pain that cuts away the pain diffuse your senses.'''

'But you didn't let him?'

'God no, but I wanted to, for an instant I wanted to.'

Anne-Marie was crying in earnest now, her shoulders shaking beneath my arm. I gave her a reassuring squeeze and she turned her face into my chest. She continued talking, her voice muffled, broken by sobs.

'I told him I was expecting someone. He paid me my money and left. Christ, it's a sin, but I was never so happy as when you told me he was dead.'

I squeezed her shoulders again. 'You've nothing to feel guilty about.'

She raised her face. There was a damp patch on my shirt

where her tears had soaked into the cotton. She touched it and laughed bravely. Her face was close, very close. She raised her lips to mine and then we were kissing. Tongue touching tongue, tenderly, tip to tip. I opened my eyes and saw that hers were closed. I ran a finger down her spine. She moved closer, small breasts pressing into my chest. I kissed along her cheekbones, tasting the salt of her tears. Her hands strayed anxiously towards my belt.

I stayed them. 'No.'

She sat up, breath heavy. 'Am I going mad?'

I kissed her again, this time on the cheek. 'No more than anyone else.'

We sat quietly, holding each other for a while, me stroking her hair, then it was time to go.

Anne-Marie came with me to the door. 'Will you tell me what you find out?'

'You'll be the first to know.'

We kissed a platonic goodbye, then, as I turned to leave, she said, 'Oh, I almost forgot. Derek's been desperate to talk to you. Wait a second.'

She ran back up the hallway to the kitchen and returned with a telephone number scrawled on a scrap of paper.

'Why don't you give him a call?'

I kissed her again and went out into the darkness.

18

Trophies

THE ENTRYPHONE BUZZED in the middle of the night. I awoke with a jolt, my body twisted in the sheets. Two drunks stumbled up the stairs, their voices indistinct and booming. On the floor above a door opened and an argument began. The illuminated numbers on my alarm clock read 04:05. Upstairs a dog lent cadence to the shouting. A door slammed, the drunks fumbled with keys and complaints, another slam and then silence. The dawn chorus began as if also awoken by the row. My hands reached out in the dark, found tobacco and Rizlas and started rolling. In the apartment above someone said something and the Rottweiler harumphed, settling back into slumber. All hope of sleep seemed lost. Then it was 7 a.m., there was ash on the sheets and a half-burnt cigarette dead between my fingers.

I rolled another smoke, got up, washed, dressed, made myself porridge that looked like paste, forced it down, lifted

the telephone and brought it to the table with another smoke
and a mug of coffee. My fingers hesitated, then started to dial.

HOSPITAL: 'Your aunt is stable, but I'm afraid there's been
no improvement.'

ANDERSON: 'Inspector Anderson is unavailable. If you tell
me the nature of your inquiry, I'll see if another officer can be
of assistance.'

JOHN: 'You know me, Rilke, I'd buy from the De'il
himself if there was a profit in it, but I'm no so sure about
you. What exactly happened between you and my brother the
other day?'

ROSE: 'Your presence is required, here, today. You've
been on an extended skive since the start of this job. Perhaps
you've forgotten how important it is? This sale could make or
break us. That reminds me, how's the old lady doing?'

LESLIE: 'What the fuck kind of a time is this? You've burnt
your bridges this time, big man. I'd just about forgotten you.
Now piss off before I remember too much and get annoyed.'

DEREK: Good to hear from you, man. You timed it well,
I'm free today.'

I asked Derek if he wanted to earn some pin money helping
move the boxes from the attic. He sounded pleased to hear
from me but didn't say what he had wanted to talk about. We
agreed to meet later in the day outside the McKindless house.
My motives were dishonourable and varied. I wasn't sure
what I was going to do with the books, but I was certain,
whatever I had promised, I wasn't going to burn them. I
needed help from someone unconnected with the auction, and
who better than this boy? A boy I wanted to spend time alone
with, a link, however faint, with McKindless. I wished I had
asked Anne-Marie more about Derek but, after what had

passed between us the night before, it hadn't seemed possible. I thought about the complexities of desire. How many years since I had been with a woman? I tried to conjure up Anne-Marie's image and to my relief saw her as she had been the night before, cosy and barefoot, in her tracksuit.

The remains of my hangover made everything an edge out, a second beyond anticipation. But it only hurt a little bit and the pain was a pleasant distraction from the rest of my problems. I forced my concentration on space, distance and driving: especially driving. Accompanying my despondency was an excitement, a recklessness probably not unconnected with the alcohol still in my bloodstream. Who cared if your friends deserted you and your employer alternately wanted to land you in jail or sack you, when the pressure on your temples made the whole world surreal?

Inside the house things looked as I remembered, the empty hallway, the stained glass reflecting a pool of coloured light onto the parquet floor. The smell was different, though, a slight dampness which hinted already at abandonment and dereliction. It was still early in the morning. Shadows lurked in the turn of the landing, in the half-open doorways. For some reason I shouted, 'Hello?' into the emptiness and paused for a second. It struck me I would rather be anywhere than here. And, though I don't believe in ghosts, I sang to keep my courage up as I climbed towards the darkened guest bedroom at the top of the house.

> 'I went down to St. James Infirmary,
> Saw my baby there;
> Stretched out on a long, white table,
> So sweet, so cold, so fair.

> '*Let her go, let her go, God bless her,*
> *Wherever she may be,*
> *She can search this wide world over,*
> *But she'll never find another sweet man like me.*'

The words didn't make sense. How could his baby search the world for another sweet man if she was dead?

I hooked down the ladder to the attic, unlocked the trapdoor and heaved myself in, noting that the height no longer bothered me. The room was in darkness. I felt for the light switch, clicked it on and looked around. I don't know what I had expected, but the unchanged quietness of the room was an anticlimax. Everything was as before: the rows of boxes, the bookshelves neatly stacked with volumes, the desk and chair, the almost empty bottle of malt tumbled on the floor. I lifted the bottle, measured its contents, two good swallows, then placed it upright on the desk, resisting a pull for good luck.

I had promised twice to destroy the contents of the attic, but promises are easily broken. John had said McKindless would be revealed through his library, but John was a bookseller; he formed his opinion of everyone through their books.

I ran a finger along the spines, wondering why I hadn't returned before. What was there to fear? Discovery? It was true I didn't want to share my knowledge or my fee. But I had managed deceptions in the past. That the sale would be cancelled? It would make a difference. Bowery Auctions was trembling on the edge of ruin and this sale could be our salvation, our future if Rose was to be believed. But we had looked into that abyss before and survived. Was I senti-mental about the printed word, paralysed by the sanctity of

books? No. I have tipped shoals of books, pitched encyclo-
paedias, out-of-date bestsellers, book-club-choice-of-the-
month and Reader's Digest Condensed into the council
dump, sent novelists' dreams of immortality somersaulting
into the refuse without a qualm. Anyway, I had no intention
of destroying these books. They were rare volumes, im-
moral, but some so scarce I had only glimpsed references to
them in dated catalogues. There was no way I would consign
them to the flames. They were coming home with me,
legitimate pochle.

What I had been avoiding was the truth. Like a child
hesitating before a keyhole, I wanted to discover hidden
secrets, but was frightened that the knowledge, once gained,
wouldn't be to my liking and could never be lost. Accent-
uating the fear was a delicious anticipation, the thrill of terror,
before the plunge. It was the thrill that scared me most.

I rubbed my hands on a clean handkerchief, making sure
they were dry, then set to work, examining the titles I knew
first, easing myself gently into the task, leaving the unknown
till last, checking each book methodically, holding it loosely in
the palm of my hand, fanning softly through the pages,
searching for ephemera or esoterica hidden between the
leaves. There was nothing. McKindless had been a true
collector. No acid leeching paper, no bookmarks, revues
or folded obituaries interrupted the progress of the pages. I
grew absorbed, stopping occasionally to read a phrase or
confirm an edition, packing them into the small cartons I had
brought with me. An hour and a half later I was sweating,
dusty and thinking of the whisky. But it was time for the
unknown volumes and I was determined to face them sober.
The calm induced by the routine sorting left me. Once more
it felt eerie to be all alone searching through a dead man's

secrets, and I wished I had brought a radio to drown out the sounds an empty house makes.

I eased a leather-bound quarto volume from the shelf and stroked my fingers lightly across its thirsty boards. The title page announced, *A Description of Merryland*, by Roger Pheu-quewell (1720), *A Topographical, Geographical and Natural History of That Country*. I closed the covers, then opened them again, letting the leaves settle where they willed. A faint, peppery smell fanned from the pages, finest rag paper, white as an egg after two and a half centuries.

Two hundred and sixty years ago an artist had laid a sheet of copper on his desk. He had lifted a pot of melted wax from a burner and painted the surface of the copper thinly with it. He waited until the wax set, then traced the outline of his subject onto the metal. Next he took a small pointed tool, his burin, poised the handle in the palm of his hand and guided it carefully, ploughing furrows. The copper plate was finally dipped in acid which ate away at the exposed cuts, leaving the rest of the surface intact, creating the template from which the engraving was printed. Etching is a difficult art. One cannot draw freehand with a burin. The final image is an accumulation of rows, dashes, flicks and dots, which grow from a simple outline into the final picture.

Rembrandt was good at it. So was this guy.

A dozen plates revealed the landscape of Merryland to be a woman's body. The quantity of plates suggested this was a first edition, but it was hard to concentrate on imprint. The engraver had not confined himself to the exterior of the country: a thorough conquistador, he had explored the new land entirely, stripping away the woman's skin, delving deeper as the book progressed, exposing her like an anatomical Venus or a cadaver left to the mercy of anatomy students. The series climaxed in a detailed rendering of her reproductive organs. A man not satisfied with looking up women's skirts, he wanted to get closer, ever closer, until he took the object of his desire apart, breaking it in an effort to discover how it worked.

I turned to the other books. Death reached out from their pages. Death was a woman, and women were dead. She hid her skull face behind a dainty mask, danced jigs with skirts raised high and wormy thighs exposed. She leant over the old, the young, embracing them like a mother. Mother Death. Dead Mother. Death stalked with a dissecting-bisecting knife, cutting woman from sternum to pubis, unfolding her skin, raising it reverently like the most fragile of altar cloths, revealing organs glazed with blood, exquisitely curled in-testines, ovaries branching heroically from uterus cradled over bladder, a miracle of engineering revealed. Death splayed across the pages in white-faced charades. Death etched, stippled, blocked, stamped, impressed itself. It tinted, printed, scraped and scrawled. Death criss-crossed the page, engraved the grave. Death whispered in monochrome, screamed in Technicolor.

I wondered how long it was since the old man had been able to climb the stairs. How many evenings had he sat below thinking of these images, teasingly out of reach, reassembling centuries of cruelty from memory?

John said I would know the man through his books.

Anne-Marie said folk have strange fancies.

The pornographer said there are many people with dubious morals, but few psychopaths.

The books told me McKindless's fantasies, nothing more.

It was time for the boxes. I sat for a minute looking at them. Eight. I had examined three on the previous visit and found one envelope of photographs. That left five. What were the odds that there was something else? The envelope I had found might have been a moment of carelessness. A forgotten image lost because it meant nothing. A photographic mirror of the etching. But then there was Anne-Marie's experience.

No watcher would mistake my movements as careless this time. I searched with care unmatched, unfolding every page, reading letters that yielded nothing.

When I saw the case, I knew, even before I opened it, that this was what I had been looking for. What it held originally I wasn't sure. Something feminine, I guessed, from the silvered shapes that decorated its surface. It was made of thick cardboard, compacted for strength, in a process rendered obsolete after the seventies. The design, though abstract, owed more to Braque's cubist complexities than to pop art or acid trips. I raised it beyond eye level. Stamped on the bottom, *Judy Plum Wigs, Mitchell Lane*. The lettering confirmed the other signs. Virtuosa II, a typescript issued by Hermann Zapf in 1953. The case felt light but there was something inside. I set it on the desk, took a seat, flexed my fingers like a pianist and lifted the lid. Three small tissue-paper-wrapped packages nestled among more crumpled tissue paper. I lifted them, one by one, placed them on the desk, then carefully slit the fastenings on the largest package with my penknife.

It was a powder compact. Not expensive, but pretty all the same. The edge of its lid decorated by a green and white Celtic design. Barely legible, entwined in the Celtic border was the word *Eire*. In the lid's centre, in case you hadn't got the message, was an Irish harp. A present from Ireland to a sweetheart? A holiday souvenir? I clicked it open. China white face powder trembled in the air, then drifted across the desk, gentle as snow in a globe. How many years since it had been opened? I looked inside. Almost full, and there was my own face, unsmiling and distant, reflected in the mirror.

I slit open the second parcel, a Bakelite hair clasp with a brass clip. A plain geometric design, the height of fashion round about the same time that Bakelite plastic was as expensive as tortoiseshell. A single long red hair was trapped in its hinge.

The objects, like the case they were stored in, were both feminine. The clasp expensive and in fashionable good taste. The compact a pretty souvenir. None of them looked special enough to warrant such careful storage.

I took my knife and cut carefully into the final package. This was the smallest of the four, twisted and taped in a way that made me suspect it might be all paper and nothing else. A prank. Except nothing so far had suggested this man liked a jest. I pierced the wrapping and shook out a delicate silver bracelet. Tiny charm like medals shivered on its chain. The ten commandments. Top of the list, before murder, *Thou shalt not take the name of thy Lord God in vain*.

'Jesus Christ,' I whispered.

I took the photograph of the girl from my pocket and scrutinised it through my magnifying glass. It told me what I already knew. There was no doubt. It was the bracelet that hung from her bound wrist.

I was parked outside the house, seat pushed all the way back, dark glasses blocking out the light, feet on the wheel, when Derek rapped against the window. I saw him vivid, sharp against the haze of the day. It wasn't exactly sunny, but there was an early-morning freshness to the damp and a glare in the grey sky that might count as good weather. Derek's hair was slightly wet, as if not long out of the

shower. I'd warned him to wear clothes he didn't mind
getting dirty and he'd taken me at my word. An old denim
jacket, frayed at the seams, black T-shirt bearing the legend
CRIMINAL, worn Levi's and Doc Martens boots. He looked
like a handsome actor masquerading as a workman for the
sake of an advert. Whatever he was selling, he had a
customer. I peered at him over the top of my shades.
He mouthed, 'Hello,' through the glass and my heart did a
flip that tugged my balls.

I untangled my legs and slid out of the van. 'How're you
doing?'

'Good, man, good. So what's the story? Is this the place
you were telling me about?'

'This is it.'

'Some size.'

'Aye, not bad.'

'So this is where the bodies are buried?'

I gave him a look.

He grinned back at me. 'Sorry, bad taste.'

His smile would slay me every time.

'Don't worry about it.'

I unlocked the front door and we went into the house
together, me explaining what I wanted him to do.

'Just grunt work, I'm afraid.'

Him being charming: 'Well that's what I'm good at.'

I led him up the staircase, towards the bedroom and the
attic beyond, aware of the irony of the situation. Circum-
stance mocked me. I had thought the task might bond us. That
a session getting hot and sweaty as we moved the boxes might
result in a hot, sweaty session between us. Now I just wanted
to move the stuff, lock the door to the house behind me and
never come back. The bracelet was the Rosetta Stone of the

quest, a definite link between McKindless and the girl in the photographs.

Derek broke into my thoughts. 'You know, this is probably the biggest house I've ever been in.'

'Yes?'

'What did he do, the man who owned it?'

'That's a good question. I should have asked it before I accepted the job.'

'My dad used to say, ''A rich man is either a thief, or the son of a thief.'' '

I took a seat on the top step. 'Sounds like a wise guy, your dad.'

'Still worried about the photos?'

I countered his question with one of my own. 'Anne-Marie said you wanted to speak to me.'

Derek's smile died and I realised that beneath the cheerful façade was an anxious boy. He settled himself beside me and gazed down the staircase as if fascinated by the swoop of its curve.

'I've got a bit of a problem. It doesn't tie in with your pictures – at least I don't think it does – but I'd like to run it by you, if you don't mind.'

'Go ahead.'

The conversation took on the rhythm of a catechism.

'Have you ever done something you regret?'

'Of course. Everybody's done something they wish they hadn't.'

'I mean really regret. Something you're ashamed of?'

'I'd say the same answer holds true.'

'Do you believe there are bad people and good people?'

'I believe there are some bad individuals, but most people do their best to be good and everybody slips up sometimes.'

'Will you tell me the worst thing you've ever done, the action you most regret?'

'No.'

He smiled with dour satisfaction. 'Fair enough. Well, I'm going to tell you the worst thing I've ever done.'

I wanted to ask him to stop, to say I knew enough of men's wickedness. Instead I braced myself, ready to eat his sins whole. 'Go on.'

He drew a finger through the recent dust on the step, then rubbed it clean against his jeans. Stillness closed over us. Me and the boy in the empty house, his voice wavering now and then, as he related his confession.

'When I first started to work in the shop it was exciting. It gave me a real feeling of power, you know what I mean, probably a bit like you with the auction.' I nodded to show I understood. 'I was part of another world. A secret world most people are too squeamish for. I mean, I was just selling dirty magazines in a basement record shop, but it gave me a buzz. I think my enthusiasm amused Trapp. Sometimes he was away for days and I'd be left to get on by myself. But when he was around we talked. I bought everything he told me. How we were freedom fighters in a war against regulation. Democracy isn't about the majority, it's about the minority, too, and as long as you hurt no one it's nobody's business what you do.'

'It all sounds very plausible.'

'Would you have believed it?'

'Perhaps at your age. The most convincing lies have an element of the truth in them.'

'I fell for it big time. I worked there for a few months, taking phone calls from his other operations, speaking to people abroad. I mean, all I was doing was screening his calls,

"Yes, Mr Trapp is in. No, I'm sorry he's unavailable at the moment," but you'd have thought I was James Bond or something the way I carried on.'

'So what happened?'

'I got promoted. I wouldn't say we were friends, him and me. He's not the kind of guy you make friends with, but I looked up to him.' Derek gave a tight laugh. 'I considered him a mentor. He'd gone for it, made lots of money and remained a rebel. On the wrong side of the law in defence of freedom. What a joke. He asked me all about myself and I was happy to tell him, my ambitions, my short films.'

Suddenly I could see what was coming. 'Oh no.'

'Oh yes.'

'He asked if you'd be interested in making a film for him?'

'It's so obvious I didn't even see it coming. He probably thought I'd been hinting for weeks.'

'And you said yes.'

'I guess it wouldn't be much of a confession if I'd walked away.'

'What happened?'

'I suppose it was simple. Trapp explained he didn't want anything too slick. He said amateurish was good. More convincing. I was a bit offended at that.' He shook his head. 'As if it mattered. We drove to a flat on the south side. Trapp was in a really good mood, a holiday mood. I think me being there gave him a kick. Like a dad taking a son out for his first pint or something.'

'And you?'

'I was shitting it. If I could have thought of a way of escaping without losing face I would've. We were the first to arrive. The flat was more or less empty, as if someone was halfway through moving out. Trapp showed me a bedroom. I set up my lights and stuff then we sat waiting and smoking. The only thing in the room was a big double bed so we sat on that, side by side. Trapp made a joke about it. The longer we waited, the sicker I felt. I kept making up sentences in my head, exit lines, but nothing fitted. Finally after about half an hour there was a ring at the door and the ''actors'' arrived.'

'What happened?'

'I went through with it. Fairly straightforward I suppose. A man and a woman had intercourse on the bed and I filmed them. End of story.'

'Sounds like it could have been worse.'

'Aye, but it was horrible.' His voice faltered. 'I'd begun filming when I realised the woman didn't want to be there. Tears streaked down her face. She was crying without making a sound. All those lies Trapp told me about freedom and democracy. I close my eyes and I still see her. She was foreign. Fuck knows where from. The whole way through she looked right into the camera, right at me, her eyes staring into mine as I stared back through the viewfinder. You know it made me angry. I wanted to slap her, tell her to look elsewhere, look at the man who was fucking her, he was the rapist not me.' His voice dropped to a whisper. 'I felt like I was killing her.'

'Didn't you do anything?'

'No. No, I did nothing.'

'Were you frightened?'

'Fucking terrified. It's no excuse, but yes. The kind of guys who'd do that, yes it petrified me.' Derek shook his head. 'Afterwards the couple left and Trapp gave me a lift into town. He paid me fifty quid. Fifty quid. I went straight to a bar where I knew I'd meet people, and spent it getting wrecked.'

'Why are you still working there?'

'Good question. You'd think I'd shift my arse quick-style wouldn't you?'

'Want my advice?'

'I think I can guess: leave. Well it's out of my hands. The police came looking for him yesterday. I hadn't seen him for a couple of days, but that's nothing unusual, he's often away. After he'd gone I tried the filing cabinets. They're usually locked, but they slid open like a dream. They were empty. I think he's done a bunk.'

'What do you think I should do?'

We had moved up to the attic and for the last hour had been working in shifts, one of us passing the cartons through the trap, the other carrying them down the ladder. We'd paced ourselves, working in silence, both dwelling on Derek's story.

'Keep shtoom.' I steadied a box as Derek balanced it on one shoulder. Les's advice came back to me. 'These guys are the real thing. You should have legged it after the video episode.'

Derek descended the ladder slowly. 'I thought about it. I thought of going to the police, sticking him in, but I was frightened.'

'You were right to be frightened. If I was you, I'd get myself an anonymous manila envelope, put on a pair of rubber gloves and post the keys back.'

'What if the police come looking for me?'

'Is there any reason why they should?'

'I don't know.'

'Then cross that bridge if you come to it.'

I passed him down the final box. The attic was empty, save for the furniture. That could wait there for the next occupiers, for all I cared. I clattered down the ladder and joined him beside the stack of books and boxes.

'If they do turn up, tell them as little as you think you can get away with, but be sure what you do tell them is the truth. And for God's sake, whatever you do, don't let on about your directorial debut.'

'Do you think I should go to the police anyway?'

I'd been pondering that very point while we shifted the contents of the attic. I wanted to protect the boy. Was telling him to run the best advice or just a reflex? But experience told me that when the police came looking for someone else it was sheer foolishness to step forward.

'What would you tell them?'

'What I'd seen.'

'Well, that would have the benefit of clearing your conscience. But it'd get you into a lot of trouble and very likely tell them nothing they don't know already. If I were you I'd keep a low profile, buy a daily newspaper and keep your ear to the ground.'

Derek leant against the pile of boxes, looking more relaxed than he had since starting his story.

'You know, it's funny how things work out. When you came into the shop I thought you were just another punter, then, when you showed me the photographs, I wasn't sure. I thought you might be getting your thrills in another way. When you showed me Anne-Marie's card I decided, well, here's a chance to test out whether you're a sleaze or not.'

'Don't you think that was a bit unfair on Anne-Marie?'

'I knew nothing would happen with Chris there and you had her card. It was inevitable you'd look for her. Better you found her when Chris and I were around. Anyway,' he laughed, 'you were so majorly uncomfortable with the set-up it was obvious you were genuine. Then when you passed round the photographs it was clear you really were bothered. That's when I first thought you might be able to give me some advice. You seem to know your way around. I got the feeling you'd understand, wouldn't judge me.'

'Why didn't you ask me sooner?'

'I wanted to think things over, then when the police came round I knew I had to talk to someone. Thanks.'

'Any time.'

I wanted to prolong the intimacy between us. I lit a cigarette and offered one to Derek. He turned it down and took a pull from a bottle of Irn Bru he had brought with him.

'You smoke a lot don't you?'

'Yes.'

I took a drag, hoping he wasn't going to start lecturing me.

'Ever think of giving up?'

He passed me the bottle and I put my lips where his had been.

'No.'

'You know it suits you, the shape of your face. It looks good when you inhale, very sculptural.'

I hadn't blushed in thirty years, but there was an unfamiliar glow creeping across my face. I turned away to check one of the boxes. The one where what I was beginning to think of as trophies were stored.

'What's that?'

I hadn't meant to tell him, but in the warmth of the moment and the aftermath of his confession, I found myself opening the wig case and passing it to him. He lifted the objects one at a time, examining each in turn, then placing them back in the tissue. Too late, thoughts of fingerprints flitted through my mind.

'So, I know nothing about antiques, man. Are these valuable?'

'Not in themselves, no. But I think they're connected to the photographs I showed you.'

'Really?'

He looked sceptical and there and then I was taken by a need to impress him, to show I wasn't an obsessed eccentric. When I think on it now, I sting with shame. I took out the photograph and my magnifying glass and handed them to him.

'Look at what she's wearing on her wrist.'

Derek raised the glass awkwardly to his eye and squinted at the picture. 'Jesus.' He lifted the bracelet slowly, examining it against the light of the window, returned to the photograph then raised his eyes to mine. 'What're you gonna do?'

'Sit tight until after the sale.'

'I know this sounds weird after what I've just told you, but don't you think you should do something sooner? Like now?'

'Possibly, but the man's dead, he's not going to be harming anyone where he is and, quite frankly, we need this sale. His sister's ill, like to die. We can't afford a delay.'

He nodded, abstracted, deep in thought.

'I guess they've waited a long time, a few days won't make so much difference.' He looked at the photograph again. 'When you think about it, the word ''snuff'', it sounds like a gentle way to go. Turn out the light, snuff out the candle.' He leant against a box. 'Here comes the candle to light you to bed. Here comes the old man to chop off your head.'

Derek laughed nervously and somewhere someone walked across my grave. I shivered and stood up.

'Let's get this show on the road.'

*　　*　　*

Loading took us another hour, then we were sitting in the van, next to each other, tired and dirty. I wanted to ask him to come out with me, to go for a meal, something to drink. Instead I handed him thirty pounds and asked where I could drop him.

He hesitated. 'You said you were short of money.'

I was touched. 'Everything's relative. You more than earned that, and you don't have a job any more.'

I didn't start the engine, sensing more was to come, but unsure of what it was.

'You know, I would have got in touch even if it wasn't for the video. D'you mind that I said I'd rather you owed me one?'

I attempted to mask my excitement with a note of caution. 'Yes?'

'There's something I'd like more than money from you.'

'Yes?'

Derek looked straight at me, his Weimaraner eyes clear and guileless. 'God you've got the perfect face.' My lips tingled. His voice dropped a fraction, growing serious. 'I told you that my dream was to make horror movies?'

'Yes?'

'Well, I think it could happen. I think I could make it. I've a bit saved and God knows I've got time on my hands. I've made a lot of small films. I've even won a couple of competitions. I'm good at it. I just need a break, the right vehicle, the right actors and I think I've found them.'

I smiled, sceptical, as the old will be of the young, but infected by his enthusiasm. 'Congratulations.'

'Cheers. But this is where you come in, if you're willing.'

I was expecting him to ask to borrow props, perhaps even

use the auction house as a location. Whatever it was, I decided
I would help.

'I'll do what I can.'

Derek flashed me a grin and asked, 'What's the most
popular horror film ever?'

'*Dr Jekyll and Mr Hyde?*'

'Good guess but no.' He lowered his voice like a fairground
barker reaching the climax of his spiel. '*Nosferatu.*' Then,
seeing my bewilderment, '*Dracula*. Things went all wrong
with Bela Lugosi. After him it was suavity and Byronic
aristocrats, Christopher Lee, Peter Cushing. Fine for a laugh
but nothing like the originals, *Nosferatu*.' He drew out the
word splitting it into syllables. '*Nos-fer-a-tu*. F. W. Murnau
had Max Schreck, Werner Herzog had Klaus Kinski. I'm
going to make my own version and you would be perfect for
the title role. The ancient vampire, end of his line, left to
moulder, alone and friendless. The bemused monster who has
lived too long. What do you say?' He put on an American
accent, 'C'mon baby, I could make you a star!'

I realised I had leant towards him. Now I pulled back. The
shrill of my phone pierced the silence. I answered it in a daze.

'Hello. Mr McKindless?' announced an authoritative voice.

'He's dead,' I said in a whisper too low to be heard across
the radio waves.

The voice continued. 'This is the Royal Infirmary. I'm
sorry to have to tell you that your aunt is in a critical
condition. I think it best that you come here now.'

19

Downhill from Here

AT THE INFIRMARY I lost my bearings and asked a white coat
for directions. He eyed me hungrily, then related a shortcut,
which led me down the gentle gradient of echoing basement
corridors, past porters wheeling trolleys laden with blanketed
mounds of the seeming dead. The nose has a way of
remembering what the brain has forgotten. There, in the
scent of Infirmary disinfectant, was every hospital visit I had
ever made. My madeleine. A stooped man in a soiled
towelling robe shuffled by without raising his eyes. An
attendant, looking like a prison guard, took him by the crook
of the arm and led him round a corner. I walked on. The
traffic of people seemed to be lessening. The walls melted
from piss yellow into eau-de-nil. The overhead pipes of
Victorian plumbing grew denser. I halted at a branch in
the corridor, unsure whether to go left or right. A small man
in grey overalls hurried by, carrying a pendulous plastic

rubbish sack in each hand. I started to call out, to ask the way, but he disappeared through a swing door. I caught the door on its return and followed him through.

The small man bent towards the open doors of a furnace. He had unfastened the bags and was scooping their contents quickly and efficiently into the flames. A wall of heat leapt towards me. My back and forehead prickled and I caught an impression of pale, fleshy softness. The hospital scent was gone. The man and I locked gazes. He made to speak and I let the door swing to, blocking out the sight.

I retraced my footsteps then propped myself against a wall, resting my face against cold, porcelain tiles, trying to erase the pictures in my head. Later there was a brisk approach of footsteps. A nurse turned the corner. I straightened myself and told her I had lost my way.

'Geographically or emotionally?' There was an Irish lilt to her voice.

'Both.'

'Ah,' she laughed, 'I can only help you with the geography. Some things are beyond cure.'

I twisted my lips into an impersonation of a smile and told her she might be right.

This time the sister had sympathy in her eyes.

'I'm sorry, your aunt suffered a second heart attack at three fifteen this afternoon. She passed away forty minutes ago.'

She had led me into her tiny office, seating me next to her opposite a neatly regimented desk. Through the glass windows I could see a nurse guiding a spoon into an elderly patient's mouth. Some of the contents of the spoon escaped and slithered down the old person's chin. I turned my gaze away.

'Your aunt was over eighty. I'm afraid there was no chance of her surviving a second shock to her system so soon after the first. The end came swiftly and painlessly. I'm sorry we weren't able to reach you any sooner.'

In the ward the nurse was wiping the patient's face. She reloaded the spoon and prepared to try again.

Miss McKindless had died while I was moving her brother's books, breaking my promise to burn them. I felt bad, bad that she was dead and bad that I had lied to her, but I knew I would have felt worse had I destroyed them. She and her brother were both dead. The books survived as they had survived the deaths of other owners. Still, I hoped they hadn't caused her distress in her last hours and I hoped she wasn't hovering where she could see the boxes piled in the back of the van.

'You did your best. It's the kind of end we all hope for.'

Sister looked relieved by my stoicism. 'Is there anyone you would like me to contact?'

I shook my head.

A young nurse chapped softly on the office door then entered. 'We're finished.'

'Well done. Thank you, Eileen.'

The nurse closed the door gently and Sister turned to me.

'Your aunt is ready. Would you like to see her?'

I'd nodded and she had led me briskly towards an ante-room. Fluorescent light shone through a yellow screen erected around the bed, casting a sunflower glow. There is a change that comes after death. The pale body washed, scented and tucked beneath the sheets was no longer Miss McKindless. Whatever it was that had made her herself, the essential spirit, vital spark, soul, call it what you will, had departed. I touched her hand.

'I'm sorry.' I whispered. 'I hope you'll forgive what I have done and what I am about to do.'

Sister stopped me outside. 'Are you okay?'

'Yes, fine.'

There was genuine concern on her face. 'You look terribly pale. Even when it's expected death comes as a shock. Why don't you have a seat in the office? I'll bring you a cup of tea.'

'No, I'll be fine, thanks.'

'Are you sure? I don't want you crashing on the way home and making more work for us.'

Some of the old sharpness was back, but I saw it for what it was now. Tiredness edged a crosshatch of premature lines around her eyes.

'Don't worry, I'll take it easy. Thank you for taking such good care of her.'

'It's our job. Let me know what arrangements you make. She can stay with us for three days but after that . . .'

'It gets a bit crowded?'

She gave me a sad, last smile. 'Unfortunately.'

I took the lift up to Bowery, squeezed in beside Niggle, two young porters, and the desk Miss McKindless had sat behind at our first meeting. In the saleroom preparations were under way to transform the damp, dead expanse into an emporium of rare delights. McKindless's Turkish rugs hung, an exotic backdrop to the podium. Ranks of furniture, once united under the same roof, were beginning to assume separate identities, marshalling themselves for auction. Trestle tables laden with bric-a-brac glittered along one side of the room. Jimmy James, armed with a catalogue and muttering small oaths, was labelling lot numbers. Jewellery and other pocket-sized desirables had been tucked safely into display cases. A boy, balanced casually at the top of a ladder, crowed a triumphant 'Yes!' as he fitted a small oil into the last space on a wall now covered in paintings. Glass shades hung from the ceiling on wire sharp enough to cut you. Objects to bewitch and beguile, assembled together and available for purchase, tomorrow, for one day only.

Rose stood in the centre of the room, posed like a monochrome 1950s *Vogue* model: back erect, hand on hip, pelvis thrust forward, feet at right angles, cigarette poised mid-air, mistress of all she surveyed, talking to Anderson. She heard the lift doors opening and turned.

'Ah, the wanderer returns. How good of you to grace us with your presence and it only three o'clock in the afternoon, the day before the sale. You know, the rest of us mere mortals have been here since eight this morning—'

'Rose,' Anderson stepped towards me, 'can you not see the man's all in?'

Jimmy James looked up from his task, shook his head and continued labelling. The boys manhandled the desk from the lift. A chandelier trembled, casting tiny, rainbow sparkles. The world seemed to sway and me with it. Anderson placed a steadying hand on my arm. I caught a glimpse of Rose's frightened face and went through to the office, too tired to explain.

'Rilke, what's happened?' She followed me and started opening and closing the drawers of the desk. 'Where do you stash that bloody bottle of whisky?'

Anderson joined us. 'Spirits are the worst thing you could give him. A cup of strong tea with plenty of sugar's what he needs.'

Rose looked flustered. She opened the office door and shouted, 'Niggle, away and get Mr Rilke a cup of tea. Nice and strong, with plenty of sugar.'

Anderson looked at her. She shrugged, lit a second cigarette and passed it to me. I drew on it hungrily. The world pitched again, then straightened itself and I felt better.

'A dram would be welcome.'

'A cup of tea first and then we'll see.' Anderson's voice held a comforting authority. 'When was the last time you ate anything?' He didn't wait for a reply, but stepped beyond the office, caught Niggle on his way out, gave him instructions and a couple of notes.

He returned, lighting a cigarette of his own and inhaling deeply, 'So been overdoing it, have we?'

'The old lady's dead.'

Rose sank into the chair beside me. 'I think I could do with a whisky myself.'

Anderson retrieved the bottle from its hiding place among the envelopes. He poured Rose and me a small measure each and watched in silence while we drank. Niggle arrived with hot rolls and sweet tea. We ate, no one saying anything until we had finished. It was Rose who broke the silence.

'When?'

'This afternoon, before I came here.'

'Were you there?'

I nodded.

'Shit.'

She reached across the table and took my hand. I squeezed hers, then drew away.

'It's all right. She was gone before I arrived.'

'All the same.' She made a sympathetic face. 'Well, I guess eighty's a good age. If any of us make that we'll be doing well.'

I nodded. 'I suppose so.'

Anderson drank the last of his tea. 'Can I ask who you're talking about?'

Rose apologised, 'Jesus, Jim, I'm sorry,' and explained.

His face creased into an expression of concern. 'So presumably this is the end of the sale?'

Rose answered before I could speak. 'No, no I don't think so.' She gave me a stern look over the top of Anderson's head and continued. 'Miss McKindless was aware of her failing health and appointed a nephew to oversee the sale. As far as I understand it, he'll be her executor so, if he's agreeable, there's no reason why the sale can't proceed and the money be lodged as part of the estate.'

'That seems very efficient.'

'It's in the interest of the estate.'

Rose was thinking on her feet. I hoped she wasn't going to overdo it.

'After all, if they delay there'll be a bill from us plus storage charges and then they still have to dispose of the goods. No, I'm sure they'll want to go ahead.'

Anderson stood. 'Well, sounds like you've got a busy afternoon ahead. I'll leave you to it.'

Rose got up, ready to walk him to the door.

'James.' It was the first time I had used his Christian name in thirty years. The surprise registered on his face.

'You mentioned there was a story attached to McKindless. You found a file. Will you tell me about it, now that they're both dead?'

'I don't know. It's not really for public consumption, know what I mean?'

Rose leant into him, putting an arm round his waist. 'Ach, you're not on duty now. Rilke's hardly ''public consumption". Go on, put him out of his misery or there'll be no work from him today.'

He smiled at her. 'You're a hard taskmaster, Rose. If he was in my squad I'd be sending him home for a rest.'

She lowered her eyes. 'You like it. Anyway, you told me you were at a loose end. Why don't I send you in a couple of coffees? You can have a good chat while Rilke catches his breath. I've got plenty to be getting on with.'

'Aye.' Anderson looked serious again. 'You'll be wanting to phone the executor and find out if the sale is to go ahead.'

Rose's smile was tight. She gave me another warning look.

'You read my mind.'

Once Rose had gone Anderson settled back in his chair and shook his head.

'She'll get me into trouble one of these days if I'm not careful. Still, I suppose I'm partly to blame for your interest, asking you to keep your eyes open for anything suspicious. Just remember, what I'm about to tell you is in strictest confidence.'

'My lips are sealed.'

He gave me his policeman's stare to show he was serious.

'See that they are. Remember, it's not my case, but I had a quick shufti at the file when I heard you were clearing the house. Not pleasant reading. Basically, it's something and nothing. You could say I got a hunch when you showed me that Japanese toggle. Eighteen months ago a major investigation was launched into vice in Glasgow. Since the collapse of communism in Eastern Europe there's been a flourishing trade in the trafficking of young men and women for the purposes of prostitution. ''White slaving'' they called it when we were young. Not just in Glasgow but all over Britain. The powers that be decided they weren't going to put up with it in

Glasgow. An initiative was launched and essentially failed quite spectacularly. Some minor players were caught, a face-saving operation, but the big boys walked away with just a warm breath on their collar.'

'And you think McKindless was involved in that?' I felt suddenly ashamed for not coming forward.

'McKindless's name had been mentioned by a few people over the years. Enough for there to be official interest in his activities. Truth is, he's dead and you can't prosecute a dead man. Whether he was involved directly or not, it's hard to say. He had one conviction for importing pornography. He convinced the judge it was an aberration, paid his fine and on the face of it learnt his lesson, never saw the inside of a courtroom again. On the other hand, maybe he just learnt how to be careful. My contacts in Vice were happy to hear he was dead. One less to worry about. They seemed pretty certain he was a long-term player. A behind-the-scenes man. What's sure is he was a regular associate of several individuals who, detectives on the case seem sure, were deeply involved.'

'So what happened?'

'Ultimately, very little. A couple of arrests – small fry – a couple of people disappeared, left the country, and now your man's dead.'

'Why was it such a disaster?'

'Part of the problem is the international nature of such crimes. The criminal will cross any border in pursuit of their crimes, while police tend to be trapped within narrow jurisdictions.'

'But isn't there international co-operation, Interpol and the like?'

'True enough, in theory. In practice, it's no so easy. Before you can persuade a foreign police force to begin a major investigation, there's a burden of proof. Get over that hurdle and there are differences in laws and procedures. Surmount them and you find there's not enough manpower or money. Finally, most importantly, there's just not the will. Different if it was drugs. The war against drugs is highly funded, highly publicised. But rape, abduction, even possible murder of the poor and the dispossessed; young women promised good jobs abroad; children found on the street; runaways out to teach Mum and Dad a lesson; there never seems to be enough money to fight that.'

'Shit.' I put my head in my hands. 'I swear to you, Jim, I never found anything like that.'

'Hey, don't let it worry you. Neither did we. The reason I thought you might find something is these guys are different from your run-of-the-mill professional criminal. They're not just in it for the money. They're into the stuff. They make a commercial business out of a sexual obsession. You can put up sentences all you like, throw away the key, who'd object? But they keep on coming, like dragon's teeth. It's a horrible compulsion. Don't ask me why, some kind of moral bypass, I don't know. Anyway, I thought that if he was involved you might have found something, not necessarily the key to the operation, just some sign that he was a deviant bastard, but there we are, I was wrong. Dinnae worry yourself, though, we'll get them. The business is getting too big. We may only have put the wind up them this time, but next time we'll be putting them behind bars. For all I know, Vice is sniffing around them again. They got egg on their face last time, that'll make them more determined. It's a matter of when, not if.'

Now was the time to do it. To tell him about the

photographs, the library, McKindless's visit to Anne-Marie. The door opened and Rose came through.

'Right, you two, break time's over.'

'You were going to tell him something there, weren't you?'

'No.'

'You were, I interrupted you. I could see it in your face.'

'Rose,' I lied, 'I wasn't intending to say anything. What could I say? It's not like I've agreed to anything.'

It was ten in the evening. The sale was set up and we were alone in the building. For once there was no bottle of wine open on the table.

'Please, Rilke, please don't screw this up for me. I really like him, and at my age I don't suppose I've got too many chances left. If Jim finds out about this scam, that'll be the end. He doesn't even like me smoking joints. He's serious about law and stuff. It's strange but that's one of the things I like about him. He's honest. I can trust him.'

'Don't you want him to be able to trust you?'

She looked indignant. 'He can! About things that matter. Anyway, he'll never know.'

'Rose . . .'

'Oh come on, you know you want to.'

And I did. I was fed up with my life. Fed up of working and never having anything. Tired of searching my pockets for the price of my next pint. I'd sat next to Death that afternoon. Why not take a risk? The only people who might get hurt were us, and weren't we used to that? I wanted something good for a change. And if the money was going begging, well, why shouldn't we have it? From what Anderson had said, it was dirty money anyway, ill-gotten gains that could do us some good. I should have known better. Dirty money contaminates. It never goes begging and there's always someone else who can be hurt.

'How?'

She sat on the desk and shook my hand. 'Glad to have you on board, partner. From my vast reading of crime fiction and viewing of American movies I have decided that in crime' – I winced at the word and she patted my hand – 'in using one's initiative, simplest is best. Did anyone at the hospital know that you were from here?'

'No, they thought I was a relative.'

'Good. So unless we hear otherwise, and I doubt we will, the sale being tomorrow, we go ahead. Now, it'll be no secret that we held the sale. That doesn't matter. In my study of initiatives, it's the greedy who get caught. We're not going to pocket the lot. We'll just take a significant percentage.' She was enjoying herself now, getting into the swing of playing the glamorous girl gangster, a role she'd been preparing for all her life. 'What proportion of our sales would you say are in cash?'

'About sixty–forty, cash to cheques.'

It was true. Antiques is a cash business. Not just for reasons of tax avoidance, though it is a significant consideration. Antiques dealers have overdrafts which, grouped together, would surely rival Third World debt. Many dealers hide purchases from their bank manager with the anxiety of a teenage daughter wearing a forbidden dress beneath her school uniform. Some like to feel their money close to them. They hide their roll against their body. Carry it around like a security blanket, crooning to it, calling it pet names: lettuce, spondulicks, filthy lucre. Secure in an inside pocket or a shoe, incubating it in the hope it might breed.

'Okay, so all we have to do is reduce the hammer price of

lots that are paid for in cash by a consistent percentage, and pocket the difference. Twenty per cent, say. Mind, we also get twenty per cent of the commission from the seller and the purchaser, split it fifty–fifty and at a rough guestimate I would say we were in for a relative fortune. What do you say? Are you in?'

She spat on the palm of her hand and held it out to me. I did likewise and we clasped hands, sealing our bargain.

'Bugger that,' Rose laughed. 'Come on, give us a kiss!'

I woke in the middle of the night. There was someone in my room. I knew it as sure as I knew I was alive. I lay still, convinced that if I reached out to turn on the light, a clammy hand with a grip like iron would grab my wrist. Into the silence broke the sound of breathing. I cried out loud and lunged for the lamp. It toppled and as it fell light cast about the room, revealing no one. I lay back on the pillows, listening to the sound of my own staggered breath.

20

Sale of the Century

My pictures blacken in their frames
As night comes on
And youthful maids and wrinkled dames
Are now all one.

Walter Savage Landor,
'Death of the Day'

GOD KNOWS WHAT ROSE had promised in her publicity:
dancing girls, marijuana, a chance to buy your own piece of
the One True Cross. Whatever she'd done, it was working. It
was 11 a.m., the auction was heaving, and we were like to run
out of vin de pissypauvre before the sale began. It was a dank,
dark morning, in a month of dark days. Outside the sky was a
palette of grey, from the palest of charcoal to the leaden
gunmetal of the approaching storm. But inside the lamps were
lit, there was free drink, old adversaries and the best stuff we

had seen in an age. I moved through the multitude, like a smooth-tongued Judas, shaking hands, giving advice, smiling all the way back to my two gold incisors, unsure if what I had agreed to do was worth it for a bag of gelt, but Hell-bound anyway. There was a glass of warm white wine cradled in my hand and a bottle tucked behind the rostrum because, although it tasted like piss, and urine has never been my cup of tea, I knew from experience that it was alcoholic. The bottle may have (often) let me down, but I was willing to give our relationship another try.

I was used to being host of this strange party. Master of ceremonies for a legion of rapscallions and slubberdegullions. Antique dealers, collectors, drop-outs and delinquents, all ages, all persuasions, the high and mighty and the merely high. I wasn't nervous about conducting the sale. I was nervous about afterwards.

Rose shone from the thick of it, hair pulled back in a torture bun, so tight it raised her eyebrows in surprise. She held an arts and crafts vase up for inspection, describing it to a more-money-than-taste couple, in a professional manner lifted from *The Antiques Roadshow*. She felt my stare and turned, giving me a music-hall wink. I scowled back and continued my perambulations, looking over the heads of the crowd, no one matching my height but the Irish bhoys, already in position along the back in a fug of cigarette smoke.

Jimmy James stood hunched close to the Calor gas heater, mindless of the singe marks that already edged the hem of his dust coat, taking proxy bids, shaking hands, slipping tight folded bungs straight into his pocket with a magician's sleight of hand. No now-you-see-it-now-you-don't, just a whispered, 'Here's for your trouble, Jimmy' brief incline of the head, acknowledgement so slight you might miss it, into the pocket

and no guarantees. Later he would stand against me, bidding
mournfully, shaking his head at every response. Everyone was
there. Barras traders and Paddy's Market pedlars had left
long-faced relatives to freeze at the stall that Saturday.

> In galleries and book shops,
> Junk yards and antique marts,
> In strip and dip warehouses,
> Mother-in-laws 'cleared out all that rubbish',
> Assistants played ragga-ragga-hip-hop,
> Lovers peered tentatively round doors,
> Tea was made,
> Feet placed on desks,
> Cigarettes smoked,
> Kisses stolen,
> Customers ignored,
> Phones left unanswered,
> Because the boss was at a sale.

Textile dealers fumbled through boxes of napery, holding
whites and not-so-whites in the air, rubbing the stiffened
fabric of stains between their fingertips, sniffing with trained
nostrils to see if they could discern coffee, say, from something more sinister, a mark no stain devil could dislodge.

Skinny Liz, no glamour girl, no, not any more, though
once perhaps, who knows? Daughter of a rag-and-bone man,
one of the old school, brought up on the cart – though she'd
deny it; proprietrix of Forgotten Moments; not second-hand
or used, no; Vintage Costume and Evening Wear. Had slipped
down to her back-lane establishment; breathed in the early-
morning old-clothes smell; the Saturday-night sweat of
party dresses; unmentionable odour of inside legs;

long-unlaundered shirts; woollen bathing costumes (sink like a stone); down-at-heel dance shoes; and scuttled through her racks, until she found the right shade of black, pure bombazine. Skinny Liz, not skinny at all, who dreams of peach satin and bias cut, who sews slender young things into barely there gowns for 'the loveliest night of the year'. Poor Liz, only ever seen in her shop, down Paddy's, the Barras, auction sales and bar rooms. Who names her frocks after film stars: Greta, Bette, Audrey, Grace, Marilyn and Joan. Skinny Liz clicked open the enamelled clasp of a bugle-beaded evening bag and searched its pockets out of habit.

Frederic the carpet man was at floor level inspecting pile, checking for infestation.

'I spend more time on my knees than a hoor. It's no joke. There's an African moth can eat a whole house in a week. Tiny moth, big appetite. Teeth, too, perhaps. Never met one but seen its picture in a book, bloody terrifying. No joke, this game. Not a game at all when you think on it. As hard as pulling a sailor off your sister. Then there's weevils and fleas, beetles, roaches, lice, nits, ticks, mites, bugs and cockchafers – they're the worst. Beasties and creepy-crawlies of all sorts. Bloody entomology, carpet dealing. That's me, entomologist and rug specialist. No fun having some wife come back to the stall complaining her house is louping. Tell you, I find a flying carpet, I'll fly away.'

Over at the jewellery cabinet, Niggle – his mammy'd sent him out smart today – passed a string of pearls to Edinburgh Iain. Iain rubbed them against his front teeth, checking for the telltale graininess that only the real thing has.

'The texture of a woman's nipple, that's what you look for,' he whispered to Niggle. 'Soft, aye, but there's a roughness there that feels good to the tongue.'

The boy blushed. He's been weaned a while and had no contact since, but he's interested all the same.

Henry the coffin chaser was wearing a new-to-him black coat.

'Looking good, Henry.'

'It's a fine one, eh? Beautiful bit o' Aquascutum.' He drew it wide, showing me the inside pocket, the original owner's name and measurements sewn inside. 'I got it from an auld bid out Mount Florida way. Husband died, Lord rest him. Gave her a hand disposing of his bits and pieces. Fits like a glove. Aye, he had a smart suit, too, insisted on having him buried in it.' He shook his head at the waste.

Henry has a circuit of churches that keep him busy all day Sunday. He starts first light and is busy till evensong. An assiduous reader of local obituaries, Henry is as ecumenical as a banker. He ferries old ladies, of all denominations, from home to church, monitoring their health and their treasures.

A young tatterdemalion, whose father is a top advocate and regular tea-room trader, brushed against me. His curls in dark disarray, wearing a long patchwork coat sewn out of a hundred hamster skins. He smiled with rotten teeth and dropped something gently into my jacket pocket.

'Brighten up your weekend, man,' he whispered in an accent they never taught him at the Academy.

Two old duffers, collectors both, hail-fellow-well-met one another and the room relaxed, as rooms do when bores find each other.

'How're you doing? What's with the suit? They caught up with you at last?'

'The daughter's getting married this afternoon. Rose Bowery phoned me about a wee railway item I might be interested in so I've jumped ship. I'll no be staying long, mind. Her and her mother are up in the house the now, faces tripping them.'

'Well, you ken women when it comes to weddings. It's a big deal for them.'

Father of the bride raised his eyes to the ceiling in miserable agreement. 'It's not even as if I like the chap,' he muttered, helping himself to wine.

Young Drummond, not so young these last ten years, is under constant observation. A dozen dealers follow in his wake, touching what he has touched, searching for clues. Voices whisper, 'There goes young Drummond.' Young Drummond who 'has a good eye', who, 'knows his stuff' and is 'nobody's fool'. Young Drummond, ex-art-school boy, who still wears paint-stained jumpers, two brown, one green. Who has a shop called '21st Century Toy' selling: Spanish dolls, sunburst clocks, valve radios, flying ducks, shellac records, prints of green ladies and crying boys, kidney-shaped tables and balsawood chairs. Young Drummond, with an encyclopaedic knowledge of television from 1965 to 1979, the records of Dusty Springfield, Meccano, military badges, the Beatles, *Oor Wullie* and *The Broons*. Young Drummond, who wishes he was born in another age. Who wishes he didn't have to grow up and tries hard not to. Who glimpses Pablo Picasso in 1950s tableware and God in Bakelite. Young Drummond, famous in charity shops from here to Govan. Who sells irony to thirty-somethings. Young Drummond, who cannot make a bid without a dozen hands rising in imitation; the best form of flattery. Young Drummond, who stays in his shop until ten every night, then retires to his cluttered bedsit, climbs into his single bed alone and dreams he is a fisherman netting a mermaid from a sea of cod. Young Drummond searched boxes of sundries, eye lingering here and there, laying false trails for his admirers.

Rab the shagger leant towards his new paramour and, in a voice as intimate as a late night DJ's, expounded the design virtues of the 1930s cruet balanced in his hand. He tilted it this way and that, showing her the maker's mark, comparing it to a grand ocean liner; salt starboard, pepper port. He conjured the jazz age: flappers dancing on the wing of a plane, cocaine in silver boxes, cocktails at Maxim's, dinner at the Ritz, bright young things dizzy with the threat of war. An aroma of romance from the simplest of spices. The woman at his side swooned. Later she will buy the cruet as a love gift and Rab will convey it to the salerooms of London. Before or after he breaks her heart? It depends how broke he is. How far he has stretched the elastic of her affection. He introduced his companion and I smiled, shaking her hand, as if I had not lost count of his conquests, who are always left enlightened in the arts of love and lighter in the bank.

'Rab,' I whispered, 'is this the one?'

'Ach, you ken me, Rilke. I need two on the go because they always dump me.'

'Aye, Rab, because you always two-time them.'

Some, though, would pay double to have him back, just for one night.

'We fucked you right up the arse, bent your lot over and gave them a right good shafting.'

'Ach, you were jammy, luck, pure luck. What about last time? Who took it up the arse then, eh? Our boys rammed you, really rammed it right in. You were truly fucked, my man.'

I turned to see who the speakers were. Two Barras dealers,

Big Vince and Davie B, crouched half under the bric-a-brac table, sorting through the cartons of mixed lots stored beneath. Davie B noticed me and began to haul himself to his feet using the table for support. Ornaments and glassware trembled. I clenched my teeth as he navigated his beer belly free of collision.

'Mr Rilke, big sale the day.'

'Not bad.'

'Did you catch the match last night?'

The penny dropped. 'No, too busy getting this thegether.'

'You missed yourself. I was just saying to Vince here, we really shafted him.'

Vince broke in, 'Aye and I was telling him it's only a fortnight since Celtic fucked Rangers in the Old Firm game. First of the season and we fucking screwed you.'

Faint, in my head, a distant bell rang, but it was too faint, too far away. I shook their hands, wished them well and moved on, wondering if they greeted orgasm with a shout of 'Goal!'

Rose smiled from across the room, puckered her red lips, set her hand as a runway and blew me a kiss. She put her arm round a man's shoulders and nodded in my direction. The man's head turned and I saw Les.

I scanned the congregation from the rostrum, charting the crowd, identifying faces, mapping who stood where. There had been no time to discover the purpose of Les's visit. He and Rose had been laughing together like old friends, but when I crossed the room to greet him, his face had closed.

Jenson's ring hard-faced, the Irishmen.

Rose whispered in my ear, 'This is going to be the best ever. After last week Jenson is going to run the Irish

sky-high and it doesn't matter to us who gets the stuff
because they both pay in cash.'

I ignored her and continued my preparation. Les had said,
'We need to talk.'

But Rose had taken me by the arm. 'Sorry, Les, he's mine
for the next few hours. You can have him after the sale.' And
she hustled me towards the podium, calling over her shoulder
at him to 'Have some wine.'

He'd looked exasperated. 'Look, I'll meet you here after
you finish.' He headed towards the exit. 'Don't forget, and if
I'm late wait for me. It's important.'

I tried to remember if Les had ever told me anything was
important before. He had, but I didn't think he was coming
back to remind me always to cleanse, tone and moisturise. I
tried to focus on the sale. A list of four hundred lots, each
with brief description and estimate price, lay on the lectern
before me. Jimmy James stood in place, shaking his head at
life. I brought the hammer down, three sharp blows, hard
enough to kill a man.

'Welcome, ladies and gentlemen, to Bowery Auction for
today's sale of fine art and collectables. Viewing is now over. I
must remind those of you who have not already done so to
register for a paddle number. Lot number one is an ex-
ceptionally fine example of Scottish craftsmanship . . .'

Jimmy James grudgingly indicated the lot: 'This one
here.'

And we were under way.

There was a thought running through my mind, a thought I
couldn't get hold of, slipping in and out of my consciousness,
slithering between the bids.

One hundred,
An idea . . .
One hundred and twenty,
Rose nudged my arm, indicating a new bidder.
One forty,
One sixty,
TWO HUNDRED . . . *Something I had missed . . .*
The bidding faltered. I scanned the room . . .
That's two hundred pounds for this lovely . . . *It*
was bothering me . . . Something about . . . **Two hun-**
dred pounds, ladies and gents . . . Two hundred
pounds . . . *time . . .*

Rose nudged me again. 'Keep your mind on the bloody job.'
And the thought went.

21

The Reckoning

THE SALE WAS OVER. The last dealer had shuffled from the building, last carrier manhandled his load from the goods lift into the street. Rose and I were alone with hulks of furniture too awkward to move until later, and a lot of money.

In Gilmartin's the after-sale drinking would be starting, they'd be pushing the tables together, drawing up chairs, buying rounds, telling tall tales of treasures bought and sold. They'd be washing off the week in pints and nips, sluicing away their troubles. I wished I was with them.

Rose locked the door, turned down the lamps and we retired to the office, an oasis of light in the afternoon gloom. She looked at me.

'Are you sure about this? Still time to back out and no hard feelings.'

But she was wrong. The die had been cast and there was no going back.

'I'm sure.'

She eased the cash drawer free and tipped its contents onto the desk.

'Jesus,' she whispered, 'it's a lot.'

And so it was. The scuffed blues, browns, pinks and purples of bank notes splayed across the table. English and Irish mixing with Scottish in happy union. We sat for a minute, staring at it. Neither of us suggested a drink. Then we set to, counting in silence, folding fives into bundles of fifty, tens into hundreds, twenties into five hundreds and fifties into grands. Our hands grew black with the reckoning.

After a while Rose asked, 'What are you going to do with your share?'

'I don't know. Sit tight, I suppose.'

'Me too.'

She caught my eye and we smiled conspiratorially, each knowing the other for a liar. I wondered what glossy magazine dreams floated in her head. Clothes and holidays, delightful *objets*, perfumed, sunny days.

'You've not to become an alcoholic, mind.'

She laughed. 'Well, if I do I suppose I can afford the Priory now.'

We drifted back into silence. I knew what I was going to do with my share. I was going away. I'd had forty-three years of grey skies and dreich days. One risk begets another. I would go where the sky was blue and I was going to ask Derek to come with me. We had almost finished when there was a rattle at the door.

'Christ!' I toppled a pile of notes.

Rose looked at her watch. 'That must be Jim.'

'Jim? Rose, Jim's a policeman. What's he doing here while we're committing larceny and fraud?'

'I know, but he said he'd come and get me after the sale, I got all flustered and didn't know how to put him off. Anyway, he's early. I thought we'd be finished by the time he got here.'

'Well, get rid of him.' We were talking in hissed whispers. 'Tell him I'll walk you round to Gilmartin's after we've locked up.'

'He'll think it strange. He'll wonder why I'm not just letting him in.'

'Make an excuse.'

'Like what?'

'I don't know. Tell him your period's started.'

She gave me a look. I shrugged. My mobile started to ring and the door rattled again. Rose muttered, 'Oh for God's sake!' and hurried from the office into the darkened saleroom.

The display panel on my phone showed a number I didn't recognise. I laid my jacket carefully over the money, then, instead of pressing the Off button as I'd intended, answered the call.

'Rilke?' Derek's voice triggered the usual somersaults in my stomach. 'Is it all right to talk?'

'Sure.' I could be hanging from a cliff by my fingernails and I would still reach out to take a call from him. 'It'll have to be quick, though. I'm still at work. Everything okay? No visits from the police?'

'Nothing so far. Anne-Marie phoned. She said she'd been trying to get you all day.'

I could hear Rose stomping to the door.

'Aye, it's a sale day. We pull the plugs on all the phones while the auction's on. What did she want?'

'She asked me to give you a message. She said she's getting a visit from someone you'd like to meet.'

'Who?'

'She didn't say.'

Dread crept over me, an impossible foreboding. 'Repeat what she said, word for word.'

'She just said, ''Tell Rilke that guy we were talking about is coming round at four thirty this afternoon. It'll be a chance for them to meet.'' '

The thought that had slipped away from me during the sale came back. It was in the timing. Anne-Marie had told me McKindless visited her on the day of the Old Firm game. Rab said the first game of the season was a fortnight ago, a week after McKindless's death.

'He's not dead. Sweet Jesus,' I whispered, remembering Anne-Marie's ordeal, the temptation she had felt to give herself up to the knife, her wish for revenge I cursed her stupidity and mine. My watch showed four fifteen. Rose was pulling back the bolts, fumbling with her keys, cursing at the rattling door as she muddled key and lock, shouting, 'All right, keep your hair on!' Anderson was impatient.

'Rilke, are you still there?' asked Derek.

'Ring Chris and get over to Anne-Marie's as fast as you can. I'll call the police and meet you there.' My heart sounded loud in my ears, beating out the seconds, a clock close to midnight.

The boy's voice reflected my panic. 'What is it?'

There was a sound in the hallway, a wounded whimper. I whispered, 'Hold on.' Dropped the phone onto the chair and looked up. What happened next is frozen in my mind like a photograph. Rose came first, her lips arterial red against the sudden white of her face. Confusion rendered me stupid. My first thought was, Why is she walking like that? Rose's assured stalk was gone. She faltered into the room. There were two men with her. Men without faces. One of them was helping her. Holding her up. Holding her back. Holding her arm twisted behind her back. Their features were blacked off, concealed behind balaclavas. My muscles tensed, ready for attack, but the gun each man held in his hand stayed me. I raised my hands and came round from behind the desk, saying, 'Whatever you want, just let her go.'

'The money.' The intruder's voice sounded loud after our silence and whispers.

'It's yours. Just let her go, then you can have it.'

Spittle spluttered from his lips. 'We're not fucking around. Give us the fucking money.'

He put his gun to Rose's temple, drawing his other arm around her neck, lifting her from the ground. Her eyes rolled in her head, feet scrabbled like a hanging man's.

'Okay, anything you want, just don't hurt her.'

The second man patted me down, taking the bundle of keys from my pocket.

'Don't get excited, pal.'

He shoved a hold-all at me. I began to sweep cash into the bag. Rose was set on her feet again.

I glanced up at her. 'You okay?'

She nodded, trembling with the effort of keeping still.

The intruder ran the muzzle of his gun down the nape of her neck.

'Keep calm, do what you're told and your girlfriend'll be fine. We're just here for the money.'

His companion pointed his gun at me with a steady hand. I bundled notes into the bag, wondering if Derek was on his way to Anne-Marie's or if he was still on the line listening.

'You're getting the money, there's no need to frighten her more.' I raised my voice hoping it would carry across the air waves.

'Aye, but it's fun.' The man laughed, then leant over Rose,

keeping the gun at her brow. 'Don't worry, doll, I wouldn't hurt you. Not unless your old man does something stupid.'

The bag was full. I glanced quickly at the phone concealed on the chair beside me. The light had vanished from the display. The line was dead.

'Okay.' I slid the bag towards them, the gunman pushed Rose from him, then she and I were embracing.

'Right,' he said, 'that was easy, wasn't it? Now, where's your storeroom?'

The possession of the money seemed to make the men high. I'd held Rose's elbow tight, feeling that if anything went wrong it would happen now. They'd laughed at the mountains of junk piled in the storeroom, then padlocked us in.

The door to the saleroom slammed behind them and Rose said, 'I need the toilet.'

I was feeling around blindly in the junk, hoping I didn't start an avalanche, looking for something she could pee into, when we heard a commotion of male voices, slamming doors and crackling radios. Derek had come through. I handed Rose a brass planter, heard the rustle of her skirt, then, just before the hiss of her stream, 'For God's sake don't shout for help until I'm finished.'

22

The Final Cut

Shot? So quick, so clean an ending?
Oh that was right, lad, that was brave:
Yours was not an ill for mending,
'Twas best to take it to the grave.

A. E. Housman,
'A Shropshire Lad'

SURROUNDED BY ALL THE vice of the city, cruelties under my nose, and all I had thought about was the past. History tells us why things are the way they are. It shows the constancy of human nature. Unfortunately, it doesn't tell us what to do about it. I'd been a fool. I looked at my watch. The hand was leaving the half-hour. Time travelled on, putting us all in the past, but I still couldn't reach back and put things right.

Anderson pushed through the policemen and took Rose in his arms. He looked at me. 'Why do I feel you're to blame for this?'

Rose put a trembling hand into his jacket, removed his cigarettes and helped herself to one. Anderson lit it for her and she took a compulsive draw.

'Leave him alone,' she said. 'It's my fault. Rilke would never have thought of taking the money if it wasn't for me.'

Anderson gave her a bemused stare.

'I think they were working for McKindless.' I pushed past Anderson and Rose, heading for the door. 'Somehow he's not dead. He put his money into antiques, easy to sell if he needed a fast getaway. The sale money was to go into his sister's account, but she died, so he resorted to desperate measures. I think I know where McKindless is.'

'You'll stay put, Rilke. This is a crime scene and if you leave—'

The door slammed behind me, cutting off his words. I took the stairs two at a time, conscious of the echo of other feet following me. I met Leslie on the stairwell. He saw me running, heard the sound of my pursuer, turned and ran without stopping to ask why. I ground the van into gear, kicked open the passenger door. Les launched himself in as I pulled out into the road.

'Suffering Christ!' He lurched against the window. 'Are you going to tell me what's going on?'

I sped towards Garnethill, using every shortcut and cut-through I knew, jarring the van along potholed back lanes, jumping the lights at junctions, cutting in and out of traffic, ignoring the irate horns of the other drivers. As I drove I told Les the story of the last week.

He groaned. 'I told you to leave they guys alone. Jesus, they are big fucking gangsters. I should know better than to involve myself in your business. I'd heard Trapp was skedaddling and I was coming warn you to keep your nose out. Try and do you a favour and end up in the thick of it. I'm no exactly happy at being involved in all of this. In fact, when we get to this lassie's house, whoever she is, you can drop me off. I suggest you go back, face the music with James Anderson, and then you and Rose develop a dose of amnesia.'

'I thought you were a hard man.'

'Aye, well, you thought wrong.'

'Fine, do what you want.'

'Sweet Jesus!' Les swore again as I sped through a gap in the traffic, outfacing a double-decker bus. 'At least try and get us there in one piece.' He leant forward and started to fiddle with the radio. 'Let's see if we can get the police channel on this. For all we know, they've already got there and she's right as rain.'

He eased the dial along the frequencies and the cab was filled with the hiss and shriek of white noise, the beeps and booms of secret signals, punctuated by shreds of voices, scraps of music. Then into the dissonance broke a regular pulse. A rhythm that percolated everything around it. A beat that jarred the soles of your feet and spread through your body like cancer.

The big drum looked a part of the man's body. A second belly, raised high, like a proud pregnancy reaching the end of its term. The man slammed the stretched skin, hammering home blow after blow, swinging the sticks into the air, then returning to pound out a slow beat, a warning, notification of hate. Behind him, swaggering in time, followed the dignitaries of the lodge: small men all; bowler hats straight; fringed, orange and gold tabards draped over their black suits. A rank of uniformed snare drummers followed, beating out a faster rhythm. *Gonnae git ya, gonnae git ya, gonnae git ya.* Beyond the drums the piping fifes brought in the melody.

> *It's old but it is beautiful*
> *Its colours they are fine,*
> *It was worn at Derry, Aughrim,*
> *Enniskillen and the Boyne,*
> *My father wore it as a youth*
> *In the bygone days of yore*
> *And it's on the twelfth I love to wear*
> *The Sash My Father Wore.*

And beyond the flutes, the women, sanctioned followers of the camp, strutting proudly in their Mother-of-the-Bride suits and fancy hats. A police cordon edged the parade, strolling in time with the beat, full part of the ritual.

The Orange Walk is part of West Coast of Scotland folklore. Every spring in tiny towns on the edge of nothing, where the steel mill has closed and the mines have shut down, in large cities where factories lie derelict and shipyards despair of orders, men dress themselves in the raiment of the Orange Lodge and march in the name of King Billy. The parade and the mob are an accumulation of the mad, bad, poor and dispossessed. Tales of beatings by the walk are legendary. The worst trespass against them is to show disrespect by cutting their path. To 'cross the walk' is a very bad idea.

I abandoned the van in the middle of the road, flung myself through the crowd and into the march. A bandsman's baton dealt a blow to my shoulders that almost felled me, but I managed to stay upright, pinballing through the marchers and out into the crowd on the other side. A constable shouted at me to 'Stop!' I ignored him and began to run the steep gradient towards Buccleuch Street.

There was someone peching behind me, a chorus to my own laboured breath, but whether it was Leslie or the policeman I wasn't sure. A group of small children followed my progress with complacent eyes as I skirted half-dressed dolls, a pram, a tricycle, a bike. Three old ladies on the steps of the Italian chapel shook their heads and muttered to each other. An elderly Chinese man leant against the posters advertising Bollywood videos that plastered the window of his shop. He drew on a roll-up and trailed me with indifference. The queue outside the art cinema trained their eyes as one, already an audience. I was almost there. I turned the corner and halted.

Two police cars were skewed across the road. For an instant the dark street blended to crimson as if I were looking through a tinted lens. Flashing lights whirled: Blood, no blood, blood, no blood, blood, no blood . . .

The slam of the close door echoed behind me. Hollow snatches of whispers drifted down the stairwell . . . *Scream . . . Screaming . . . You hear it? . . . A scream . . . Fair chilled me, so it did . . . Murder . . . Someone said a murder . . . a scream . . . chilled my bones . . . shivered ma timbers . . . a dozen polis . . . shower of bastards . . . heard the sirens . . . heard the scream . . . He said I'll go and help, the lassie needs help and I said no you'll no, you're staying here . . . A boyfriend . . . A sex fiend . . . One o' the family . . . Foul play, right enough . . . Never heard a scream like it . . . no since the war . . . no since Faither left . . . no since Saturday night . . . frightened the cat . . . soured the milk . . . turned the soup . . . turned ma stomach . . .* I started to run the long spiral of the staircase, knowing the race was lost, but unable to stop. . . . *look at him . . . skinny cunt . . . in a hurry . . . in a rush . . . her husband . . . too old . . . her lover . . . too ugly . . . the doctor . . . too scruffy . . . a polis . . . too dodgy . . . no dodgy enough . . .* I could see myself, insignificant, a beetle crawling the curves of a conch . . . *stabbed . . . raped . . . chibbed . . . molested . . . murdered . . . kilt . . . Godsaveus . . . Godhelpus . . . God help her . . . Help and Keep Her . . .* Barking dogs flung themselves against doors as I passed. I felt outside myself. A puppet press-ganged into someone else's hallucination. The door to Anne-Marie's flat was ajar. I pushed it wide and went through.

The body looked small in death. Head thrown back, pale face raised to the sky, lips frozen in a last ghastly grin, as if caught in a final yearning for life. A red sea glazed the rough pile of the carpet, spreading into a river, a slick scarlet trail that edged into brown, where a desperate, failing effort had been made to crawl towards the door. The bloodied hands clutched at the stomach, caught in the process of trying to force something back in. There was a glimpse of entrail, a smell of corruption and decay.

'Who'd have thought the old man would have so much blood in him,' I whispered.

Anne-Marie, a blanket draped round her shoulders, tracksuit steeped in bloody splashes, heard my voice, broke away from the policewoman she was talking to and trembled towards me.

'Is it a sin to kill a dead man?' she whispered.

I held her close. We watched together as a police photographer bent his knee, focused his lens, and placed the body in the centre of the frame. There was a bright flash and Mr McKindless, the man I knew as Grieve, was captured for ever.

23

Transcript

THE POLICEMAN WHO INTERVIEWED me was younger than Anderson. He wore a well-cut suit and a superior manner which would normally have made me obstructive. I told him everything, from the discovery of the photographs to the hold-up in the auction house. Of course, when I say everything, I don't mean the entire narrative. I stressed Trapp's involvement, excluded Les, John's under-the-counter trade, Derek's dubious entrée into film making and the auction sting. But I laid myself wide open, unfolded myself on the cross and prepared to play the martyr. When he told me I was free to go I almost protested. I stayed in my seat ready to ask him, 'Don't you understand all of this is my fault?'

'Inspector Anderson would like a word before you leave' was all the young detective said as he showed me the door.

*　　*　　*

'Have a seat.' It was the same office where we had examined the netsuke while I dripped on the carpet. 'Well, you were in the thick of it this time.'

'Yes.'

Anderson looked shattered. I guessed I looked no better.

'Did it never occur to you to have a word with me?'

'It occurred.'

'It might have saved us both a lot of bother.'

'I realise that.'

'You've succeeded in putting me in the bad books. I told my contact in Vice that McKindless was dead, he took me at my word and somehow it's my fault he didn't check the facts.'

'Sorry.'

'And then there's this.' He handed me the calculations Rose had done for our sting. Master criminal that she was, she'd committed our crime to paper. 'When Rose mentioned taking the money I thought I'd better have a root around the desk and see if there was any evidence. I'd destroy that if I were you.'

'A moment of madness. It was my idea.'

He gave me a sceptical look. 'I thought it might be. Give you a hard time through there, did they?'

'I survived.'

'Aye. I didn't see any mention of your old chum Les in your statement.'

'It wasn't anything to do with Les.'

'No? I thought he'd appear somewhere, though. Makes me wonder what else you've left out. Here.' He slid a slim file across the table towards me. 'Vice have been closing in on Trapp for a while. Your statement enabled them to get a warrant to swoop on his saunas.'

As I read, it was as if the girl in the photograph had suddenly rolled over, loosed herself of her bonds, and was addressing me.

TRANSCRIPT OF EVIDENCE
GIVEN BY ADIA KOVALYOVA

DATE: 30TH APRIL 2001 – TRANS. OLYA MCKENZIE

When you have no money you'll do anything. Respectable people don't understand that, will never understand it – why should they? They think that only bad people do these things – that isn't true – it's the friendless and desperate. You make a slip and then another slip and suddenly you find that you are on your own when all you ever wanted was a decent life.

I come from the Ukraine. In my country it is very difficult to earn a living. I trained as a teacher, but still I found it impossible to get a job which would support me and my three-year-old daughter. One day I saw an advert in the paper seeking English speakers to work abroad. This is everyone's dream. A job abroad where it will be possible to earn enough to send money home. I telephoned the number on the advert and spoke to a man. He asked me some questions, my age, family situation, education, and then arranged an appointment for the next day.

At the interview everything went well. The man was smartly dressed, professional. He seemed friendly. As well as inquiring about my experience of work, he asked about my family. I had no reason to think anything was wrong. I told him everything.

Straight away he said I had got the job. I was to be a secretary working for a Ukrainian company in Britain and should prepare myself to travel that very week. I was amazed by the speed of everything, but of course this is what I had prayed for. So I packed my clothes, gave up the lease on my apartment, arranged for my daughter to stay with my parents and kissed them all goodbye. Lots of tears but happiness too. I had lived for so long without hope, thinking only of today, never of tomorrow, now I could plan a future. Leaving home was a sacrifice, but one I made willingly for the sake of my family.

I didn't know. Life in the Ukraine was hard, but if I had any idea I would have run for home as fast as I could.

In Britain I was met by another man. A white-haired man in an expensive suit. Once more he was friendly. He asked about my flight, carried my bags to a car. I was tired, I missed my daughter already, but still I was excited, happy to be there. He said he was taking me to my new flat, not very smart but clean.

At the flat everything was all right for a while. He offered me some wine. I declined, but he seemed disappointed and I thought, Adia, this is one of your new bosses, don't begin by being antisocial. So then I accepted. I asked him about the job and he said that his associates would arrive in a short while. They would tell me all about it. Soon after there was a knock at the door, he excused himself and let them in.

As soon as the two men walked into the room the atmosphere changed and I knew I had made a terrible mistake. Everything about the white-haired man altered, even his appearance became, I don't know, coarser. One of the two men said I belonged to them now, they had spent thousands of dollars buying me and I was to earn it back by sleeping with men, being a prostitute. I objected. I said that this was not what I had been engaged to do. I was educated. I had signed no contract. When I saw that this was doing no good, I tried to leave. The white-haired man blocked my way, I panicked and started to scream, hoping someone would hear. The two men restrained me. They beat me badly. When they were finished and I was subdued and bleeding, the white-haired man . . . he committed a sex act on me, I don't want to say what it was. They let me know that I was in for a difficult night. And then . . . the other two men . . . they raped me.

After that it was difficult to fight back. They said that they knew everything about my family. It was true, I had told them myself. They said that if I did anything they would take it out on my parents and my little girl. I believed them. I was taken to a massage parlour on a busy street. I worked there with six other girls. Their stories were the same as mine. We were slaves. Every day from eleven in the morning until twelve at night we were on call. Sometimes the men would hurt us bad. We were not allowed out, but I would peer through the frosted windows and see people walking by, normal people. Then I began to think, in a world where such evil exists, are there normal people? Who were the men that used us? Did they go home and kiss their wives, cuddle their daughters, with the smell of our abuse still on their fingers?

Every day another piece of me died. I thought about suicide many times, but then I would think about my family and worry that they would be punished.

When the police rescued us I was frightened. I thought perhaps they were more bad men. When I realised that they were there to set us free . . . I was relieved but I couldn't feel true happiness, feelings like that are lost to me now. The last bit of me died before they arrived. Now I only want to go home.

I put my head in my hands. 'The bastards.'

'Trapp was a kingpin in the trafficking of young men and women into the city for the purposes of prostitution. There'll be an investigation, but Trapp's gone and McKindless really is dead this time. We're going through the files, examining unsolved attacks and murders to see if any of them might have been down to McKindless. I doubt we'll ever know the full extent of their involvement. In a way the pressure's off, they're out of our jurisdiction.'

'But it's not over, is it?'

'We'll circulate what we have to other forces in Europe, but Trapp will probably start somewhere else.'

'And meanwhile there'll be someone who takes note of Trapp's absence, and slips from the gutter into his shoes, ready to start all over again.'

Epilogue

Soleil et Désolé

Let love clasp Grief lest both be drowned,
Let darkness keep her raven gloss,
Ah sweeter to be drunk with loss,
To dance with Death, to beat the ground.

Alfred, Lord Tennyson,
'In Memoriam A. H. H.'

ROSE AND I WERE walking along the rue des Martyrs towards Montmartre. Rose was fashion-model chic in a black trouser suit teamed with white silk shirt and a jaunty hat that set off her new short, bobbed hair. I was a funeral scarecrow in my long black raincoat and black suit.

Rose looked up at me. 'Bloody typical.'

'What?'

'Paris in the springtime and I'm here with you.'

'I could say the same thing.'

I smiled to show I was joking. The truth was too close for both of us.

A week ago I had walked through Kelvingrove Park towards the five-pointed spire of the university. At last the bad weather had broken. The air was crisp and fresh, the sky a cloudless Tyrolean blue. Daffodils hosted together in golden clusters and pink blossom drifted on the air. The kind of day that invokes a quickening of the heart, intimations of summer, nostalgia for springtimes past.

Over on the green students mugged a game of football. Two girls in shorts and safety helmets glided past on roller-blades. Somewhere a band was practising, the drummer a beat behind the rest. A police car cruised by, windows down, the driver's arm, sleeve rolled up, lazily half out of the open window. Three kids, hunched together on a bench, concealing a half-rolled joint. A brightly painted ice-cream van parked opposite the pond. A jakey took a swig from his can and raised his face to the sun. Toddlers clambered around the play park. An old man fed a bustling clutter of pigeons. Squirrels bolted, quick-fire, up a tree. Even the graffiti on the fountain contrived to look cheerful. Only a discarded condom by the swings reminded me that this was the scene of my near-arrest. I headed over the bridge and away towards the dark, gothic turrets. I liked it best when I was the only one wearing sunglasses.

Professor Sweetman had greeted me effusively.

'Mr Rilke, how nice to meet you at last. Before we start, what about a refreshment?' He ignored a selection of herbal infusions filed next to the kettle, saying, 'You look like a man who appreciates the hard stuff. Earl Grey?'

The professor was almost as tall as me, out of proportion with the medieval dimensions of his office. As he lifted a pile of essays from a chair, I reflected that the world I inhabited was a jumbled place with never enough space even to sit without displacing something. He passed me my tea. I looked for somewhere to put it, but the desk between us was hidden beneath a confusion of books and papers.

'So, Rose said you were interested in Soleil et Désolé?'

'I'd appreciate anything you could tell me.'

He passed me a book, open at a marked page. 'I looked this out when I knew you were coming.'

A black-and-white photograph of an undistinguished, bourgeois, four-storey house, anonymous in a row of similar houses.

'It was a place?'

'Most definitely, yes. Not very exciting to look at, is it? Now turn the page.'

The next page revealed a faded monochrome picture of an elaborate Moorish chamber, glittering with mirrors and exotically tiled mosaics.

'Beautiful.'

Professor Sweetman beamed through his beard. 'Isn't it! From the outside you would never know. Except people did, of course. In its heyday Soleil et Désolé's interior was so celebrated that society ladies would make discreet tours of it during the day.'

'What was it?'

He struck his hand against his forehead in exaggerated exasperation. 'Sorry. I get carried away. Typical academic. I work largely in isolation, so when I find someone interested in my field I get overexcited.'

I shook his apology away and he resumed his account.

'Soleil et Désolé was a house of ill repute. A brothel of the kind that could only have existed in Paris. Paris, as you'll know, is popularly called the "city of love". It was also traditionally associated with sexual excess and with good cause. In the nineteenth and well into the twentieth century, many a gentleman guarded his respectability by confining his adventures to Paris. By the end of the century the tradition was still strong, though ironically under attack from a loosening of sexual morality. Who wants to pay when you can get it for free? There was even some acknowledgement of this from the authorities in the form of licensed, short-term rooms. The kind of thing you read about in 1950s hard-boiled American fiction. *Maisons de rendezvous* where you could rent a room for an hour or so. The result was the same as in any evolving economy – the very best and the very cheapest survived.

'Soleil et Désolé was one of the very best. Part of a flowering of specialist brothels, *maisons de grande tolérance* where "particular" tastes could be catered for. It was established in 1893 and didn't close until 1952. In its heyday Soleil et Désolé could reputedly provide you with anything you wanted. There are anecdotes about clients on their way to an assignation being passed in the corridor by a nun, or a bride hurrying to her next rendezvous. It was lavishly decorated with murals by Toulouse-Lautrec. One of the beds was said to have belonged to Marie-Antoinette, though its provenance was dubious. As well as the Moorish room in that photograph, which incidentally you may have noticed was decked out like a mosque, there were rooms representing other nations, a Russian room, a Spanish room, a Chinese room, a Scottish room – not the most popular, I would imagine, an Indian room, a Persian room, and so on. It also contained, among other things, a "funerary chamber" where an obliging young lady, fresh from an icy bath, would lie very still for those with fantasies of necrophilia, an oriental boudoir and, of course, a torture chamber. This is what Léo Taxil had to say about the "funerary chamber".' He lifted another book from the mess on his desk, opened it at a section marked with a ripped subway ticket, and started to read. ' "The walls were lined with black satin and strewn with tears of silver. In the centre a very luxurious catafalque with a lady lying inert in an open coffin, her head resting on a velvet cushion. Around her, long candles in silver holders, incense-burners and livid-hued illuminations. The lustful madman who has paid ten *louis* for this seance is then introduced. He will find a *prie-dieu* on which to kneel. A harmonium, placed in the neighbouring closet, will play the *Dies irae* or the *De profundis*. Then, to the strains of this funeral music, the vampire will precipitate himself upon the girl simulating the deceased." Taxil, in common with a lot of moralists, goes into lurid detail.'

I smiled politely. I liked Sweetman. Not so long ago his account would have made me laugh. It wasn't his fault that now it made me feel wretched.

'I'm interested in the period after the war. Probably in the activities in the torture chamber.'

'Yes,' he sighed. 'Rose said as much. How is she, by the way?'

'Fine. You know Rose, she bounces back.'

'Good, glad to hear it. In the period after the war the specialisation of Soleil et Désolé began to become more . . .' he hesitated, 'specific. It takes a war to release certain emotions, don't you think? Certain impulses to cruelty, kindness, too, perhaps, but anger, rage, injustice, they're all grist to sadism. Displacement, bereavement, survivor guilt contribute towards providing the victims. And underneath it all a knowledge of death that makes life more precious to some and more disposable to others. Soleil et Désolé: a rough translation would be ''Sunshine and Tears''. Sunshine, good times, music, girls, drink and tears . . . well, Soleil et Désolé is referred to in several memoirs. Mainly from the fin de siècle, when a trip to the brothel would have been as common as a walk in the park to some gents.'

I searched his face for hidden meaning. He carried on, seemingly unaware.

'Of course, memoirs tend to be fragmentary and unreliable. There's a tendency to self-aggrandisement and sexual boasting which can make it difficult to distinguish truth from fiction. Bearing all this in mind, accounts seem to suggest that after the Second World War Soleil et Désolé catered increasingly for a clientele interested in sadism. Indeed, one contemporary chronicler described it as having ''the prettiest torture chamber in Paris'', though what exactly he meant by ''pretty'' is unrecorded.'

Outside, through the open lattice window, the university clock struck the hour. Somewhere, a million miles away, a blackbird was singing.

'Rose explained to you about the photograph?'

'Yes. After we talked on the telephone I did a search of anything relating to Soleil et Désolé in the post-war period. There was nothing about torture unto death. It was a real place. It existed at the time your photograph was taken and was associated with sexual cruelty at a time when all over Europe people were disappearing. It isn't beyond possibility that your young woman was one of those who disappeared.'

'But we will never be sure.'

'Are the police any help?'

'No, they're having difficulty tracing people trafficked by McKindless and the pornographer in the last couple of years. I gave them the original photographs and the trophies. Officially the file stays open, but unofficially, no, there's no chance.'

'Then you're right. You will never be sure. Perhaps that's best. If you're not sure, then there is a chance.'

And there, in his last statement, he revealed what he believed.

Professor Sweetman was due at a meeting on the other side of campus. We walked together through darkened corridors, the sound of our boots resonating in the Easter holiday stillness, then out into the sunshine of Professor Square, where tubs of hyacinths scented the air. As we passed the chapel a wedding party emerged. The groom a dashing young Lochinvar. The bride a sacrifice in white. Confetti caught on the breeze and drifted across the lawn, landing on our shoulders, catching in Professor Sweetman's dark hair. We had walked on, through cloisters where students stood in anxious huddles around lists of freshly posted exam grades.

He gestured towards them. 'A new generation.'

'Yes, life goes on.'

We entered the West Quadrangle and paused, our long shadows facing each other at the parting of the ways. I prepared to shake his hand.

'I wonder' – he gave an unprofessorial blush – 'if you would like to meet up for a drink one evening.'

I'd looked at his shy, clever face and not had the heart to turn him down outright.

'Perhaps when I get back from Paris.'

*   *   *

It was as if Rose was tuning into my thoughts.

'Why don't you give Raymond Sweetman a phone when we get back?'

'I might.'

'You should. He's a nice man.'

I harumphed.

'What's wrong? Too nice for you? You might have to make a go of it?'

I didn't reply. We walked in silence for a while, past pavement cafés where cheerful continentals sipped civilised cappuccinos. Rose halted in front of a row of pavement artists' tourist traps. She gestured towards a Degas ballerina.

'That's rather good.'

'Too saccharine. Seven out of ten.'

'Ach, you're a miserable old sod. How are Derek and Anne-Marie getting on?'

'Love's young dream.'

My true feelings must have shown on my face because Rose laughed and said, 'Oh, come on! He was far too young for you. At least with Raymond you'd have things to talk about.'

'I could talk to Derek.'

My gaze shifted to another painting. *Marat's Last Breath*. The revolutionary, head thrown back, flesh blanched against the oxblood backdrop, wrist trailing, dead in his bath, stabbed in the head and chest, draped in the wet towels David had used to slow the decay of the corpse-model. We walked on, away from the main drag, down cobbled streets where the cafés were shabbier, more appealing.

'Sorry about you and James.'

'So am I. I guess it was doomed from the beginning. Can you really see me living with the law?'

'Perhaps.'

'Well there's no chance now. Jim left our attempt at big crime out of his report but that was the end of it. I can't believe I let slip we were going to cream off the money. Christ, we'd barely started seeing each other and I compromised him. I've a flawed personality.'

'That makes two of us.'

'We'll come to a bad end.'

'Let's hope we enjoy it.'

I realised we had reached our destination and stopped laughing.

From the outside the house had changed little except for the neon CAFÉ-BAR sign above the door. The waiter moved briskly across the floor, skirting a table of expectant diners, to attend Rose. She gave him her movie-star smile and ordered two glasses of red wine.

'What do you think?'

She gestured to the room. It was the opposite of what I had expected, blond wood and clean, modern lines, not a sign of crimson velvet drapes or languorous courtesans.

'I don't know. I don't feel any mystical tingling down the spine if that's what you mean.'

'What are you going to do?'

'Wait here. I'll be back.'

The basement was graveyard damp, a storeroom for beer barrels and racks of wine. I took the photocopied images from my pocket and walked towards the bare brick wall, my heart pounding in my ears.

I tried to think of an excuse, a reason I could give for my presence if detected. I could think of nothing but the truth. I was hoping for a miracle. That if torture and murder had taken place here there would be a memory of it. A scream trapped in the atmosphere. An echo of the past, locked in the walls, like a medieval cathedral prayer.

I could tell nothing. The photograph revealed too little. This might be the place but I felt no truth. No new connection. I sat on a barrel, bowed my head and let the tears come.

'I cared,' I whispered. 'I cared enough to try. I'm sorry I never knew your name.'

And I found I wasn't crying for the girl in the photograph. I was crying for other victims, present and future. I looked once more at the images, then took out my lighter, touched flame to paper, dropped it on the earth floor, watched it curl into ash, then stamped on the embers. I sat for a moment longer, wishing there was someone to pray to, then wiped my face and went back to the bar.

The waiter was talking to Rose, asking if she would like to try the *spécialité de la maison*. I noticed she had got a little of her colour back. Rose inclined her head saucily, telling him she would think about it. She had finished her wine. Mine sat before her, half a glass lower then when I had left. She looked up as I crossed the floor and the waiter stepped smartly away.

'You okay?'

'Yes, I feel better.'

'You look worse.'

I smiled. Deep down I love Rose.

'Despite all appearances to the contrary, I'm in the pink.'

We left the bar and walked slowly along the cobbled streets with the aimlessness of tourists. It started to rain.

'I don't know,' said Rose, putting out her hand palm up,

catching the raindrops. 'All this way from Glasgow and it rains.'

But it was a different kind of rain. Warmer, softer, with a promise of watered plants and freshly washed pavements.

Rose put an arm round me and gave me a hug.

'Come on, then,' she said. 'We're in Paris. Let's find somewhere swish and have a good drink.'

FOR A TASTER OF LOUISE WELSH'S LATEST
THRILLER, READ ON . . .

Naming the Bones

Part One

Edinburgh & Glasgow

Chapter One

MURRAY WATSON SLIT the seal on the cardboard box in front of him and started to sort through the remnants of a life. He lifted a handful of papers and carefully splayed them across the desk. Pages of foolscap, blue-tinted writing paper, leaves torn from school jotters, stationery printed with the address of a London hotel. Some of it was covered in close-packed handwriting, like a convict's letters home. Others were bare save for a few words or phrases.

James Laing stepped out into an ordinary day.

Nothing could have prepared James for the . . .

James Laing was an ordinary man who inhabited a . . .

The creature stared down on James with its one ghastly fish eye. It winked.

Murray laughed, a sudden bark in the empty room. Christ, it had better get more interesting than this or he was in trouble. He reached into the pile and slid out a page at random. It was a picture, a naïve drawing done in green felt-tip of a woman with a triangular dress for a body. Her stick arms were long and snaking. They waved up into a sky strewn with sharp-angled stars; the left corner presided over by a pipe-smoking crescent moon, the right by a broadly smiling sun. No signature. It was crap, the kind of doodle that deserved to be crumpled into a ball and fired into the bin. But if it had been deliberately kept, it was a moment, a clue to a life.

He reached back into the box and pulled out another bundle of papers, looking for notebooks, something substantial, not wanting to save the best till last, though he had time to be patient.

Pages of figures and subtractions, money owed, rent due, monies promised. A trio of Tarot cards; the Fool poised jauntily on the edge of a precipice, Death triumphant on horseback, skull face grinning behind his visor, the Moon a pale beauty dressed in white leading a two-headed hound on a silver leash. A napkin from a café, printed pink on white *Aida's,* a faint stain slopped across its edge – frothy coffee served in a glass cup. A newspaper cutting of a smiling yet serious man running a comb through his side parting; the same man, billiard-ball smooth and miserable on his hirsute double's left side. *Are you worried about hair loss?* The solution to baldness carelessly cut through and on the other side a listing for a happening in the Grassmarket. No photograph, just the names, date and time. *Archie Lunan, Bobby Robb and Christie Graves, 7.30pm on Sunday 25th September at The Last Drop.*

Then Murray struck gold, an old red corduroy address book held together by a withered elastic band and cramped with script. A diary would have been better, but Archie wasn't the diary-keeping kind. Murray opened the book and flicked through its pages. Initials, nicknames, first names or surnames, no one was awarded both.

Danny
Denny
Bobby Boy
Ruby!
I thought I saw you walking by the shore

Lists of names with the odd phrase scribbled underneath. There was no attempt at alphabetisation. He was getting glimpses already, a shambles of a life, but it had produced more than most of the men that went sober to their desks at nine every morning.

Ramie
Moon
Jessa* * *
Diana the huntress, Persephone hidden, names can bless or curse unbidden.

Murray would have liked photographs. He'd seen some already, of course. The orange-tinted close-up of Archie that showed him thin and bestraggled, something like an unhinged Jesus, his hands knuckled threateningly around his features, as if preparing to tear the face from his head. It was all art and shadows. The other snaps came from a *Glasgow Herald* feature on Professor James's group that

Murray had managed to pull from the newspaper's archive. Archie always in the background caught in a laugh, squinting against the sky; Archie cupping a cigarette to his mouth, the wind blowing his fringe across his eyes. It would be good to have one of him as a boy, when his features were still fine.

Murray pulled himself up. He was in danger of falling into an amateur's trap, looking for what he wished for rather than what was there. He hadn't slept much the night before. His mind had got into one of those loops that occasionally infected him, information bouncing around in his brain, like the crazy lines on his computer screen-saver. He'd made a cup of tea in the early hours of the morning and drunk it at the fold-down shelf that served as a table in the galley kitchen of his small flat, trying to empty his brain and think of nothing but the plain white cup cradled in his hand.

He would divide the contents of the box into three piles – interesting, possible and dross – cataloguing as he went. Once he'd done that he could get caught up in details, pick at the minutiae that might unravel the tangled knot of Archie's life.

Murray had handled originals many times. Valuable documents that you had to sign for then glove up to protect them from the oils and acids that lived in the whorls of your fingertips, but he'd never been the first on the scene before, the explorer cracking open the wall to the tomb. He lifted an unsent letter from the box, black ballpoint on white paper.

Bobby
For God's sake, find me some of the old!

We'll wait for you at Achnacroish pier on Saturday.
Yours, closer than an eye,
Archie

No date, no location, but gold. Murray put it in the important pile, then took out his laptop, fired it up and started
listing exactly what he had. He picked up a discarded bus
ticket to Oban, for some reason remembering a hymn they'd
sung at Sunday school.

God sees the little sparrow fall,
it meets His tender view;

Even this simple ticket might have the power to reveal
something, but he put it in the dross pile all the same.

Murray's interest in Archie Lunan had started at the age
of sixteen with a slim paperback. He could still remember
the moment he saw it jutting out from a box of unsorted
stock on the floor of a second-hand bookshop. It was the
cover that drew him, a tangerine-tinted studio shot of a
thin man with shadows for eyes. Murray had known
nothing about Lunan's poetry or his ill-starred life, but he
had to have the book.

'Looks like a baby-killer, doesn't he?' The man behind
the counter had said when Murray handed over his fifty
pence. 'Still, that was the seventies for you, a lot of it
about.'

Once he owned the book Murray had been strangely
indifferent to its contents, almost as if he were afraid they
might be a let-down. He'd propped it on the chest of drawers
in the bedroom he shared with his brother until eleven-

year-old Jack had complained to their dad that the man's non-existent eyes were staring at him and Murray had been ordered to put it somewhere where it wouldn't give people nightmares.

He'd rediscovered the book the following year, when he was packing to go to university, and thrown it in his rucksack, almost on a whim. The paperback had languished on the under-stocked bookshelf in his bed-sit through freshers' week and into most of the following year. It was exam time, a long night into studying, when he'd found himself reaching for the poems. Murray supposed, when he bothered to think about it, that he was looking for a distraction. If so, he'd found one. He'd sat at his desk reading and re-reading Archie Lunan's first and only poetry collection until morning. It was an enchantment which had quietly shadowed Dr Murray Watson in his toil through academe, and now at last he was free to steep himself in it.

It was after six when Murray stepped out from the National Library. Somewhere a piper was hoiching out a tune for the tourists. The screech of the bagpipes cut in and out of the traffic sounds; the grumble of car engines, the low diesel growl of taxis and unoiled shriek of bus brakes. The noise and August brightness were an assault after the gloom of the small back room. He took his sunglasses from their case and swapped them for his everyday pair. A seagull careened into the middle of the road, diving towards a discarded poke of chips. Murray admired the bird's near-vertical take-off as it swooped up into the air narrowly missing a bus, its prize clamped firmly in its beak.

It dawned on him that he was hungry. He hadn't eaten since the Twix he'd had for breakfast on the Glasgow to

Edinburgh Express early that morning. He crossed the street, pausing to buy a *Big Issue* from a neat-pressed vendor who readjusted his baseball cap when Murray declined his change. There was a faint scent of salt in the breeze blowing through the city from the Firth of Forth. It suited Murray's mood. His mind still half on the island where Archie had been born, Murray began to walk briskly towards the city centre. The Edinburgh Fringe was well under way. The town had taken on the atmosphere of a medieval fête and it was hard negotiating a path through the crush of tourists, rival ghost-tour operators, performers and temporary street stalls that swamped the High Street. He sidestepped the spit-spattled Heart of Midlothian, at the same time avoiding a masked Death, cowled in unseasonably warm black velvet. On other days the crush and stretched smiles of performers trumpeting their shows might have irritated Murray, but today their edge of cheerful hysteria seemed to echo his own optimism. He turned into Cockburn Street, his feet unconsciously stepping to the rhythm of a busking drum troupe, each stride on the beat, precise as a policeman on duty at an Orange Walk. Murray accepted leaflets shoved at him for shows he had no intention of seeing, still thinking about the papers in the box, and keeping his eyes peeled for a chippy.

In the end he settled for pie and beans washed down by a pint of 8o/- in the Doric. He ate at one of the high stools by the bar, his eyes fixed on the television mounted on the wall above the gantry, watching the newsreader relaying headlines he couldn't hear. The screen flashed to soldiers in desert fatigues on patrol then to a crease-eyed correspondent packed into a flak jacket, the background behind him half sand, half blue sky, like a child's what-I-did-on-my-holiday drawing.

Murray slid his hand into his rucksack, brought out his notebook and read again the names he had copied from the red corduroy address book, wishing to God it had been a diary.

> *Tamsker*
> *Saffron*
> *Ray – will you be my sunshine?*

It was a misnomer to call it an address book. It had contained no addresses, no telephone numbers, simply lists of unfamiliar names occasionally accompanied by phrases of nonsense. If he knew the identity of even one of them he'd have something to work with, but he was clueless, the knot still pulled tight. Murray folded the words back into his pocket, feeling the pleasure of possession, the secret thrill of a man on the brink of a discovery that might yet elude him.

His plate was cleared, his pint nearly done. He tipped it back and placed the empty glass on the bar, shaking his head when the barman asked him if he'd like another. It was time to go and do his duty.

TAMBURLAINE MUST DIE

LOUISE WELSH

London, 1593. A city on edge.

Under threat from plague and war, strangers are unwelcome,
suspicion is wholesale, severed heads grin from the spikes on
Tower Bridge.

Playwright, poet and spy, Christopher Marlowe walks the
city's mean streets with just three days to find the murderous
Tamburlaine, a killer escaped from the pages of his most
violent play.

Tamburlaine Must Die is the searing adventure of a man who
dares to defy both God and the state and whose murder
remains a taunting mystery to the present day.

'Brilliant . . . Utterly engrossing.' *Sunday Telegraph*

'Pungently atmospheric.' *Observer*

'A taut, seedy novella scraped off the undercarriage of
Elizabethan England.' *Arena*

£6.99

ISBN 978 1 84195 604 6

ISBN 978 1 84767 694 8

THE BULLET TRICK

LOUISE WELSH

Magic is murder when dying is just part of the act.

When down-at-heel Glasgow conjurer William Wilson gets
booked for a string of cabaret gigs in Berlin, he's hoping
his luck is on the turn. There were certain spectators from
his last show who he'd rather forget. Like the one who's
now a corpse.

Amongst the showgirls and tricksters of Berlin's scandalous
underground Wilson can abandon his heart, his head and,
more importantly, his past. But somehow secrets have a habit
of catching up with him.

'Her most thrilling yet . . . An electrifying journey into one
man's heart of darkness.' Kate Atkinson

'A tour de force.' *Independent*

'Breathtaking.' Jake Arnott

£7.99

ISBN 978 1 84195 890 3

ISBN 978 1 84767 639 9

NAMING THE BONES

LOUISE WELSH

Some secrets are best left buried.

Knee-deep in the mud of an ancient burial ground, a winter
storm raging around him, and at least one person intent on
his death: how did Murray Watson end up here?

Loaded with Welsh's trademark wit, insight and gothic
charisma, this adventure novel weaves the lives of Murray
and Archie together in a tale of literature, obsession and
dark magic.

'Saturated with dark imagery, which colours even the most
ordinary of settings.' *Times Literary Supplement*

'A smart and horribly funny slice of campus gothic.'
Guardian

'It's not magic that takes us to another world – it's story-
telling. And Louise Welsh is mistress of that dark art.'
Val McDermid

£7.99

ISBN 978 1 84767 256 8

ISBN 978 1 84767 902 4